Mildred Penniwink

Hazel Warlaumont

Mildred Penniwink is a work of fiction. All names, characters, places, and incidents are the product of the author's imagination or used fictitiously. Any resemblance to current events or locales, or to living persons, is entirely coincidental.

Special thanks to my steadfast readers who poured over this novel with diligence offering support, suggestions, and insight: Sydnee Elliot, Gail Scriven, Carrie Nasti, and Pat Leahy.

*Our greatest pretenses are built up
not to hide the evil and ugly in us,
but our emptiness. The hardest thing
to hide is something that is not there.*

Eric Hoffer

(1902-1983)

One

A LAVENDER SKY eased into daylight as Mildred Penniwink readied herself for work unaware she would be fired later that day. Staring into an old tarnished mirror in the bedroom of her small midwestern bungalow, she brushed her hand across the surface to wipe away the minuscule remnants of dust that accumulated when she left the back door open. A faded plastic flower lei dangled from the mirror next to a shelf with family photographs - including one of her as a child; a serious, hesitant little girl, face tight, eyes looking away, a smile that could have been painted on her small face.

Leaning closer she examined her face; simple, everything in its place yet nothing extraordinary. Her ash-colored hair, mostly light brown but showing signs of gray, was naturally wavy and sat carelessly away from her face which was round and cheeky to match her frame. Built sturdy, as if her purpose was to be well grounded in life, she bought her clothes in the full-size section especially in the winter, when she added barley and noodles to her homemade soups.

She finished dressing and packed a tuna-salad sandwich, and left for work humming show tunes as she pulled her rusty Ford Fairlane out of the garage. Mildred settled long ago for jobs in retail. Working at the "five and dimes" or *variety stores* as they're called, was typical in small towns in the late 1990s. Eventually, she moved up to a job in the lingerie department at JC Penney on Main Street. When asked, she always said her job there was "fine, just fine," but she never raved about the company and the feeling was mutual.

Her termination occurred shortly after she returned from lunch while the *Monteur de Corset* was on a break - that's what Mrs. Blanchbury, the snobbish corset fitter liked to be called. The problem began when Winifred Adams ran into the store saying she needed a corset right away to wear with a new dress to the Elks' dance.

"What do you mean the corset fitter's at lunch? What kind of a place are you running here?" she said, raising her voice. "I just want a simple slip-on girdle, nothing with laces or those damn bulky fasteners. You work here don't you?"

"Well, yes but we're told never to fit corsets," Mildred said, feeling her face flush. "I mean, we're just salesgirls." Mildred remembered the stern warning from the finger-wagging *Monteur de Corset* about fitting corsets, as if it required some kind of magic. Mildred sighed as Mrs. Adams stood tapping her toe.

Cripes, it can't be that hard, she reasoned, so holding herself erect she squeezed into the dressing room to help Mrs. Adams wedge into a deluxe pink sateen corset. She was surprised how easy it was, *not technical at all,* she mused. She did have to tug and pull though, and appreciated the corset fitter's work as the perspiration began to form on her own upper lip.

"Oh, I think this might be too tight," Mrs. Adams whined, as she sucked in enough air to blow up a balloon and then started panting. Mildred tried to slide the corset down, stretching and tugging with all her might.

"It was easy to get on, why doesn't it want to come off?" she said to Mrs. Adams in a comforting tone. But she too was getting out of breath.

"Maybe if you get on the floor and tug from the bottom," Mrs. Adams offered.

"Yes, that's it! Get on the floor," Mildred said, as she lay flat between the woman's legs looking up for a place to get a firm grip.

"I really need to be going, can't you get it off?"

"I'm pulling as hard as I can."

"Well, what about the other woman who usually fits corsets? Can you get her?"

"She's at lunch right now," Mildred said, her voice growing weak.

"The manager?" Mrs. Adams asked.

Mildred sank lower into the floor, realizing she would have to take Mrs. Adams to the lunch room to find the corset fitter. "Good lord almighty," she whispered under her breath.

Draping Mrs. Adams in a robe off the rack, Mildred marched her to the break room while the poor woman gasped for air. As they entered, the room became silent. When Mildred saw the look of horror on the corset fitter's face she knew that would be her final day working at JC Penney.

"My god, woman! What have you done?" were the last words she heard. Later, with the manager and the other clerks standing nearby, she left with the *Notice to Terminate* in her hand after the corset had been cut off Mrs. Adams, and she had been refitted with a new one by the *Monteur de Corset*.

Mildred stood outside on the sidewalk that day squeezing her fingers until the ends turned crimson. "Now what?" she mumbled as she scuffed her brown and white oxfords along the cracked sidewalk.

TWO

BORN LATE IN HER parents' lives and an only child, Mildred never really knew her parents when they were youthful, only after they'd aged with weathered skin and stiff backs. Her most vivid recollection was seeing her parents with drawn faces and eyes that had seen about all they wanted. They were predictably quiet people, always sitting apart, she with her needlework and tiny glasses that slipped down her nose, and he with the newspaper held close to his face by gnarled fingers, uttering only an occasional grunt about something he'd read, neither of them talking, only mumbling half sentences, but mostly not. They never imagined having a child so late in life; shocked really when the country doctor announced that her mother's indigestion was actually a pregnancy.

Mildred was born at home on the kitchen floor, a reality not uncommon in farm communities in 1940s, nor was putting an infant in the oven, sometimes known as the "country incubator. Neighbors could never fathom oldsters like Maude and Jacob having a child, as if it was dropped by a stork from the sky after everyone had gone to bed one night. When asked, even the doctor whispered, "Imagine that, and she's sixty!" Her mother's response was always the same. "Yes, well, I'll be darned."

When Mildred was young, and once she'd seen dirty pictures from the kids in the neighborhood, she too wondered how she was ever conceived. She'd never even seen her parents touch, except when her mother draped a napkin under her father's chin before supper. There were times though, after the lights went out in the

Hazel Warlaumont

house and everyone had gone to bed, that she'd hear her father grunting and straining like he was working on the lawnmower or lifting something heavy, but there was never a peep from her mother. Mildred never really knew what to make of that until much later, and even then she couldn't quite imagine it.

As an only child, Mildred listened to the radio in her room, and when the weather permitted, she'd follow her mother around the yard near the clothesline watching her prune plants and step on snails.

"Can I help?" she'd ask her mother.

"There's nothing to do Mildred, and don't just dawdle under foot."

So, mostly Mildred watched. In the late afternoon she'd follow her mother into the kitchen while her mother - with sleeves rolled and apron tied - prepared supper, a ritual that usually began with chopping on the old oak chopping block while occasionally glancing at the splattered pages of a cook book on the table beyond the jam pot. It seemed to a small child, the chopping went on all afternoon. In fact, Mildred could even hear "chop, chop, chop" later in the day when she played hopscotch in the street.

An exciting new world opened unexpectedly for Mildred when she was six years old and sent to school, a world totally different from the quiet isolation she'd known at home with her parents. At first, all the chatting and interacting in school both pleased and frightened her, but she soon fit in when she discovered and started playing with other children her age.

One day she returned home with a note pinned to her pinafore. It seemed students were encouraged to participate in some musical activity that would require home practice. Her parents selected tap dancing to avoid any "blaring horn or squeaking fiddle practice," plus the school had tap shoes to loan. Mildred practiced in the street in front of the house after school since the garage had a dirt floor and there were too many throw rugs in the house. The sound of her tapping in the street strangely coincided with her mother's chopping. It was about the only activity they ever did together.

Whatever Mildred learned from her parents in those days was from watching them. They never talked about their lives or passed down stories from their own parents or siblings, or what they had learned in life. It seemed to Mildred they were just there to fill the seats at the table, her mother in her apron, her large blank face and small hands pushing the bowls closer instead of inviting second helpings, and her father in some distant orbit that even he didn't recognize, raising the fork to his otherwise silent mouth. There were no bedtime stories or kisses goodnight. Mildred just went to bed whenever she felt tired.

Each night she'd say to herself, "now I lay me down to sleep I praise the board my soles to keep," because she'd heard it on a radio show once but really never knew what it meant or why kids were supposed to say it at night. It would be years before she realized the prayer was "Now I lay me down to sleep I praise the Lord my soul to keep."

Mildred was ten years old the night her father failed to come home. A group of people came to the house bringing meat casseroles and baked apple cake. She was told her father passed on to heaven and wouldn't be coming back. Nothing more was said. Her mother continued to set a place for her father at the table each night, although she did cancel the subscription to the newspaper.

Graduating some years later with her classmates, Mildred left home to take secretarial classes at the Sawyer Business School in the city. At eighteen, a young woman was expected to prepare herself for some sort of work even though most married and wore aprons the rest of their lives. Mildred struggled however with fingers that seemed too short and too slow for typing, so she dropped out, taking odd jobs in retail and moved back home. She rode the public bus to work each day and that began her love affair.

She told her mother one day, "I'd rather ride the bus than just about anything in the world. You sit up high and everyone talks to each other."

Her mother sighed and wiped her hands on her apron. "Good thing. You won't be affording a car working at the five and dime.

Better be looking to get married, Mildred. Settling down is what women do."

That was about the most her mother ever said to her so she assumed it was all her mother had to say. Later, she wondered why her parents didn't teach her about life other than how to reheat leftovers or fix the lawnmower, but she came to realize that each person has to figure it out for themselves.

One evening on a chilly autumn night some years later, Mildred came home to find her mother gone. A neighbor said her mother had taken a taxi to the hospital to die. The only thing her mother left was needlework, boxes of it in the closets and under the beds, and her apron folded neatly on the kitchen table.

That year Mildred tried to absorb the immense fact of her mother's death, but it just seemed too removed from anything she'd learned about life so far. At twenty-seven, she still hadn't figured out what she was supposed to be doing in life.

Three

SHORTLY AFTER HER mother died, Mildred bought a modest two-bedroom, one-bath bungalow with her meager inheritance. It was 1968 and she had enough for a down payment on the house, and a little cash for the dinette set she saw at the annual Daughters of the American Revolution rummage sale. She filled the rest of the house with older furnishings from the local thrift shop not because they were cheap, but because she thought of herself as old fashioned and liked old things. She was still trying to understand life, let alone keep up with "modernization," as she put it.

Living in Myers Junction - a small Midwestern town anchored between long stretches of farm land that went on forever, she likened the town to a watercolor, the kind she'd seen in museums depicting fertile soil and pastoral farmland that had coaxed farmers to the area for decades, along with those with nothing else to do but admire the charm of a town quintessentially part of the Midwestern landscape. Myers Junction was like many other small towns that hadn't quite caught up with the times but were still All-American. The winters were thick and white, and in autumn the leaves blazed to glory before blowing off in a northwester. Summers were so fierce they could melt the soles of your shoes but no one left.

Mildred kept busy with her jobs at the "five and dimes" and volunteered at the hospital and branch library, and even bowled in a league at the Riverdale Alley. But on weekends her passion was her small garden near the worn wooden steps to her front porch where she pruned and shaped her flowers to keep them smart and perky. That same year, Burt Stillwell moved in across the street. He bought his house with a military pension and payed his monthly mortgage from his disability check since he'd left one leg on the beach at Normandy thirty years ago. Like Mildred, he kept to himself, flew the flag on every occasion, and took in stray cats if they happened to come his way.

They exchanged a few words every so often, like the day her hose sprung a leak and spun out of control.

"Whoa Mildred, what are you doing?" he yelled from the curb as the hose whipped in circles, each spin drenching him as he tried to get closer.

"I can't stop it," she yelled, soaking wet and standing in a puddle on the lawn.

"Put it down, put it down, Mildred. Turn it off at the faucet," he hollered.

She dropped the hose and it flew high into the air with a mighty burst of pressure before flopping back and forth out of control. She tried to dodge it, but each time it switched direction drenching her already-soggy clothes. Finally Burt was able to stand on the hose while she ran to the faucet.

"Sweet Jesus," she said, throwing off her embarrassment like sowing seeds in a field.

"Hmmm." Burt scratched his head and went back across the street, water dripping from his soaked clothes.

Mildred and Burt were private neighbors over the years and never asked about each other's lives, appreciating the distance between them more than any obligatory neighborly friendship that neither wanted. She'd watched him gradually grow small and quiet, and occasionally she'd put his newspapers on his porch if she saw them piling up on the lawn.

They almost always waved, except a few years ago when he was pulling into his driveway in his light green Chevy the day Mildred sat on her porch steps in the rain. It was 1991, the year of the great floods. There was so much rain that year even the yards flooded along with everything else. It was the same day the gentleman left who had been living with her briefly, his coat thrown over his old brown leather suitcase to protect it from the rain as he walked up the street toward the bus stop.

That was the day the water crept up to her second step and she sat there as it inched up over her shoes. She saw Burt watching from across the street, and was always grateful he didn't ask her about that day. She couldn't even talk about to herself. Her garden sat dormant that year and she stayed in most of the time. She was sure her neighbors suspected something since her wheelbarrow showed signs of rust. That was three years ago, about the time she began to turn the light on during the night, her shadow roaming from room to room.

When she and Burt did talk it was mostly about snails or why the postman walked across the lawn and not up the path to the mailbox.

"I don't get it, Mildred. Why does he have to walk across the lawn?"

"Burt, is that the most important thing on your mind today and every day?"

"Well, sure enough is," he said raising his brow.

It was hard to understand his strange ways at times, Mildred thought, but he did make for a decent neighbor.

On the other hand, the neighbor who lived next door to her, Angus Baumgartner, was a "pain up the rump," she liked to say. One morning after she bought two bags of daffodil bulbs from the country store along with a sack of planter mix, she gathered what she needed and set out to work in her small garden next to the porch. Pushing her heavy feet into a pair of yellow rubber boots with daisy designs, she reached for the thorn-proof gloves from the top shelf in the garage, along with a can of Dog-Off repellent she'd bought at Simpson's hardware. She sorted the bulbs by color and made small sticky notes on which she wrote the color and row number, and scribbled the planting instructions for each one . . .

daffodil bulb, yellow, four inches deep, row three . . . until all were accounted for.

"Yesiree," she said to herself and clapped her hands. She smiled as she spaced her plants equally apart. But before actually digging, she scanned the neighborhood looking in all directions before spraying the Dog-Off on her backside, holding the can awkwardly while bending over.

"There we go!" she mumbled with satisfaction and raised her chin, already doubled on her short and full-bodied frame.

It happened when she was finishing the red tulip bulbs in row four. He bounded on her like a locomotive connecting to a passenger car at full speed. Her hands flew forward to keep from going face down.

"Get off! Get off you beast!" she bellowed.

Buster, Angus Baumgartner's big lumbering oaf of dog held tight, his paws like claws squeezing into her waist while his hips jerked with such violent gyrations his back legs actually left the ground.

"Help! Somebody help!

Her yellow-brimmed garden hat swung violently back and forth, until it flopped forward and hung like a food trough while her head bobbed in and out like a hungry wolf at meal time. With a purposeful lunge, she pushed forward and rolled on her side, destroying a full row of newly planted fuchsias but unlocking Buster's amorous grip. With her hat blocking all but a sliver of her view, she watched Buster run off after stopping to lift his leg on the porch railing.

"Disgusting," she muttered to herself while untangling herself from her petunias.

~~~~

Angus Baumgartner, a tall man with thinning hair and dry skin, stood barely inside his old post-war bungalow, one that resembled everyone else's on the block. As Mildred's neighbor almost from the beginning, she remembered him as awkward and grumpy but lately combative. She waited for him to open the door and when he did her eyes went straight to the stain on his shirt.

"Your dog mounted me again this morning!" she yelled, still trying to untie the garden hat from under her chin.

His false expression of surprise - an insidious stare, mouth half opened, eyes blinking - was offset by the slight smile he tried unsuccessfully to hide. She didn't know him well and never wanted to, but she knew he drove a long car and wore a suede jacket shiny at the elbows. She also knew that Angus was really his middle name, first name Robert. She saw that on some mail put into her mailbox by mistake and after she held it up to the light to see what was inside. She steamed open the envelopes addressed to him if they were in her box, but always with good intent; that is, to see if the contents were really for her, but put in an envelope addressed to him by mistake.

"Well?" she said, tapping the toe of her grass-stained garden boot and he, tapping his finger against the door while he held it open. As in a duel, they both stood in a standoff waiting for each other to break the silence. When neither did, she stomped her rubber boot and turned in a fit of pique leaving him holding the door.

"That dog of yours should be snipped," she yelled over her shoulder in a departing shot as she huffed off across the lawn.

"You both should," she added, when she was out of earshot.

Four

"OH, BOSH TURDS," she grumbled, as she plucked the Myers Junction *Tribune* from her row of petunias next to the porch. "Why does he have to throw this into the garden?" she grumbled under her breath while shaking mulch and dried leaves from the newspaper.

Sitting with her morning tea she scanned the front page and then the headline: *Transit Company to Add New Bus Route.*

Hmmm . . . She sat tapping the sugar spoon on the table.

Mildred's dream had always been to drive a public bus. As a child she marveled gleefully at their gigantic size, looking like giant caterpillars crawling along city streets. When she grew up, she enjoyed the camaraderie of people sitting together on a bus talking in hushed tones as if in church. She had applied several times for a job as a bus driver in Myers Junction, but much to her disappointment she was repeatedly rejected.

"I'm sorry Miss Penniwink, but your arms are too short," was the usual response although she secretly suspected it was because she was a woman. Back in the 1960's and 1970's, women had their jobs and men had theirs.

"My arms are too short? What do you mean too short? It's not like I'll be hanging wash up on the clothesline," she said at one point, trying to hide her disappointment.

Unfortunately, she soon discovered on her own why she was rejected. Sitting in the driver's seat of an empty bus one day, she felt like a small child hugging a large donut. She couldn't even get her short arms around the steering wheel let alone see over it.

She put her cup down that morning reading the headline more closely and then again. *Hmmm . . . looks like the transit company might be hiring a new bus driver for the new route.* She turned the pages to the classified ad section and there it was! She read it twice. *Hiring male bus driver, will train.* She mumbled, "Well, now I have three strikes against me. My arms are still short, I'm now fifty-three, and the ad says MALE DRIVER WANTED!

On the other hand . . . .

~~~~

The stout man behind the counter at the Brown County Transit Authority hesitated. "You'll have to pass both the written and driving test before even being considered, and you might not because quite honestly you're short and your arms even shorter, and . . . well, the job is for a male driver."

She remembered the incident in the vacant bus when her arms wouldn't reach. "Hmm . . . is it possible to get a smaller steering wheel for my driver's test?"

He rolled his eyes and shuffled some papers pretending not to hear.

"May I make an appointment?" she said, feeling her body stiffen.

"I . . . well I suppose. But . . ."

"Any day this week will work for me," she said firmly.

~~~~

That afternoon Mildred bought some weights to strengthen and stretch her arms and upper body, and in the evenings when the local playground was empty she hung from the jungle gym bars convinced it would make her arms longer. She was sure it was working since her arms surely *felt* longer to her.

On testing day she sat in the bus transit terminal with the other applicants, all young males, and she squeezed her palms together

Hazel Warlaumont

waiting to see if she passed the transit company's written test. She stood and let out a loud "whoopie" when her name was called as one of three who passed - a prerequisite for taking the driving test. *Oh my god!* She felt her heart racing. She waited, twisting her watch band, and then walked over to the large window and pressed her face against the glass. The large blue and white bus was parked just outside. *Good lord, I don't remember them being THIS big!*

"Miss Periwinkle . . ." His name tag read, Roger Studebaker, Supervisor, Brown County Transit Authority.

"It's Penniwink, Mildred Penniwink."

They stood at the desk while he looked over her written test. "To be quite honest, Miss Periwinkle . . ."

"Penniwink."

"Uh huh, well whatever," he mumbled with a forced smile.

"While it seems you had the highest score on your written test, well . . . well let me put it this way. This really is a man's job, a young man, as you must know." A few in the office looked his way.

"No, no I don't know."

"You see," he said smirking, "there's really no need to do the actual driver's test. We don't want to waste your time and I see where you applied years ago and were told you didn't have the physical ability to drive a bus. That's enough for us, but we thank you for applying nevertheless."

Mildred felt her throat tighten. "But I'd like a chance to take the test. I do believe I have the physical ability."

Supervisor Studebaker flipped through her test pages again. "Unfortunately, we just don't think . . ."

"Excuse me Supervisor Studebaker." A tall black man who had been standing by the door interrupted. "We've got 'er all ready. The bus is running right outside the door," and he took Mildred's arm leading her in that direction. "Come quickly," he whispered, leaning closer. "And your arms are short so scoot the seat up all the way forward once you sit down. Then drive it just like a car . . . a big car."

Supervisor Studebaker growled, "Alright, alright, let's get this over with," he said, grumbling something under his breath while following them outside.

I can't believe I'm actually doing this! After fumbling for the knob, she slid the seat forward a couple of times with some effort and a noticeable groan. Pursing her lips she threw herself over the giant steering wheel with arms outstretched and wide apart, her blouse pulling loose at the waist and her eyes staring at the dashboard. *Oh good grief! How will I ever . . ."*

Her knees quivered and at one point she slapped her hand on one and forced a deep breath. "Ughhh," she moaned quietly when stretching her leg to reach the pedal. When the bus moved forward, she let out a sigh that sounded more like a gasp.

Okay, brake release, shift in gear . . . She fumbled with the seat adjustment knob again and heard the seat click in place even closer to the pedals. *Halleluiah! Oh, my god. We're moving!* She wiped her face on her sleeve and clenched her teeth as she made all the turns, stopped at every light, and followed all the instructions. She even parallel parked the bus in front when she returned it to the building.

"Wow, looks like we have us a new driver," the tall black man said to Supervisor Studebaker as they got out of the bus. "Highest written scores and a perfect driver's test! No doubt about it, she's the most qualified," he said, looking squarely at the supervisor who muttered an obscenity under his breath.

"Oh, crap. Alright, but a temporary hire only! I'll give her six months." He threw the paperwork on the clerk's desk. "A middle-aged female bus driver, for god's sake. It's highly unorthodox," he grumbled. "We'll be the laughing stock of everyone." He turned to Mildred. "Let me remind you, Miss Perriwinkle, this is just a temporary hire."

"Penniwink, Mildred Penniwink."

"On probation for six months if even that," he said, storming off. "You can be sure we will be watching you closely. Any accidents or issues will mean an immediate termination, is that clear?" he yelled over his shoulder. "Training, first thing Monday morning and don't be late."

"Yes, sir. Thank you, sir." She pinched her fingers to keep from screaming.

Just then the clerk stepped up. "Oh, Miss Penniwink, there's just one minor correction needed on your application. Under *body art* you listed a beaded necklace from your trip to Hawaii and blinking Santa Claus earrings at Christmas.

"Yes?"

"Uh, we meant any tattoos," the clerk said as she crossed out Mildred's answer.

"Oh no, I don't do tattoos. Can you believe what people draw all over their bodies these days? My goodness, pictures and snakes, and the like."

The tall black man standing near the door laughed and walked toward her. "I'm Spencer, the mechanic and maintenance man. You'll be seeing a lot of me. Welcome, Miss Penniwink."

"Ah, Spencer, thank you, and thank you for the tip about the seat, and . . . well, everything else. Really, thank you."

~~~~

The lights burned bright that night in her small bungalow and music blared from every room in the house. Those passing by could see the silhouette of a woman in a long but tattered silk robe dancing through the house with a glass of wine held by her fingertips.

Five

WHEN THE ALARM rang, she was already up and standing over her uniform on the bed. *Everyone is nervous on the first* day, she reminded herself as she stood looking at her regulation grey shirt and pants. "I get one chance," she whispered, pulling her hair back and away from her face.

Leaning over the bed, she ran her hand over the crisp blue blouse with the Brown County Transit Authority logo above her name stitched in yellow. On the floor, two neatly shined black leather shoes with thick rubber soles sat waiting. She bent down, nudging them closer together.

Twenty minutes later she looked in the mirror. "Oh my!" she said to herself, stretching her shoulders back and standing straight. Her gray pants, just touching the tops of her shoes hid her thick ankles and hung smartly. When her blouse was tucked in she looked in the mirror and raised her chin, then her arm to salute, a little embarrassed but giggling at the silly pleasure of wearing a uniform for the first time in her life.

~~~~

On her first day, Mildred slipped a little card under the visor that said: *One chance, work hard, be kind to everyone.* That became her mantra and she glanced at it faithfully every morning before putting her regulation black lunch pail with her peanut butter sandwich and Oreos under the driver's seat.

Spencer trained her well, but she still got the gears mixed up

Hazel Warlaumont

on her first day and had trouble getting the doors to open each time. She kept running her hand over her new uniform and stuttered when introducing herself to the riders although she knew many already. Living in a small town was like that. Yet she was shy at first and blushed often. But she learned her riders' names, and every day it all became easier.

With Spencer's help she also got to know the bus, its noises, the inner workings, and how to keep the seat adjusted. It wasn't unusual to see her sitting in the bus an hour before her scheduled departure or staying late after returning it to the Bus Bay where it was cleaned and stored for the night. She drove it slowly at first, and when cars honked at her she just flashed the peace sign and waved happily out the window.

It wasn't long until Mildred became known affectionately around town as the *bus lady* since almost everyone rode the Crosstown #2 at one time or another. Her riders included senior citizens in the community who had long given up driving on icy roads to enjoy the comradery of seeing each other on the bus, a meeting place of sorts. They used the time to catch up on what was happening in Myers Junction, plus Mildred never told them to keep the talking down like the other drivers did. At the end of the day, she looked forward to returning the bus to the Bus Bay, out on Bray's Corner next to the Waffle House and chatting with Spencer.

"Hey, you don't have to do that Miss Mildred," Spencer shouted as he watched Mildred cleaning the inside. "That's what they hire me to do, girl."

A tall man from Zimbabwe, Spencer Matima came to Myers Junction several years ago with his wife and daughters under the sponsorship of the local church. The transit company gave him a temporary job but kept him on because he was a good worker and a trained mechanic.

He cleaned all the buses at the end of each day, but Mildred still climbed out of hers every evening looking for a bucket of water and some rags.

"You can clean windows Spencer. I'll just tidy up a bit

inside," she usually said.

"You say that every time Mildred and then end up cleaning the whole thing," he said, needling her. "Oh, by the way, I found old Herb Frank's glasses last night. They were under the seat in the last row."

"Ah! They must have slid to the back during one of the stops. I'll call him at home tonight. We looked high and low yesterday. Even Bessy Sinclair and Nate Jennings were down on their hands and knees looking under seats. I'll drop them off to him on my route tomorrow. "

"Now Miss Mildred," he stood with his hands on his hips. "You know he lives six blocks from your route, and you'll never get this bus down Spurgeon Road, even if you were allowed to leave your route, which you know you are not."

"It's only a few minutes off course. Here, take these cookies from one of the riders as a reward for not telling. We had a little party today."

Spencer raised an eyebrow and laughed. "I can see that. Your riders like you, but you haven't forgotten the scolding you got last week when you took Mrs. Peeples to her house because the sole of her shoe came off."

"Oh horse feathers, Spencer, how was I to know one of the managers, Mr. Banks, would be driving down that same road at the same time? What a coincidence! He did give me a scolding though, didn't he?"

Spencer taunted her. "I can't remember, what did he say again?"

"You know. He screamed as he stood in the middle of the road, 'Christ Almighty, Mildred, we're not the Yellow Cab Company. Get this bus back on your route!' Thankfully, he didn't file a report or tell Supervisor Studebaker."

Spencer laughed and shook his head. "I like your spirit Miss Mildred. Try to stay out of trouble on the way home."

Hazel Warlaumont

She could still hear him laughing and mimicking her as he locked up the bus.

"Christ Almighty, Mildred . . ."

Six

AT THE END OF THE DAY Mildred normally lugged her groceries from the car and braved the chill as she walked out to the mail box. She'd wrap a scarf around her face to ward off the cold and looked forward to fixing a simple meal of hash or sweet potatoes before turning on the television or playing one of her favorite Duke Ellington LPs. A basket of yarn sat near her chair at night. She knitted hats for the newborn at Mercy General. But that night when driving home she got a queasy feeling in her stomach, like *monkeys playing inside,* as she described it to herself. She decided to stop by Thelma's Thrift Shop up on Main Street, a favorite place of hers when she was feeling a little blue.

Mildred met Thelma Giordano a number of years ago during a class at the Farm and Garden store on gastropods, including snails and slugs. When Mildred discovered gastropods were capable of being either male or female, possessing both the egg and sperm to allow them the opportunity to self-fertilize, she dropped the course, saying their sex life was way too much information when all she really wanted to know was how to keep them out of her garden. She decided it was easier to keep stepping on them.

They remained friends after that and Mildred stopped by Thelma's Thrift Store regularly. Thelma was always there with a kind word of support on those days when Mildred came in with worry written on her face.

Hazel Warlaumont

"Mildred, I was hoping you'd stop by! I saw your bus go by this morning." Thelma bent down and looked at her.

"What's going on with you tonight, are you feeling like an empty shed? I can see that look."

"Oh I don't know. Maybe I'm just a little restless tonight," Mildred said, looking around the shop and taking in the familiar smell of mothballs and old wicker.

"Take a little something home, just something for a shelf or for the kitchen table. I do the same once in a while; you know, something to fill the space or an empty drawer." She lowered her head and looked at Mildred over the top of her reading glasses. "You know, we can't always expect to fill all the emptiness ourselves. Pick something and I'll put it in a bag for you. My treat tonight."

Mildred went home with a small saucer to add to the myriad of thrift-shop items stacked throughout her house and felt better for it. Even then, she woke that night with a dream she couldn't remember. For her, dreams mysteriously seemed to fade once she's out of bed. At times she imagined seeing a glimmer of light beneath the closed door to the spare bedroom but when she opened it, the light had disappeared and all she saw were boxes of baby furniture unopened. On those nights she often sat in her chair pulling the basket of yarn to her lap and letting her eyes fill.

~~~~

The following night, black ice had already formed on the road as she drove home from the Bus Bay. She was glad to be at home and pulling her old blue Ford into the driveway. "*Hmm, these cold nights are getting to me,*" she thought to herself, shivering as the frost bit her cheeks when she followed her breath up to the mail box. She stopped to look at the stars scattered across the sky and took a deep breath before going in.

She turned on the heat and heard the hissing from the radiator as she poured herself a small jelly glass of Chablis, which she pronounced with two "s" at the end. Changing into her pink chenille robe after carefully hanging up her work uniform in the closet, she stood looking at the top shelf and then reached for a worn box containing a pair of tap dancing shoes, a gift to herself a few years ago when she began to stay in more. She hesitated but then put the box back on the shelf, instead wandering into the kitchen with her portable player and her *Duke Ellington* tape. Within minutes she was shuffling around in her old slippers to songs like *Satin Doll* and *Mood Indigo* and twirling her chenille robe like a satin gown, dancing late until the day faded.

~~~~

In spite of long hours on the bus, Mildred was eager to start each day. She was at the height of glory driving the bus through Myers Junction. Every encounter was a chance to learn something new and make everyone glad they were riding "Mildred's bus." She was mindful however, that Supervisor Studebaker saw his army of drivers to be men and not women. *Hog's breath,* she thought, *he'll get over it.* But she vowed to do the best she could in all situations to make sure she made it past her probationary period with just four months to go.

"Good morning, Mildred, You're looking chipper today," Harriet Pierce said, as she climbed up the last step and dropped her coins in the box. She'd been riding the Crosstown #2 practically every day so Mildred had had a chance to get to know her. She knew that Harriet's husband, Freddy, used to ride with her before he left for a more peaceful place, and knew they were both salt of the earth. Harriet showed Mildred a photo of them together, both tall and lean with a squareness to their jaw so typical of hard-working people.

"Good morning, Harriet, are you still losing weight? You look like you don't weigh more than a sack of potatoes."

Harriet laughed and headed for her favorite bus seat where Mildred had put a red acrylic blanket. Mildred watched in her rear-view mirror as Harriet sat snuggly with the blanket over her knees, looking out the window or talking to old Ted Thompson and his wife Vera.

Most of the riders on Mildred's bus had known each other for years, as far back as school for some and as fate would have it, the bus brought them together again at this time of their lives. Mildred noticed a certain civility among them, taking seats next to each other, nodding politely, sharing space, talking in murmurs as if in church. She liked to think she was watching over the flock more or less, although she never thought of them as needing to be led, only as friends traveling together.

"Here's your stop Mr. Thompson," Mildred shouted, looking in the rear view mirror. "Your stop, Ted." She waited for a minute. "Uh, Vera?"

Vera gave Ted a nudge and he jumped up with a start. Mildred waited patiently for him to gather his wits and his cane, and ease himself down the steps to the sidewalk with Vera following close behind. Mildred noticed his pants were too short and he was thick in the middle. She also noticed Vera's hair was redder than last week. *Why would anyone want red hair on purpose? Oh, well, I guess Vera does,* she thought. They waved as she pulled away from the curb, and Mildred watched as Vera put her arm through his, pulling him close and putting her head on his shoulder.

At the stop after the bridge, Maude and Elmo Mansfield waited by the bus sign to board. Maude stood gracefully as usual, and straightened her hat before putting on more lipstick. Mildred thought perhaps she wore too much makeup for a woman her age, but then probably not since she was on the Board of the Public Library and organized the yearly Toys for Tots campaign. Elmo's double chin looked tripled that morning and his hair was slicked down too pat, but Mildred thought they were still an attractive couple. Maude was considered one of the more sophisticated residents of Myers Junction. As Mildred pulled closer for them to board, she noticed the glowing tip of Maude's cigarette when she turned her head to blow a stream of smoke over her shoulder. *Oh my, just like in the movies,* Mildred thought. Maude dropped the cigarette butt on the ground grinding it into the pavement with her leather wedge sandal. The bus belched and lowered almost as if bowing to the glamorous Maude Mansfield.

"Good afternoon, Mildred," they chirped in unison while

dropping some change in the box.

"How are you two doing today, off for some shopping?"

Maude leaned a bit forward and whispered with her lip curling, "hearing aids," she said, as if they were dirty words. She nodded toward Elmo.

"I see," Mildred said almost apologetically.

Mildred's eye followed them in the mirror as they walked to the back of the bus, Maude's dress clinging to the backs of her legs. The Manfields were among the wealthier citizens in Myers Junction; banking or some such thing Mildred had heard, but she liked them anyway.

Seven

RAIN PELTED THE SIDE of the bus as she pulled out of the Bus Bay that November morning for her first stop of the day, arriving four minutes early at 2nd and Elm. She let the bus idle while waiting. Mildred had stacked several umbrellas by the back door for rainy days and for patrons to borrow. Some were returned but many were not so she made it a point to buy a few each week when she went to Thelma's Thrift Shop to buy a nice saucer or two, or just to visit. Most of the early morning riders were on their way to the Senior Center to play bridge or weave baskets, so she looked forward to hearing their comforting chatter that morning. Later in the day, others headed to the barber shop or the hardware store. Matt Rogers was taking his watch to the jewelers because the minute hand fell off.

"Goodness, what a shame, Matt!" Mildred said, in order to show some compassion.

That afternoon as she neared the stop by the high school, she felt a rush of adrenaline and it wasn't just the usual *monkeys* in her stomach again. For the past few days a group of rowdy teen-age boys had been riding the bus, usually four or five of them, all noisy and rude with pasty complexions, except for one she thought looked more ethnic. They sat in the aisle seats reserved for senior and disabled riders, all elbows and legs blocking the seniors and raising havoc with riders entering and exiting the bus. Music blared from their boom boxes while they gyrated in the aisles making obscene comments, especially to the female passengers. Mildred assumed they were from the new Gang Intervention

Center getting so much recent attention in the newspaper. Just last month the mayor officiated at the ribbon-cutting ceremony at the Center and hailed it as an asset to the community. *Hmmm, can't say much about the program judging by these nincompoops!* she thought, as she let the bus idle and followed them to the back.

"Excuse me, but these seats are reserved for seniors and the disabled as the sign indicates," and she pointed above. "They face the aisle and have easy access for those who need the extra space." The boys stared but didn't move. "You can find plenty of other seats in the front or in the back."

Finally, one jumped up moaning, "Oh, I'm old, I'm so old," he said, limping in a circle. Another contorted his arms and hands dancing around making unintelligible noises while the other four chanted, "retard, retard."

Mildred took a deep breath, the color rushing visibly up her cheeks. "I'm sorry but if you want to ride the bus you need to follow the rules," she said before hurrying up front to get to her next stop. But the noise and antics continued. She glanced at the note near her visor: *One chance, work hard, be kind to everyone.*

~~~~

Much to her disappointment that week the gang of thugs, as she called them, rode the bus every day and took over the entire back including the senior section. She asked them repeatedly to please take other seats, even announcing the policies over the loud speaker when they boarded the bus, but they just got louder and more obnoxious. After a few days of that she got off the bus with them and talked quietly on the sidewalk while the other passengers peered through the windows.

"Look gentlemen, I need to ask for your help. We need to accommodate the older passengers on the bus and that's why we have special seating for them near the rear exit. I'm happy to block off some seats for you so you'll have your own section. What do you think?"

They looked at each other saying nothing, and then broke into fits of uproarious laughter. She rubbed her forearms and got back on the bus.

The following day they were even worse, taunting her as she approached them again. "Bus bitch, bus bitch, here comes the motha fucker bus bitch." One hung from the overhand handles, his pants held up only by the bulge in his torn jeans. Music blared from the ear buds hanging over his shoulder while his head bobbed to:

Bitch why you lyin, bitch you've been cheatin.
Now I gotsa to give your motherfuckin ass a beatin.
I punched her in the . . .

Mildred walked to the back of the bus. "Turn the music off please," she said, her voice cracking, "and these seats are reserved for seniors and the disabled as the sign indicates and as I've announced before. Thank you for your cooperation." She tried not to bite her tongue.

"Whoa, little bitch, what's you gettin' so upset about?" said one of the boys. "We're not diss'n anyone, just havin' fun, mamma girl."

She stared at his greased-back hair and acne. "Have you ever tried to broaden your vocabulary? Where did you learn to talk like that? It's not becoming." Her face was burning from the neck up. "You're in violation of the Riders Code of Conduct. If you want to continue to ride the bus you need to follow the rules."

One smacked his knee laughing. "The rider's code of what? Now don't be pickin' on us cuz we just riders."

"Yeah, and we got our own code, mamma bitch," said the one wearing a gray stocking hat.

"I don't want to file a report, gentlemen. I know it's important for you to use the bus, and we welcome you to the Brown County Transit System, but you are taking seats reserved for seniors, the disabled, and all of those who need easy access to the aisle. And you are disturbing others with your music. I know you want to be good citizens."

"Huh? No shit mamma boss."

"Hey bitch, why 'yo dressed so funny?"

"Yeah, look at yuh."

She glanced at her watch and rushed back up front while they laughed and clapped in unison as one chanted, "Walk da walk, mamma bear. Don't be a snitch, bitch."

"They're disgusting Mildred," Patsy Parker said as Mildred passed by her seat. "Can't you do something about it?"

"Yeah, throw 'em off the bus. They shouldn't be riding the bus if they're going to act like that," Jack Paulson said.

"Sorry folks," she said to the other riders who were now crowded near the front. She sat for a moment and read the card above the dash again: *One chance, work hard, be kind to everyone.* She grabbed the steering wheel like a sumo wrestler and pulled the bus back onto the street.

At the end of town and before turning to go back in the other direction, Mildred glanced back to make sure all passengers had left the bus, including the unruly gang, before pulling into the spot reserved for the buses' "recovery time" where drivers took a break. Running her hands down the sides of her face she let out a long sigh and took out the T-key, or toilet key for the small comfort station, but put it back and retrieved her lunch box from under the seat. She opened it, looked at her sandwich, then closed the lid. Instead of eating lunch, she locked the bus and took a short walk in the park.

To her, viewing her town and the people in it every day on the bus was a gift. Yet, her mind kept drifting back to the gang of thugs disrupting her life and that of her riders. She didn't want to jeopardize her probation but she wanted at the same time to get the vandals off her bus. For the first time she almost wished she was back in JC Penney selling lingerie.

~~~~

That evening she stopped by to see Thelma who was just putting the *Closed* sign in the window of the Thrift Shop. Poking her head in the front door, Mildred said, "Are you getting ready to close Thelma? I can come back another time."

"No, absolutely not. You get yourself in here girl," she said, pulling Mildred in by the sleeve. "It's been slow so I thought I'd close early and just mess around the shop. I'm glad to see you, but jeeze do you look awful! Bad night again last night? What's going on?"

"It's my job I suppose. I'm actually wondering if I can keep it. I'm on probation and I have this unruly situation on the bus that I can't seem to handle myself. Maybe this job just isn't for me."

Thelma sat shaking her head when Mildred told her about the gang of thugs and how helpless she felt.

"My dream job now seems threatening, menacing even, unlike at first when it was fun and comfortable, and I felt like I was a part of something. Know what I mean?"

"Tell me about it. What is it you like about this job? What makes it so special"

"I don't know, it's just been a few months now but I like the anticipation of seeing people I know and learning about Myers Junction. I've felt like the luckiest person in the world as I watch the town and people coming and going and living life, and waving. I wait for the riders rushing toward the bus bundled in hats and scarves cradling cups of coffee to keep warm, and how special it's been to keep the bus warm for those waiting in the cold. I hear them say, 'Burr, it's cold out there today, Mildred,' or 'Gonna be a blizzard tonight,' before tugging at their scarves and removing their gloves or covering their knees with one of my blankets."

Thelma leaned closer. "You started driving the bus toward the end of summer. What was that like?"

"You know, Thelma, it's always wonderful when the ground bursts open with a fury and flower stands appear on nearly every corner and shop doors stay wide open all day, but it seems special to see it all from the bus. The stores show cotton dresses in the windows instead of down jackets, and thrift stores pull out BBQs and croquette sets to lure in buyers. Of course you already know that." She thought for a minute and looked out the window.

"I love seeing the flowers decorating the parkways, and when Simpson's hardware puts out red wheel barrows and galvanized watering cans. Then you know it's actually spring. And toward the outskirts of town, I see the neighborhood kids sitting cross-legged playing games, and young girls wearing roller skates or running and laughing through sprinklers. Miller's Market usually has bins of sweet corn and ripe watermelon, and fireworks stands are all over in parking lots and the parks. Gosh, I even see splashing in the community pool up on Third Street on my last run back to the Bus Bay. It just all looks so different from the bus, so wonderful. I feel like I'm seeing my town for the first time."

Thelma looked at her over the top of her glasses. "With all that, Mildred, do you really want to quit your job? You've just started. Give it some time."

"I just didn't know it would be this hard."

Eight

THE OVERHEAD SUN warmed her shoulders but no shadows at noon when she took her "power walk" as she called it. Dressed in red spandex tights and pink trainers from the big box store, she walked in the direction of the Myers Junction public library after struggling her way into the tights that morning. She felt trendy since drivers slowed to look when she wore spandex. "It must be the bright colors," she mumbled under her breath that day when they honked and waved. The Brown County Public Library was just four blocks from her house and she considered the walk her "workout" for the week. *Must get in some athletics*, she reminded herself.

Housed in an old red brick building formerly used as a bank, and across the road from the old Kress' five and dime, the library was a source of contention in Myers Junction. The city wanted to tear the building down for a modern structure but the residents protested by camping on the sidewalk one summer evening. The sight of a whole block of brightly-colored tents along Oleander Drive brought the press and television cameras so the city decided to keep the landmark rather than get the people riled up. Mildred had carried a protest sign herself but didn't spend the night since she feared her pajamas were becoming threadbare, and she didn't own a tent.

The library was quiet when she entered through the double doors except for the usual steam flowing through the radiator and the thud of a book or two on a nearby table. Mildred spotted Velda

Cromwell, the librarian and a friend of hers, standing behind the check-out area. Velda barely stood a head above the top of the counter. If it weren't for the pencils she stuck in her bun she might not be seen at all. Her diminutive stature belied her expansive knowledge of books, but the tight bun that held her hair close to her head and the glasses she wore low on her nose added an air of intelligence she didn't necessarily have.

Their friendship began when Mildred volunteered at the library several years ago because she enjoyed shelving new titles, choosing ones she liked before patrons put holds on them. She and Velda would occasionally go for *cocktails*, as they liked to say, but in reality it was a glass of wine and a meatloaf sandwich at Louise's Diner. When Velda met Stewart Vanderhoff in the Elks Club bowling tournament and they married, he wanted her home fixing dinner rather than going out for cocktails with friends. So she and Mildred chatted in the library, and went for cocktails only on their birthdays, even though Stewart sulked for days.

Velda spotted Mildred in the fiction section and walked over quickly when she could finally get away from the busy checkout counter. "Here for another book to read this week Mildred, or just out for a walk?"

"Actually both. It's been sort of a stressful week."

Velda looked at her over the top of her glasses. "Stressful? Somehow I don't think of you getting stressed."

"Oh, I have some difficult riders from the Gang Intervention Center and they're upsetting my other riders."

"And you."

"Yes, and me. I'm not actually sure how to handle it, Velda. They don't and won't follow the rules. I've thought about talking to someone at the school, but I don't really want to make trouble for them."

"You would rather they make trouble for you and the other passengers?"

"Yes, well when you put it that way I see your point, I guess."

"Why not just tell your boss and let him take care of it? Isn't that his job?"

"Oh, goodness, I can't, Velda. I'm on probation to see how I handle this job. If my boss thought I couldn't deal with problems on the bus he'd let me go for sure. I imagine he's just waiting for me to put the fly in the ointment."

"You have flies on the bus too? Gee, Mildred, you've got a lot going on. Hmm, flies."

"No, no . . . oh, just forget I said it."

"Well, get tough with those . . . those delinquents. And the flies too," Velda added.

The check-out line was getting longer so Velda disappeared back behind the counter. Mildred looked at the new titles, but left empty handed. She did feel somewhat better after talking to Velda about the gang of thugs, as she had come to think of them.

~~~~

Mildred always treated Saturday nights as if they were special, *kind of like date night without the date,* she thought. And even more so that Saturday night after her disappointing week with the gang of thugs. She dressed in the green satin robe she bought on sale at Gulliver's Department Store after Christmas three years ago, the one she kept on a satin hanger in the closet near the front where she could see it. She wanted to feel special that night, so when she put it on she ran her hands down her sides and twirled a few times in front of the mirror. "Scoobie do, not bad!" she said to herself before pouring a glass of *"chabliss."* Stepping into her satin slippers, she did a little soft shuffle floating across the floor to the tunes on her Perry Como record and dancing into the bedroom and back through the living room . . . "til the end of time . . . la te da te da . . . *"*

Later that evening she turned on the television set but disgusted, she soon turned it off. *Good heavens, so much negative information . . some nincompoops killing someone, or an awful war somewhere.* She wiped off the sticky marmalade jar and the chrome-rimmed Formica table in the kitchen and put another record on the turntable, this time the Andrews Sisters. *So hard to find newer tunes on LPs, and I'm sure not going to buy some newfangled kind of player when the one I have now works perfectly fine,*" she thought, as she waltzed through the house swishing her satin robe.

Since it was too early for bed, she sat in her recliner and pulled the yarn basket onto her lap looking at the pastel colors she used for knitting stocking caps for the newborn at Mercy General Hospital. When she had a dozen or so, she took them to Nurse Eloise in the Neonatal ward. She put her hand on the yarn feeling its softness, and left it there for a while. "I think this can wait until tomorrow," she said to herself in a half whisper.

Nine

A SUMMER RAIN splashed against the sides of the bus and a gale-force wind rattled the oleander bushes alongside the road as she backed the #2 bus out of the Bus Bay early Monday morning. Seeing everyone's hair blowing wild in the wind and men holding their hats meant the storm was coming from the south bringing hot and humid weather. After turning on to the main road she opened her window feeling the air already warm. Mildred enjoyed stormy days when everyone on the bus felt cozy and chatted about what mattered. Much to her disappointment though, the gang of thugs were waiting at their usual stop, this time accompanied by a young woman with orange hair and black fingernails.

"Good morning," she said, greeting them as cheerfully as she did the other riders. She had copies of the Riders Code of Conduct and handed one to each as they boarded the bus. She also put copies on the seats so they would have one every time they rode the bus. Most were turned into paper airplanes or wads to be thrown, but at least she made an attempt to inform them of the rules.

She'd learned their names by now, at least what they called each other, but not wanting to encourage conversation she just nodded when they got on the bus. Salvador was probably the oldest, maybe eighteen, and wore his pants so low she feared they would drop to the dismay of the other passengers. His white T-shirt, wet from the rain, held an unopened pack of cigarettes in the rolled sleeve.

Sonny wore his jeans low as well and had the cuffs turned up. The gold chain looped in his jeans hung down below his knee. She fantasized about yanking it from his trousers and chaining them together before throwing them off the bus. Bruno looked young. His baseball cap was turned backward and only partly hid the frizzy hair bursting from beneath. He dressed in black every day. Leon wore oversized plaid shirts and large pierced earrings that looked like bottle caps. They all made some remark as they boarded the bus.

"How you goin', bitch?"

"Hey motha' fucker."

The one they called JR was last to board. He reached over and twirled Mildred's hair. "C'mon back for a little gang bang mamma bitch," he said gyrating his hips while dropping coins in the box and laughing.

"Up Gramps." Leon was standing over an elderly man seated in the senior and disabled section and holding a cane in his lap looking confused. Leon grabbed his cane and tapped him on the head with it. "I said get up Gramps." The man rose and stumbled up front to a different seat. Mildred seethed and reached for the fire extinguisher. Walking to the back, she pointed it at Leon but then thought twice. Walking back up front she pulled back into traffic, her stomach churning.

In the next block, one of the passengers leaned over to Mildred and said, "Someone's smoking pot. I can smell it." Mildred pulled the bus over and walked to the back just as Salvador stepped on something and blew smoke at the same time. The passengers took the opportunity to move closer to the front before Mildred drove to the next stop. She dropped the ramp for one of her riders, Albert Parks, a young military amputee who lost both legs in combat. He regularly rode the bus in his wheelchair. Mildred lifted one of the aisle seats and fastened his chair to the wall with hooks.

"How are you today, Albert? Where are you off to?"

"Doctor as usual, Mildred. Nothing special, just a checkup."

Hazel Warlaumont

"Well, I guess we all need to do that from time to time," she said, putting her hand on his shoulder. By now most of the passengers were either sitting or standing in the front of the bus, and Mildred hoped for more road noise to drown out the loud conversation coming from the back.

"Wassup my homie G?"

"Nuttin, boy. What 'bout 'ju?"

"S'all good."

"Man, there was dis black boy, tryin' to act gangsta so I popped a cap in his ass."

"Dat's how we do it, boy!"

"Well, dawg, ya got my weed?"

"Uh... No..."

"No? You fucking son of bitch!"

"I'm sorry. Yo, my baby mama found it and tossed it."

"What? Why?"

"She be like, 'I don't want none of 'dis pot around my baby, no sir.'"

After that it got quiet and Mildred's breathing slowed. A few minutes later she heard loud voices in back. She heard one of the thugs calling Albert "gimpy," and Albert telling him to bug off. Then she heard Albert's voice yelling "stop it, stop it." She glanced in the mirror and saw one of the thugs by his wheelchair as it rolled down the aisle toward the back. She pulled on the hand brake and emergency flasher, and ran down the aisle in time to grab Albert by his shoulder before his chair slammed into the back row of seats.

"Are you alright?"

He shook his head for a while. "Mildred, you have your hands full here, and I'm not telling you anything you don't already know. But if I had a gun . . ."

"Shhh, don't talk like that," she said, wheeling him up toward his spot again. As she passed the gang of thugs, she noticed the orange-haired girl perched on the lap of the one smelling like tobacco and menthol while he gyrated up and down to the hysterical laughter of his friends.

"Hey, momma boss, you wanna be next?" and they laughed and cheered.

She felt the perspiration on the back of her neck and both hands were shaking visibly when she got Albert back in place and his wheelchair fastened to the hooks again.

She pulled the lever to open the back door and walked to the rear. "Get off, get off the bus right now. All of you, all of you get off, get off!" she yelled. Her body shook along with her voice. She remembered reading in the manual that drivers cannot touch or assault passengers.

"I said, get off this bus."

The gang of thugs broke out in laugher.

"Come sit on my lap bitch and I'll get it off," one said, and they all laughed and danced around her, taunting her, pulling her hair, chanting "get it off, get it off."

She stumbled backward and ran to the front, her hands still shaking as she closed the doors and pulled out in traffic, almost hitting the car next to her. As the riders filed off at their stops, Mrs. Leary stopped for a moment.

"Too much testosterone in the world these days, Mildred. And don't look at what they just did to the back of the bus."

~~~~

At the Bus Bay later that afternoon Spencer watched as she backed into her spot. She saw his look of concern as he caught sight of her through the windshield. Glancing in the mirror she saw herself, hot, tired, and strands of hair stuck to the perspiration on her face just below her hairline. She pulled her damp blouse loose from her waist and wiped her face on her sleeve, and then waited for Spencer.

She looked toward the back and then opened the door. Spencer stared. Her posture was different, her face flushed with angst.

"What happened, Mildred?"

They walked to the back looking at the graffiti scratched on the metal seat frames and scribbled on the walls and ads above the windows.

"You don't need to put up with this. They're hoodlums and should be treated that way."

"They unhooked Albert's wheelchair and I caught him just in time, Spencer. I told them to get off the bus. I lost my temper, something I said I'd never do but I did. They just laughed."

"Is Albert alright?"

She gripped her mouth and tears ran down her hand.

"Oh, Mildred."

"He doesn't have any legs, Spencer, and they unhooked his wheelchair," she sobbed.

"Let's go outside," he said, and they walked to the front of the bus and out to the lot. Spencer took a deep breath. "You need to talk to Studebaker, Mildred."

She shielded her eyes from the sun. "I know. It's just that I'm trying to keep my job. I can't physically remove the thugs and I don't really have the authority to do that anyway. A few of the men offered to throw them off the bus but it's my job to keep the peace. And it's more than just throwing them off the bus. They can sue me if I touch them in any way, according to the driver's manual."

"But something has to be done. Your safety and that of your riders . . . this just can't go on."

"I know. I know. I just don't know what more I can do. I'm reporting this every day on my daily log. I called the police last week and they said it's generally a matter between the private bus company and the vandals, unless it's a physical assault, and then it becomes a police matter. If the damage is severe enough, the owner can file a report with the police department but the complaint must come from the owner."

"Mildred, Mildred. Then go to Studebaker. He'll see it's not your fault, and maybe he'll even have a solution. At the very least, he needs to file a police report. "

"Argh, you know what a prim pit he is. But, you're right. I'll make an appointment to see him."

"I can go with you."

"I think I should do this alone, Spencer. Jeeze, we don't want him to fire you as well. But . . . but thank you."

Ten

MILDRED WAITED for Roger Studebaker to look up from his desk. Looking around the room, she sat with her hands in her lap and hooked her feet around the chair legs, As minutes passed, her eyes finally settled on the top of his bald head. Some of the other drivers suspected his wife, Peggy, rubbed face powder on his head each morning to take away the shine, but Mildred couldn't tell from her angle. Studebaker studied the papers in front of him and mumbled something under his breath before looking up.

"So, what is it you wanted to see me about? We're all quite busy here as usual," he said, glancing at his watch. The small fan on his desk ruffled the papers in front of him, lifting each one in waves until he slapped his hand on top of the stack.

She forced a smile and murmured, "Oh, swell," under her breath and shifted in her seat. *Just my luck he's in his usual foul mood.*

"I appreciate you taking the time to see me. I hate to bother you with this right now, Supervisor Studebaker, but I have an important matter to discuss. You see, I have a problem on my route I think you should know about."

"Hah!" He smiled and shook his head knowingly. "Well of course you do, Miss Pen . . . er Mildred. What did you expect?" He glanced to make sure the door was closed. "This is a man's job, my dear, and I don't know what your problem is but of course you can't handle it." His sarcastic grin settled on his face.

She resisted the urge to slouch in her chair. "I think this is a matter for management sir, since I've gone as far as I can without exceeding my limited authority." He sat back in his chair looking at his watch while she explained, at length, the situation with the gang of thugs, but then corrected herself, calling them *young men* instead.

"I've written a report as required, according to the operations manual, and documented the situation. I think the passengers' safety is at stake as well as the safety of the bus, sir. The disruptions are getting worse, the smoke from the marijuana is bothering the passengers, and the bus is being vandalized."

He sat cold as snow with one eyebrow raised. "Were they really fornicating, I mean the girl with the orange hair and one of the young men?"

"I don't honestly know sir, but their other offenses are of a more serious nature. I mean, Albert Parks. That situation could have been disastrous. Their language and behavior are driving all the passengers to the front of the bus, many standing in the aisles. I've studied the Driver's Manual and know I don't have the means or the authority to remove them from the bus. The manual instructs . drivers to consult a supervisor in these matters."

He ran his hand over his head and she stretched to see if there was powder on it when he put it down on the desk. There wasn't.

"Of course you realize this kind of behavior would not happen if a man was driving the bus – which is of course *normal*. These boys see your weaknesses, your lack of . . . well, let's just say 'know how.'"

"What I'd like to suggest sir, is for you to file a police report outlining the repeated incidents. This has to come from you as a representative of the company. It can't come from me. I'm not sure what the police will do, but it seems a step in the right direction, sir. Maybe if the delinquents knew about the report, it might be a deterrent."

"What? Have you gone mad? You expect me to broadcast this absurd situation to the town and the mayor just because you are incapable of handling a group of little boys on your bus?" He slammed his hand down on the table. "This can't go any further than this office, do you hear? The entire community is behind the new Gang Intervention Center. I mean, even the mayor was at the ribbon cutting ceremony and has encouraged us all to be supportive. You do know he's up for re-election?" He ran his hand over his head again. "I've made a small donation to his campaign and . . . well, I might even be running for the city council in the near future," he said with a prissy grin, looking up as if posing for a portrait. "This embarrassing situation is strictly between us, do you understand?"

She blew her nose.

"You must put a stop to this behavior on your bus without turning this into some kind of public embarrassment or media circus! If this were to get out, along with news we've hired a woman driver, we will be the laughing stock of everyone, and . . . and come into disfavor with the mayor." He leaned forward and growled, "I don't need to remind you that you are on probation with this company. I warn you, this situation must be handled quietly and discretely as soon as possible, or you will get your two-week notice, is that clear, Miss Per . . . , oh, whatever?"

She sighed. "Yes sir, but may I ask how I might do that? There are five or six of them all intent on causing trouble and too big to be handled physically. It's difficult to change their behavior without knowing how."

"Miss Periwinkle . . ."

"Penniwink."

"If you don't know how to do your job, then you will be let go immediately, and without a two-week notice!" He slammed his hand on the desk and reached for the fan, switching the power to high indicating the conversation was over.

Her thick, rubber-soled shoes thumped as she walked from the room.

Roger Studebaker stared, and then picked up his pencil and

went back to work.

"Well, Scooby do, that was a bust," she said to the secretary in a sarcastic tone as she tucked a glob of hair behind her ear and left.

~~~~~

Spencer had his hands on his hips. "And he didn't offer any help or agree to file a police report?"

"No, the jackass just said handle it and don't make a fuss or he'll fire me."

"Isn't this his job, to supervise? Is there a plan B?"

"Ahh . . . not really Spencer. At least I talked to him about it. That's what I'm supposed to do according to the manual. My job is even more insecure than ever. He threatened to fire me even without a two-week notice. I don't know what to do at this point. Cripes, I feel like a tractor with its wheel in a ditch."

~~~~~

Mildred watched Sumo wrestling when she vacuumed. She thought it gave her more energy. The grunts and groans seemed to coincide with her own as she pushed and pulled the vacuum through the house. That night she dragged out the vacuum and turned on the television, changing channels until she found the wrestling. Then she sat and watched up close with a new interest. The most intriguing part of Sumo wrestling, she discovered, was the goal, and that was to force the opponent out of the ring.

"Hmm, force them out of the ring?" she said to herself. "Force them out . . ." She began to picture herself in a loincloth and barefoot.

In the weeks to come, Mildred became a Sumo wrestler determined to force the gang of thugs off her bus. Since her regular riders now avoided the damaged senior and disabled seats, she started sprinkling those seats with water just before the thugs got on. She watched as they plopped down onto the seats seemingly unfazed their pants were getting wet, so she tried Dr. Pepper the following week but still no response. *They're probably too high to notice,* she surmised.

Hazel Warlaumont

After work one night, Mildred stopped at the Woolworths store and grabbed a shopping cart so no one could see all the gum she was buying. She threw in some paper towels to make it look like she was buying bulky items. Irma Snyder, the checker, looked up just then and waved. *Oh, good lord!* She'd known Irma before Irma's hair turned, her muscles softened, and her eyes got glassy. In all those years, Irma never rang Mildred's purchases without commenting on what she was buying.

"Hi Mildred, whatta ya going to do with all that gum?"

Mildred grimaced. *It might as well have come over the loud speaker!* Mildred made herself look smaller and looked down, hoping no one would recognize her. She and Irma used to play bridge at the Grange on Tuesday nights until Irma's temper got so bad no one would play with her. That was before the rule that you could only throw your cards three times before being asked to leave, so Irma had to leave soon after that. But, since she only threw her cards once at Mildred, they became friends. The two would play two-handed bridge at Irma's apartment on occasion until Irma's eyesight went. About that time the five and dime store installed scanners, so Irma didn't have to use a magnifying glass to see the prices. That's when she started announcing what patrons had in their carts, probably to let people know her eyesight wasn't that bad after all.

"The gum? Oh I just chew it when I drive sometimes to make the time go by. Nothing more than that, Irma."

Irma looked puzzled but put everything in a bag and they exchanged niceties before the next person in line moved forward.

~~~~

Both Mildred and Spencer took pride in the bus, picking up trash at the end of each day, and making sure it was all wiped down and ready for the following morning. So it was particularly upsetting for her to stick gum on the senior/disabled seats. She'd chewed several packs during the day and once back in the bus bay, placed a wad on each seat where the gang of thugs sat. As usual, the following day the obnoxious thugs filed on the bus all revved up and full of expletives. She closed the door quickly, hoping it would close on the last one.

"Oops," she said, pursing her lips to hide a smile. Leon inched in unscathed much to her disappointment.

She looked in the mirror at each stop to see if the thugs knew they were sitting on sticky gum, but it was just before their usual stop when she heard the screaming.

"What the fuck?" Salvador yelled looking over his shoulder and feeling the back of his pants. Long strands of gum stuck to his low-riding jeans and now to his hands. The others jumped up, and before long she noticed strands of gum strung everywhere.

"Stop the bus, stop the bus," one of them yelled. She pulled to the curb even though it was not an official stop. Wrapped in gooey strings of gum, they jumped off, pulling at the mess as she drove off.

Yippy! Surely, this will do it. They're not about to put up with this again, Mildred thought.

She laughed, taking her hands off the wheel momentarily to clap. She wanted to stand on the seat and honk the horn with her foot, she was so happy. *Finally, a way to keep the thugs from riding the bus!* She worked hard that night at the Bus Bay cleaning up the gummy mess but didn't care. That night she had two glasses of *chabliss* and danced around the living room to the music of the Andrews Sisters. "La de da, hmm, eight to the bar . . . boogie woogie bugle boy . . ."

~~~~

"No need to stand in the aisle, folks," she announced the following afternoon to the gleeful cheers of her regular riders. "Take whatever seat you like even in the senior and disabled section." She loved hearing the joyful chatter as people chose their favorite seat once again.

But shortly after four that afternoon she felt like she had been hit in the chest with a bag of bricks. *Oh good lord!* Ahead, she saw the thugs gyrated and yelled as usual at the bus stop. She heard the moans from riders on the bus and pounded her fist on the steering wheel as she fought back the tears. *This can't be! I was sure. . . .* After her regular riders got off, the gang of thugs bounded up into the bus.

I'll never get them off now. She slouched in her seat until she heard the line of honking cars behind her.

Eleven

THE TELEVISION blared in the background while Mildred cooked chicken and gravy. A few minutes later she turned the sound up, hoping it would drown out her thoughts as she pushed the food around on her plate.

"Twelve were gunned down before police killed the shooter. Police still don't have any idea of a motive. Neighbors painted a picture of a man who kept his lawn mowed and attended church every Sunday. This is Roger Williams from WKPK."

"Oh, for god's sake!" she said out loud. "What difference does it make if he mows his lawn?" She changed the channel and took her dishes to the sink.

"The House passed a resolution requiring all federal employees to take sensitivity training in regard to sexual harassment given the surge of molestation complaints filed by female legislators and aides."

"Swell." She changed the channel again.

"Troops are being sent to . . ."

"Really?" she yelled as she turned the television off in a huff. "Has everyone gone bollywonkers? Is everything about violence?"

She sat in her recliner and let her arms fall to the sides. A few minutes later she reached for her notepad and pencil and scribbled the word *testosterone,* looking at it while tapping her pencil.

~~~

The following morning Mildred spread her uniform on the bed as usual and turned on the television long enough for the weather report. But the screen was black and there was no sound, even when she changed channels.

"Cripes, not the cable again," giving the television set a pounding for good measure. She glanced at her watch. *Argh, at least time for one phone call.*

"I have no service, is there an outage?" she asked politely. "No sir, you may not put me on hold. Last month I was on hold over an hour." She glanced at her watch.

"No, I can't call back later, I drive a bus."

"No, there's no one else who can call for me. The screen is black and there is no sound." She walked back and forth in front of the television.

"Of course I tried different channels," she said slipping into her shoes and looking at her watch again.

"Yes, the set is plugged in." *What a nillywit! Where do they get these people?*

"No, I don't have children who tamper with the knobs," she said, raising her voice. "Please, can you just tell me the problem? Is there a general outage?"

"No, I can't make an appointment to come in. Must you continue to badger me in this way? I work for the Brown Country Transit Authority, certainly that must mean something." *Getting something out of this jackass is like nailing jelly to a wall,* she thought as she paced floor.

"May I speak to a supervisor please?" She looked at her watch again.

"He's busy? Well what about another one?"

"I don't know why you are being so hostile, and I understand you probably do have better things to do than talk to me." *Although I'm not sure what, you nincompoop!*

She took a deep breath. "What do you mean my service has been disconnected and I should have known that?"

"The prices have increased? Again? Well my service hasn't increased. I get the same lousy channels I always have. Besides, I have a two-year contract, signed just a few months ago."

"You don't offer that package anymore? What do I need to do to get my service back on?"

"How much?"

When she left that morning she slammed the door so hard the picture of Jesus teetered on the wall, and dust flew off the umbrella stand near the door.

~~~~

Mildred trudged up the steps to the library a little past noon, her eyes cast down. "Morning Mildred," Velda said, waving from behind the counter. "I haven't seen you in a blue moon."

Mildred turned toward the checkout counter and spotted the pencils in Velda's bun. They looked like little yellow antennas as Velda walked toward her.

"I've been busy I guess," Mildred said. "And I just had an argument with the cable company again since they raised my rates, and I'm also trying to get some bulbs planted when Buster's not around," she added." How about you, and did you know you had all those pencils in your bun?"

"Oh, that's where they are. No wonder I can't find any at the counter."

"Yes, hmm, no wonder."

"You sound pretty busy, Mildred. You have me worried now since my cable bill hasn't come yet this month."

"Well be prepared." Mildred nodded as if conveying a grave warning and then leaned closer, "I have a question for you, Velda."

Mildred looked around and motioned her over to the History aisle. She said in a half whisper, "If I wanted to know something about testosterone where would I look?"

Velda stammered wide-eyed. "Testo . . . testosterone? What on earth . . . I mean goodness Mildred, we all get a little fuzz on our face at our age. If you have any it doesn't show," she said in a tiny voice.

"No you ninny, it's something else," Mildred said, standing up straight. "I'm just curious about how it affects . . . well you know, behavior, things like that. Mrs. Leary said something on the bus when the thugs were acting up. When she left, she said 'there must be too much testosterone in the world.'"

Velda blinked rapidly.

"I want to know if testosterone causes antisocial behavior, Velda; you know, being obnoxious, pushy."

"Oh, does testosterone cause that?"

"That's what I want to find out."

"Well . . . the computer is a good place to start, but I know you don't use one."

"You're darn right. Just when you do find something it slips right off the machine."

Velda looked at Mildred's hands and short thick fingers. "Hmm, yes. I see what you mean."

"So what kind of book would have something like general information on testosterone?"

"Well okay, let's start with the medical encyclopedia. C'mon I'll show you."

Mildred eyed Velda's bun as they walked to the back wondering how she got her hair in that tight knot. *Hmm, I can see how it might be good for storing pencils and . . .*

"Any one of these will give you some general information on testosterone, probably all you want to know." Velda turned to face her. "Is someone bothering you, Mildred? Why on earth would you want to know all about pushy people? Is it that dog again, or that

Mildred Penniwink   53

crotchety neighbor Agnes Bombgunner?"

"Angus Baumgartner. No, it's just that those . . . those thugs on the bus are getting to me." Mildred's shoulders dropped and she let her hands fall to her sides. "I could lose my job over this."

Velda gasped and put her hand to her mouth. "But it's not your fault."

"No but since I'm on probation my supervisor said to put an end to the disruptions or he'll let me go. He didn't want to hire me in the first place, so it wouldn't take much for him to fire me. I've tried everything I can think of, but nothing seems to be working." Her voice turned to a whisper. "I'm thinking about what Mrs. Leary said in a moment of disgust about too much testosterone in the world."

"Well, she might know," Velda said. "She's president of the League of Women Voters."

Mildred narrowed her eyes. "If it's true, then there might be a fix."

"Oh my! This sounds serious!" Velda shook her head slowly, *probably so she wouldn't displace her pencils*, Mildred guessed, as she watched her.

"Well, start with these encyclopedias, and we can order more books if you need more."

Mildred swung her purse strap over her shoulder and took three heavy volumes from the shelf before staggering to a table and dropping them with a thud. She looked around sheepishly and then pulled them toward her one at a time.

Testosterone is the primary male sex hormone and plays a key role in the development of male reproductive tissues and in promoting secondary sexual characteristics such as increased muscle and bone mass, and possible aggressive tendencies.

Mildred pulled her shoulders back and wiped her nose twice with her index finger. "Humph, just as I suspected," she whispered to herself before reading more. Then she found the ammunition she'd been looking for:

Hazel Warlaumont

If your healthcare provider suspects that you have low or high testosterone, then he or she will first test total testosterone levels. Behavioral symptoms may occur when total testosterone is high.

"Aha!" she blurted out creating an echo. Library patrons looked her way, and Velda's head popped up above the counter in alarm, but she quickly looked down putting everyone's concern at rest.

Mildred sat staring at the words, *when total testosterone is high.* She slammed the book shut and almost skipped back to the counter.

"Well?" Velda said.

Mildred stood with both hands on the counter and her purse hanging from her neck. "I'm on to something," she said resolutely. "I need something more important, you know . . . beyond medical descriptions."

Velda tightened her lips and raised her finger above her head before busily pulling up titles on her computer. "Do you want books, or chapters in books?"

"Everything! Books, yes books, as many as you can find."

"We can get books on loan from the university library. Did you find something of interest in the encyclopedias?" she said still working at the computer.

"Yes, yes, some encouraging clues," Mildred said, leaning forward and whispering. "Listen to this, Velda." She opened the encyclopedia on the counter.

"As male robins enter the breeding season their testosterone level rises. They become aggressive and amorous." Mildred wet the end of her pencil with her tongue and underlined the passage with such vigor that Velda gasped.

"Mildred . . . Mildred!" Velda whispered in a high pitch.

Mildred's tongue rested just beyond her lips and her eyes were on fire as she continued underlining the passage, hunched over as if she'd just discovered the Ten Commandments. Velda grabbed the pencil and yanked it from her hand. "We can't write in the books, Mildred," she said in her loudest whisper.

She quickly put the pencil in her library apron and shook her head. "What's the matter with you? You're not yourself these days."

Mildred raised her chin a bit and patted the encyclopedia before gathering her notes. She stood for a moment with her purse still hanging from her neck, and her coat still draped over the chair.

Velda went behind the counter and sat for a moment. "Good lord," Mildred heard her say before rushing out the door.

Twelve

THAT EVENING, Mildred was in the kitchen when she saw Velda's car pull into the driveway. Velda sat for a minute before walking up to the front door and ringing the doorbell.

"Velda, what a nice surprise. Come in," Mildred said, swatting at the bugs going frantic around the porch light. "I was just pouring a glass of *chabliss* and now I can pour two. Sit down, slip your shoes off." Mildred went into the kitchen and reappeared with two jelly glasses of wine.

"You left your coat in the library today and I wanted to bring it by thinking you might need it," Velda said, putting the coat on a chair and looking around the living room with all the recent kitsch from the thrift shop.

"How nice, thank you Velda. Aren't you expected home about now? Will Stewart be worried? Do you want to call him?" They clinked glasses and Mildred sat with her shoes off wondering why Velda was really there. It wasn't like her to stop by just to deliver a coat.

"Oh, Stu can wait. Mildred we've been friends for a long time and I'm . . . well, a little concerned about you . . . the books on testosterone and today in the library you seemed upset, even obsessed. I think we should talk. You know you can trust my discretion."

"I'm really sorry about today, and disturbing the patrons in the library. I feel my life has been upended to say the least."

Velda listened to Mildred's dilemma. "And you think it will jeopardize your job if you talked to your supervisor again? What's happening is horrible and could escalate into something worse. Can't you just kick those jerks off the bus?"

"How? I'm afraid it would take Superman to get them to budge, and they just laugh at me no matter what I say. They push the other riders aside and barge on and take over the bus. Everyone's afraid of them. Besides, we take an oath to treat all riders the same and with respect. We aren't supposed to discriminate and especially now with the new Gang Intervention Center supposedly a feather in the cap of the mayor. The driver's manual warns that riders can sue us if we discriminate, but on the other hand I have a supervisor telling me to stop the disruptions and damage or he'll fire me. And he can do that because I'm hired conditionally and on six months' probation. So, I'm left straddling a rising creek."

"A creek?"

"Velda, I need to get these thugs off the bus. I'm convinced it's the testosterone, and if I can think of a way to lower it . . . well, it might solve the problem."

"But you can't be sure. I mean if that's the case wouldn't someone have thought of that before? Violence is everywhere in the world."

"There seems to be a clear connection between testosterone and behavior but the books say it's a naturally occurring hormone so no one questions it. And what man would even want it reduced if it threatened his manhood or sex drive? Normal levels are not the problem, it's when testosterone gets out of whack and causes aggression, at least that's what I'm reading."

"Gosh, Mildred, when you put it that way. So what about the creek?"

"Jeeze, Velda. Just forget I said that. I was just . . . oh, never mind the part about the creek.

~~~~~

Mildred went to the library regularly each week to pick up the books she requested on testosterone. On one occasion, Velda pulled her to the Maps section to tell her the cable company raised her rates. "And, they weren't even nice about it. Could it be the testosterone, Mildred? I know they weren't very nice to you either. Goodness, I'm beginning to suspect everyone."

"Yes, I'm seeing it everywhere too. I'm convinced the overgrowth of testosterone is rampant. Imagine even the cable company! How else can we explain the aggressive behavior and greediness for no reason? The problem is more serious than I thought," Mildred said with worry on her face.

"Oh my, that explains the clerk at Dawson's Market. You know, the man with the thick glasses. He refused to ring up my groceries because I was in the *Ten Items or Less* line. Sure, I had a few extra boxes of Jell-O but can you imagine making me go to another line? I've never heard of such a thing. I think he was just mean!"

"Hmm yes, aggression, and don't forget about control."

"Oh, no! Aggression *and* control too?"

"I'm noticing it everywhere, Velda, on the news, the wars, the mass shootings, and even Angus Baumgartner and his dog Buster. Oh jiminy cricket, especially Buster! Now I know why people get their dogs fixed when they're pups or make them stay on the porch. It makes perfect sense!"

On the way home, Mildred stopped by Simpson's hardware to buy some plants, colorful ones, the winter blooms she promised herself after thinking the house looked so bare without color. She thought if she moved about quietly Buster wouldn't know she was in the yard. The following afternoon she pulled on her gloves and gathered her spade and her value pack of yellow pansies and staked out the perfect spot near the porch. *Plenty of sun here* she mused while digging the first hole. It was then she saw him coming, tongue and lips flapping, all fours off the ground.

"No, git, no," she yelled and then rushed inside just as Buster's front paws landed at the foot of the stairs.

"Shoo, shoo," she hollered, shaking the broom through the small crack in the door. But by then Buster was sniffing in the garden and standing on her value pack of pansies.

~~~~

To take her mind off her day, Mildred walked four and a half blocks to Mercy General Hospital to deliver her knitted caps to the Neonatal ward. In her best week she could knit seven or eight little stocking caps in the evenings; some pink, some blue, an occasional yellow. In the colder months when daylight gave way to the encroaching winter nights, she'd put her slippers on over a pair of wool socks and sit in the recliner with her basket of yarn on her lap. Lately though, two or three hats were about all she could muster with all she had on her mind. The hospital had a supply of hats for infants just born, but the nurses in the nursery were always glad to get Mildred's hats.

Nurse Eloise liked to remind her. "The mothers want to think their newborn is wearing a cap hand knit by someone in the community, rather than one saying *Made in Taiwan*."

When she came through the double doors to the hospital nursery that afternoon, Mildred spotted Nurse Eloise at the nurse's station doing some paperwork. Eloise always seemed pleased to see her.

"Oh Mildred, pink this week? How'd you know we had more girls than boys today?" She held up the little hats. "These are adorable with the little crocheted bunnies sewn on. Look girls what Mildred brought," she yelled in spite of sleeping babies in the next room. Two nurses folding blankets waved to Mildred.

"How many babies born this week?" Mildred asked while straining to look through the glass at the nursery. She put her hand on the glass and pressed her face close.

"Can you believe we had eight, five girls and three boys? One boy is in the incubator but he's doing well. Just real well," Nurse

Eloise repeated and moved closer. "Mildred, want to hold one?" she whispered. "The little girl at the end of the row is going home in the morning. You can sit and hold her if you like. She's real sweet."

"No. I have to go." Mildred pulled her coat tight in front and folded her arms before leaving.

"Okay, we'll see you next week," Nurse Eloise yelled. But Mildred was just closing the door behind her.

"Bye, Mildred," another said and waved as she left, and "byes" could be heard softly from others even after the door closed.

"I thought she might stay this time," one of the nurses said to Eloise. "It would be good for her."

"Yes, yes maybe in time."

"Don't you think enough time has passed? What do you think is holding her back?"

"Well, probably herself. She hasn't yet dealt with her loss. Sometimes it just takes a long time."

Thirteen

SHAFTS OF MUTED LIGHT streamed through her car windshield as Mildred sat watching the miniscule specks of dust caught in the beam of sunlight. Recognizing the symptoms, she tried to catch her breath and wiped her sweaty palms on the cloth seat of her car, Her doctor said to come by the office the next time it happened and she knew he was working late that day. She decided to stop by on her way home from the Neonatal ward at the hospital.

Mildred settled into the brown leather chair and looked at the family photos lining Dr. Rob's desk, and the golfing trophies on the shelf next to his diplomas. She tapped her finger on the arm of the chair. She'd known Dr. Robert Phillips for years and while he was always professional in the office, they were long-time friends like practically everyone else in Myers Junction.

A few minutes later she had an answer. "Anxiety attacks? Good grief, what are those?"

"Mildred, everyone goes through times of stress and the body reacts in a protective way to prepare for battle or self-preservation. I wouldn't be concerned, but when do these happen? I mean, you just came from the hospital nursery so that must provide a clue."

"Yes, well sometimes I have them at night when a disturbing dream wakes me and I imagine the house is completely empty, like no furniture or books on the shelf, or pictures on the wall, or clothes in the closets. It seems there's an echo inside the house I can't explain, so I walk through the house at night to reassure myself that it's just a normal house with furniture and a clock on the mantle."

"Well, empty houses do have an echo, especially without rugs on the floor or furniture to absorb sound. Do these feelings usually come on at night?"

"No, not really. The ones during the day are a little different. I sometimes dread going home after work or when I've been out because I'm afraid everything might be gone. I guess it's similar to the empty house fear. Sometimes I stop at the thrift shop to buy something, even something small in case the house really is empty. It sounds so silly doesn't it?"

"No, not at all . . . not at all. What you're describing are feelings you may not be ready or willing to deal with. You've had some losses, and we all react to loss in different ways. It's healthy to get it out. Do you have someone to talk to?"

"Myself."

He laughed. "Mildred, I can prescribe something or refer you to a professional therapist if you like, but I suspect you will deal with this in your own way. Just knowing to go to the thrift shop for some household item is one way. It makes you feel better. By the way, Patti and I are having a garage sale next weekend . . ."

Mildred reached over and swatted him on the arm. "You goof ball."

"Seriously Mildred, remember that your furniture is just a manifestation of something less tangible, something deeper. When these attacks come on, try to think of what might be missing, although you probably already know but aren't ready to deal with it. Bring it out into the open when you're ready. A therapist can help with that."

"Oh, I don't know what I'd even say to a therapist. I don't have any hidden secrets."

He sat and tapped his finger on the desk. "Sometimes the most devastating secrets are the ones we keep from ourselves, Mildred."

~~~~

Thelma dropped a handful of clothes on the counter before looking up. "How are you doing, kiddo?" she asked when she saw Mildred come through the door.

"Ah, I'm doing okay. The house is feeling a little barren. You know how it is. How about you, Thelma, did you get that bedroom painted?"

"I sure did, and I painted it myself. How about those apples?"

"Oh, my, I'm totally impressed. Good for you."

Thelma looked at her askance. "We got a shipment from an estate sale yesterday. You know, those older things you like. Take a look around, find something you like."

"Oh, I don't know, I have so many things right now, truth be known."

Thelma smiled. "There are no simple truths to anyone's life, Mildred, be known or not. Do you think you're ready to bring in those things from your spare room, you know all those unopened boxes? It's just a thought. There's always a need for baby things in the store. Maybe you might sleep better at night. What do you think?"

Mildred shrugged and changed the topic. A few minutes later, Thelma rang up two colorful pillows for Mildred's couch in the living room, a dollar each.

"Thank you," Mildred said, giving her a little hug.

"You know Mildred, some days are just crappier than others."

Mildred paused at the door and smiled before leaving.

~~~~

"Clean 'er for you tonight, Mildred?" Spencer was waiting for her to pull into the Bus Bay. She didn't have the heart to ask him to clean the bus these days now that the gang of thugs had taken over and trashed it each day.

"Just the windows, Spencer, I'll do the rest."

She had a box for lost items on the bus and each night she and

Spencer gathered gloves or umbrellas that got reclaimed the following day with a wink and a smile after Mildred urged her riders to check the box. She also kept some lightweight acrylic blankets in the box up front, but no longer on the seats since the gang of thugs started using them in the back.

She told Spencer, "I don't know what they do under those blankets and I don't want to know. But some of the regular riders use them when a cool draft plays havoc with old elbows and knees. It's not unusual to see Agnes Merriweather or Darleen Fitsworth with one thrown over their lap on cool days."

He nodded. "Yes, all the more reason to keep 'em up front."

"Windows look good, Spencer, they're nice and shiny," she said, sitting on the last step filling out her daily report. She stared at the list.

☐ Violence or threats of violence

☐ Displaying a weapon

☐ Any illegal activity

☐ Unwelcome physical contact

☐ Damaging another's property or the bus

☐ Shouting, profanity, unruly behavior

☐ Use of drugs or alcohol on the bus

☐ Being intoxicated from use of drugs or alcohol

☐ Interfering with other passengers

"I'm damned if I do and damned if I don't, Spencer. Filling out the daily log is an admission that I continue to have major problems on the bus. Studebaker can use this as a reason to fire me." She checked every one and put it in the office box.

"Are you sure you don't want to talk to the supervisor again, Mildred? You've been looking awfully tired lately."

"No . . . No, I think that would be like talking to a dead goose," she said while taking one more peek inside the bus. "I guess we can put this grand old bus to bed for the night, don't you think? You have a good evening, Spencer."

"You too, Miss Penniwink. Get a good night's sleep. You carry a satchel full of burdens that seems way too big for such a nice lady."

Fourteen

THE COLD BIT her face that night as she hurried inside flinging her gray sweater and scarf on the bed, and stopping to straighten the chintz spread at the corner. "Hmm, missed it this morning," she mumbled to herself, and then remembered being rushed before work preparing one of her new perfumed concoctions to spray on the senior/disabled seats that afternoon. The *Broken Seat* sign didn't work the day before. She sighed and sat on the edge of the bed, remembering when she used to say *every day was a day made in heaven*!

She noticed the blinking light on the answering machine and detected a lilt in Velda's high-pitched voice. "Mildred, it's Velda. Guess what? Some of your books on . . . well, you know what, arrived. I'll hold them for you at the desk. Bye." Mildred looked at her watch. *Ah, I'll just make it,* she thought as she headed to the library before closing time.

Velda was dimming the lights to alert patrons the library was about to close when Mildred rushed in. "Mildred, I didn't expect you to come tonight, but glad you did."

Velda moved close and whispered, "three of your books came in! I browsed through them on my lunch break and . . . oh my, wait until you read this," She pulled a white slip of paper from the book on top. Mildred put her face right down into the book and anxiously read the passage next to Velda's index finger.

It's commonly assumed that testosterone, that stereotypically male hormone, is intimately tied to violence.

Mildred and Velda looked at each other both wide-eyed. Mildred read on silently.

Experiments demonstrate that testosterone is necessary for violence. Male violence disappears after castration.

"Aha! Snipping. Just as I suspected," Mildred said so loud that Velda gave her a nudge with her elbow and a "shhh."

"We have to be quiet, Mildred, especially about . . . you know, the *T* word." She whispered it as if the word was forbidden.

"Oh, goodnight Mr. Harmon," Velda said as the last patron left. She put the *Closed* sign in the window and when she returned, Mildred was scribbling with her pencil in one of the books.

"Mildred, no!" she said rushing toward her. "You cannot write in the books. Here, use these scraps of papers to make notes and then stick them into your books as markers."

"Oh, sorry. I forgot, but listen to this," and she pointed to a passage.

The most violent prisoners have higher levels of testosterone than their less violent peers. Scientists hypothesize that this violence is just one manifestation of the much more biologically and salient goal of dominance.

Mildred looked at Velda. "Dominance! That's what it's all about. That describes the thugs on the bus, and the cable company, and all those killers out there, and the politicians, and Baumgartner and his dog. And get this," she said, running her finger down the page and reading:

It has been suggested that the antisocial behaviors related to high testosterone are a function of dominance in these groups.

Mildred scribbled *Dominance* with a heavy hand on a piece of scrap paper and put it in as a marker. She looked at Velda for approval. Velda nodded when she saw Mildred using the scrap paper instead of writing in the book.

"This tells us what we need to know, Velda; this is exactly

what I suspected."

"Oh, my," Velda said looking confused.

~~~~

The following week, Mildred visited Dr. Rob again in his office. She followed Nurse Marjory down a hall to a room painted lime green. "It's good to see you in here again, Mildred."

"Thank you, Marjory. I have something I want to talk to the doctor about. Just a little conversation . . . you know, just a talk . . . no health problems."

"We'll let's put you in his office then. It's more comfortable there." Mildred followed, admiring her nurse's shoes with the extra thick soles, much thicker than her own regulation bus shoes.

"Mildred!" Dr. Rob said, bounding into the office with a file in his hand. He lowered his voice. "Feeling a little better about things?" he said putting his hand briefly on her shoulder.

"Yes, everything is good, Dr. Rob."

"Well, did you come for a referral or some meds for the anxiety thing?" He took out a prescription pad from a drawer.

"No, no I'm fine. I have some questions about something else today. You see, well I'm mostly curious, but I wanted to know something about test . . . well, testosterone. I've been reading some books in the library . . ."

"Mildred, Mildred, you haven't even gone through menopause, and all women change as they age; you know, a little facial fuzz and thinning hair, shifts in where they store fat. You have no reason to be concerned at all about testosterone." He sat in his chair and put her folder down in front of him.

"Well, actually my questions are more general. You know, on a worldly level. I wanted to know if testosterone is responsible for abnormal or violent behavior. I read that when male Robins enter the breeding season their testosterone level rises and they become aggressive."

He threw his head back and then stared at her before opening her chart, leafing through the pages before looking up. "Mildred, we are not the same as Robins. The prevailing view is that human behavior is regulated by higher cognitive processes. Reason cools the blood and allows us to take responsibility for our own actions. So testosterone doesn't run amok, if that's your concern."

"I know, but you can't deny aggression happens. I mean, I see it every day on the television."

He took off his stethoscope and laid it on the desk and leaned back in his chair. He was about the same age as her but graying at the temples and a bit overweight, making him appear somewhat older.

"Mildred, what's this all about? This isn't like you. You're always so rational, practical. Why are you so concerned about testosterone?"

"Well, uh okay, I have some young thugs on my bus every day, and they're disruptive and putting graffiti all over, and swearing, and obscene . . ."

"Ah, I see. And you want to understand their behavior, is that right? Can't you kick them off the bus or have them arrested? Understanding people's behavior is complicated and probably more complex than just hormones."

"But I've read in books that when convicts were given medication or castrated their aggression and need for dominance goes away."

"But Mildred, you can't castrate these young men," he said trying not to laugh but did anyway. "And some argue that the cause and effect of testosterone and violence is not clear. It could very well be that aggression and or dominance can increase testosterone instead of the other way around. And in spite of the literature, testosterone can have positive effects."

"Like what, domestic violence and raising our cable rates because of greed, or mass shootings, and invading other countries for their oil? Women don't have testosterone and don't do those things, do they?"

Hazel Warlaumont

He squinted. "Mildred, Mildred, all women do have small amounts of testosterone and work at the cable company, and for the government, and commit crimes and become aggressive."

"Oh, horse farts, Rob. By comparison, most women are not nearly as aggressive as men. You don't see them on the television news shooting at people or acting up on my bus."

"Perhaps, but it's only a small majority who cause problems in society . . . and on your bus, I might add. Mildred the fact is, serious crimes of violence occur at remarkably low rates in modern societies. This means that most young men or women never engage in any criminal violence regardless of their testosterone levels."

"That's the point I'm trying to make. It's not the normal, but those with an over-abundance of testosterone, like the thugs on my bus. And everyone at the cable company," she added for good measure.

He smiled and shook his head. "There can be a host of physical and environmental issues that can cause outlandish behavior. Still, I do agree with you, that violent crime is often perpetrated by young men and high testosterone may be a factor in their reckless conduct."

"Yes, like those wagpasties on my bus!"

"So what do you want to do about this, Mildred? I can see this is upsetting for you and for good reason. Those rogues on your bus are a pain you know where. Why don't I prescribe something to relax you so you can deal with this without ruining your health; or, do you want that referral to a psychologist so you can talk about this with someone? You know, that can be helpful."

Mildred thumped her finger on the arm of the chair and took a deep breath. "No, I guess I just needed to talk to someone who knows about these things. I'm looking for answers, Rob." She stood up half way before sitting again. "I have one last question though. Can testosterone levels be reduced? I read that female hormones or some foods or medications can reduce testosterone, is that true?"

"Well, there are medical reasons for reducing testosterone in both men and women and we have medicines for that purpose. This is a little out of my area of expertise, but some argue that diet can play a role as well. I'm not sure this has been documented, but some patients who need to reduce testosterone make changes in their diet along with medication."

"Hmm . . . is that so? Well thank you, Dr. Rob. I hope I didn't take up too much of your time."

"You know I always make time for you, Mildred."

"By the way, how was the garage sale?" she said as she stood.

"He raised his eyebrows, "Still have a few things left if you're interested."

"No need, I just made a trip to the thrift store," and she winked as she left.

Nurse Marjory came in to pick up the file. "Did she seem all right to you?"

"No." He tapped his pen on the desk. "But she did seem like the Mildred I know," he said smiling.

Fifteen

IT CAME TO HER while she was making a cup of mint tea. The next time she went out she stopped at the butcher shop up in Grover's Corner.

"Willard, can you spare a piece of that pink paper you use to wrap my pork chops, maybe just about a foot or two?"

Young Willard Turner owned the butcher shop he had taken over from his father two years ago after his father went to jail for shooting the neighbors' chickens and then dressing and selling them to customers in the shop. Of course his father denied it but the town was all abuzz wondering about the legitimacy of the meat and poultry they'd been buying from him over the years – and where it came from. Old Simon Cribbs claimed he was missing some goats and the widow Irma Brown said she was sure some of her cows were missing from her field out back.

"Sure, Mildred, we call it butcher paper," he said as he ripped a long piece from the roll on the counter. "You slaughtering something?"

"Oh goodness gracious no. I live in town; without even a cat or dog." Then she thought about what she said. *I didn't mean to imply they went missing or that I was suggesting . . . I'm sure he didn't give it a second thought. Besides, I'm absolutely certain he would never follow in his father's footsteps.* "No, just working on a project, Willard. Thanks so much."

That night she spread the butcher paper next to her glass of *chabliss* on the Formica and chrome table in the kitchenette. Bending over and with lips pursed, she carefully drew lines with a marking pen and ruler. *Hmm, I don't know if I like the pink paper for this, but I suppose it will do,* she thought. But when it started to look like a graph, she stood back and smiled.

"Yes! Yippidy do dah, not bad, not bad," she said to herself before making her list in the left column: gang of thugs, her neighbor Angus Baumgartner, cable company, and Roger Studebaker, the Chief of Operations for Brown County Transit Authority. She had one line left over so she wrote in: Buster, Angus Baumgartner's beast of a dog . . . and tried to fit it on one line.

She walked around the table looking at the graph from all angles and then sat again writing in the spaces across the top: *Licorice, Flax Seeds, Soybeans* and other dietary items suggested in the library books that might lower testosterone levels. When finished, she tacked the graph on the wall in the laundry room, after taking down an old calendar several years out of date.

"Well va-va-voom, what do you think of that?" she asked, as if someone else was in the room. For one last touch, she wrote THE PLAN across the top.

~~~~

Mildred braved the wind and pulled her jacket tight as she ran up the steps to the library. Grabbing Velda before she went behind the counter, she told her everything. Velda stood erect, her eyes large like donuts and her mouth wide open. "The Plan? What plan? What are you planning, Mildred? Food for what?" A lock of her tightly pinned hair slipped from her bun, landing over one eye and she stared at Mildred as if she were an intruder. Taking Mildred by the arm, Velda pulled her into the Ancient History aisle. "Mildred . . .?"

"Now don't be such a pussywillow, Velda. Jeepers, it's not an assassination. It's just a little food that won't hurt anyone and I'm totally convinced we'll soon see some major changes."

Velda stood gawking. "I don't even know who you are anymore. You could be wearing a flak jacket and helmet, with a rifle thrown over your shoulder." She leaned in close. "Have you thought this through, Mildred? I mean it would probably take tons of licorice to make a difference in someone's testosterone level and even then, do you know for sure testosterone is the culprit?" By then Velda's brow was high on her head.

"How can it not be? What else would explain the gang of thugs who have taken over the bus, and the arrogance of my neighbor Baumgartner who wants to rule the neighborhood through his beast of a dog. And Buster himself? What kind of dog would try to hump a neighbor if he didn't have some run-amok testosterone problem because his owner won't get him snipped, that's what."

Velda blinked rapidly and tried to stutter some words. Mildred wanted to brush aside the errant lock of hair over Velda's eye but she left it be.

"We've gone through this before," Mildred whispered. "You've been terrorized by the greedy people at the cable company. The pharmacist and the milkman don't try to run herd on you, or try to charge more for what they sell, because they have normal levels of testosterone. And the gang of thugs? What kind of boys would leave their baseball mitts at home and terrorize the elderly on a public bus? Those drowning in more than their share of testosterone! Think about it, Velda."

"Good grief, Mildred, now that you put it that way. All this time those people running the cable company have been making a killing off of us because they have too much testosterone? Honest people don't do that. Just last week the gardener offered to take that old swamp cooler to the dump where he takes his trimmings, and he didn't even charge me one cent! He must have the normal amount of testosterone."

"Yes, you see, Velda? Willard at the butcher shop gave me a piece of butcher paper and did it without charging, and Slim Butterworth brought me some squash from his garden last week when he got on the bus, just as a favor." This is how men act when their testosterone is in check."

"I'll be darned, Mildred, I think you're onto something. I've never thought of this before. Can you imagine?" They giggled softly as they left the Ancient History aisle arm in arm. Velda, still with that lock of hair covering her eye, and Mildred with another arm full of books on testosterone.

~~~~

Two weeks, later Mildred spotted her neighbor, Burt Stillwell, across the street wrestling with a new screen on his front door.

"G'morning Burt," she hollered as she approached. "Are you having problems with your screen door?"

"Yep, do I ever. Darn thing won't stay closed. Might as well just take the damned thing back but I know I'd regret it come the heat."

Mildred thought of him as a quiet and peaceful man, just the opposite of Angus Baumgartner. She thought, *he probably has low testosterone, maybe because he's aging or just built that way.*

"Burt, what were you like as a young man?"

He let the screen door swing open and scratched his head. "Am I'm missing something about this screen, Mildred? I've tried adjusting the hinges . . ."

"No, no I wasn't referring to your mechanical skills Burt, although you could look at the diagram in the instructions; that is if they're in English." She laughed to put him at ease.

"Threw 'em away. I didn't think I needed them."

"Well, what I really meant is that I'm wondering about your testosterone level. You see . . ."

"Whoa, Mildred. I like you, and I don't want to hurt your feelings but I don't want to mess around, if that's what you're getting at."

"No, no Burt, nothing like that at all. I was just curious if testosterone affects men's behavior in general."

He scratched the back of his neck. "Hmm, darned if I know, Mildred."

"Well, do you know . . . I mean, do you remember acting differently as a young man?"

"Hmm, gosh . . . it's, well it's kinda hard to recall those days."

"Well, let me ask you this. Do you ever get your testosterone level checked? I don't mean to be so personal, but I'm working on a project, you know, sort of a research project."

"No, I don't think so, but I do get my hearing checked every year. I don't wear hearing aids and sure as hell don't plan to."

"I see," she said as she watched him fiddle with the hinges. "You know, you and Angus Baumgartner are both neighbors but so different. How do you explain that?"

He grabbed his chin and gave it a good rub. "Gosh, well, I suppose some critters have stripes and others have spots, nothing more than that, I guess," and he nodded pleased with his answer.

"Uh huh, I see. Well, I hope you get the screen fixed, Burt. I don't think the heat's coming anytime soon," she said reassuringly.

"Sure enough," he said, and paused. "You take good care, Mildred," he yelled as she crossed the street.

Sixteen

MILDRED DROVE around until she finally found a parking space at the big box store and checked her list before going in. Twenty minutes later, her cart was filled with several packages of licorice candy, all black and all individually wrapped. She hoped no one saw her buy all that licorice. In Myers Junction she never knew who she might run in to. *That can also be a good thing too*, she reasoned; *that feeling of belonging.*

But she thought of this visit to the big box store as a secret mission . . . *probably like men buying condoms or women buying that henna hair dye that's so popular. One day your hair is mousy brown and the next day rust? The condoms I can understand*, she thought, as she got through the line without seeing anyone she knew.

~~~~

The next morning she hummed Broadway tunes, carrying sacks of licorice under her arm before climbing aboard the bus and tucking them neatly under her seat. When she came to the stop where the gang of thugs waited, she handed a wrapped pack of licorice to each one as they climbed aboard.

"Just a little something for all of you boys today," she said cheerfully.

"Yeah, mother fucker! Hey, look guys, our porn star bought us some licorice. Way to go little motherfucker bus mom."

"Sweet motha, a treat today instead of a treatment," the last one to board said, as Mildred handed out the last of the licorice.

The cellophane wrappers flew before the gang of thugs even reached their seats, and when she looked in the rear view mirror they were silently chewing on long strips of sweet black licorice. Although the profanity and boom boxes disrupted the ambiance as usual, there was no sign of new vandalism when she examined the bus later that evening. "Yes!" Her hands flew up in the air. "Sis boom bah! Finally, a solution!"

"You're sounding awfully happy today, Miss Mildred," Spencer said as he stepped up into the bus.

"Oh boy, Spencer, have I good news!" she said, showing him the area around the back of the bus that afternoon.

"It doesn't look like good news to me," Spencer said. "Still the usual trash back here, and they've torn down the regulation signs again."

"I know, I know, but no new graffiti anywhere, Spencer! Imagine that! All of this was from before."

Spencer looked at her askance. "It's still the usual mess no matter how you look at it, Mildred." He watched as she ran her hand over the seats. "You're right though, Miss Mildred. No new graffiti today. What a miracle!"

~~~~

"Psst, Velda." Mildred motioned with her eyes and Velda followed her to the Travel aisle minutes after the library opened. "You'll never guess what happened!" Mildred wore a bright green blouse that morning and her hair was actually combed, rather than just patted in place. Velda looked her over twice.

"What is it, Mildred? You look different today, and you're here awfully early this morning."

Mildred scanned the aisle, making sure they were alone before explaining the licorice episode in detail. Velda's mouth hung open in disbelief.

"You didn't actually give them real licorice to lower their level of testosterone, did you Mildred? Are you allowed to do that, I mean isn't it medicine? And would it really work that fast? Golly, I can't imagine, but then I don't know anything about science."

"It worked Velda, at least partially. The bus was still trashed, but there was not one sign of new graffiti at the end of the day!"

"Well couldn't that just be . . . I mean maybe they were too busy chewing licorice. Will you be giving them licorice every day from now on?"

"No, no," Mildred whispered. "I haven't worked that out yet, but I'm just glad to see it works. And maybe once or twice is all it will take. Rome was not built in a day, Velda, but someone had to lay the first brick!"

"Bricks?" Velda repeated as she stared wide eyed at Mildred as patrons lined up at the checkout desk.

~~~~

That night Mildred guided her finger down the butcher paper chart on the wall starting, with *Licorice* at the top to *Gang of Thugs* in the left column, and marked the date. *Aha, and on the first try! Yippidy do dah!*

She turned out the light in the laundry room and sang a Carmen Miranda tune as she danced into the kitchen. "Chica chica boom chica boom" . . . and she poured herself a glass of *chabliss*. The jelly glass caught the reflection of the ceiling light and twinkled as she did a quick shuffle. For the first time in weeks she danced around the kitchen making several twirls while she made chicken pot pie.

Seventeen

THE SUN WAS JUST SETTING behind the row of evergreen trees as it normally did that time of night. Tall and stately, the trees swayed with the breeze from the north, sighing as they moved from side to side. Mildred watched them as she pulled up into her driveway, wishing they were shorter so she could see more of the sunset. But she knew the trees were a welcome barrier from the howling northeast winds. She liked telling anyone who would listen, *those winds can blow the hair off your head and a wicker chair a mile from the front porch.*

"Hi Miss Penniwink."

She squinted and could barely make out Alphie Miller's outline in front of the trees. He stood on the sidewalk while she closed the car door.

Alphie Miller was only ten, but Mildred considered him one of her favorite neighbors on the street. He came every Saturday morning to mow her lawn in the summer and shovel the driveway in the winter. He came even if she didn't have anything to be done. She usually thought of some small chore since Alphie was always saving for something . . . a project for school or his Boy Scout troop. A year ago, he made a small weather vane that won him a regional science award and a special scout badge. Mildred went to the ceremony even though she was coming down with a cold because she knew she'd be the only one there on his behalf. She didn't know his parents, but on trash days she saw the empty liquor bottles sticking out of the can in front of their house so she made no effort to meet them. She intended to when they first moved in, but she couldn't find a time when she thought they wouldn't be drinking. One day passed and then another. Then it seemed the opportunity was gone. When they found out she was taking Alphie in when things weren't going well at home, they got a court order prohibiting her from taking him in, even though they let him do paid chores for her.

Every Saturday, like the one last week, she asked Alphie about his new project for the week. He lit up and couldn't wait to tell her.

"I'm putting playing cards on my bike spokes with clothes pins so my bike will sound like it has a real motor. Wanna try it Miss Penniwink? It sounds really cool."

"Thanks, I'll pass this time Alphie, but it sounds like fun."

"Well, you can try it anytime you want. If you do, be sure to go down the hill at the end of the block. Go real fast 'cause it sounds like a real race car!"

"Oh my! I'll be sure to do that." She thought how innocent and uncomplicated he seemed, and how little he knew about life at his age. "Do you have time for some homemade cookies?" she always asked as part of their regular routine. They always laughed, since they both knew the answer.

After his chores he would brush off his jeans and stamp his feet before sitting at the small table on the porch. Mildred would bring out homemade chocolate chip cookies and milk and slip off her shoes while they tried to see who could name every state in the nation.

~~~

"Alphie, is that you out there?" she said, seeing his silhouette against the trees and walking closer.

"Yup, it's me. Just me." His face was red and scratched, and his shirt looked torn where some buttons were missing. His arms were wrapped around himself to keep warm.

"Isn't it a little cold to be out without a jacket tonight?"

"Yeah, I suppose so."

The image told the story and it was not the first time he'd waited in front of her house for her to come home. She put her arms around him and held his head close, feeling the silent grief tear through him as he fought back the tears, or at least tried to. She held him for what seemed like a long time and then they went inside while she turned on the heat and covered his shoulders with the pastel afghan she'd knitted once.

"Wash your face, Alphie. I'll make us some supper." While the soup simmered, she took out the chocolate chip cookies she always kept in the freezer and let them thaw on the drain board.

He was on his second helping of soup when the doorbell rang. Sgt. Patrick McCain stood there in his police uniform, looking at her askance with his eyebrows raised. She stepped out on the porch.

"Okay, sue me . . . put me in jail, Patrick."

"Mildred, you know my hands are tied. There's a court order that you are not to take him in or interfere in domestic matters. I'm here to take him home. I know you've already seen a copy of the court order but here's another."

"Nonsense," she said swatting at the papers in his hand. "Court order, court shmorder. Those judges are a pack of mollycoddles; weak and cowardly. It's not *your* hands that should be tied, Patrick. Have you seen that boy's face, his body, when he comes here?"

She'd known Patrick McCain since he lived in her old neighborhood on the other side of town. He used to play kick the can with the other kids on her street and she'd bake cookies and leave them on the porch. Over the years many of those kids, now adults, still stopped by to chat or to see if she needed anything. Patrick was one of them, always checking the hinges on the gate or the tires on her car. When he first joined the force he stopped by to show off his new uniform and brought a friend to take his picture with her. She still had her copy on the mantle above her fireplace.

He took a deep breath and shook his head. "You're not to take him in, Mildred. That's what the court order says. You're to mind your own business in other words. I know what you're going to say, but Child Protective Services is on this but the case workers are swamped."

"You know, Patrick, Alphie will end up like those thugs on my bus. Now's the time to prevent that from happening with this boy."

"I agree with you Mildred . . . of course, but it's out of your hands; you alone can't do anything about him."

Her face reddened and her eyes teared over. "I can't? Damn it Patrick, I can't?"

He sighed and paced on the porch. Finally he said, "You have to let me in Mildred, I need to take the boy home."

She opened the door wider. "I know, I know. Come in, Patrick. You'll have to wait though. He's finishing his soup and I have cookies thawing on the drain board."

"Fair enough," he said, as he took off his hat and followed her inside.

Later that night she warmed up the soup again, leaving it on the stove with steam rising just to feel something else in the room.

Eighteen

"ARE YOU still embroidering those wild-looking tea towels, Mildred? They were such a hit at the Christmas auction last year, remember?" Gettie Mae Leary chatted with Mildred from her seat near the front of the bus, looking good in a new pants suit. Mildred already knew her to be a snazzy dresser who wore nice clothes that always seemed freshly laundered.

"To tell you the truth, I haven't embroidered anything this year. I'll make sure to have some before the Christmas bazaar though. I have some new colored threads."

"When you can, Mildred. No rush. You seem to have your hands full with what's happening on the bus these days. Can't anyone do anything about it? You've had your share of grief. With what you've been through, you sure don't need to be dealing with delinquents."

"Oh, zowie, if only someone could do something about it! Unfortunately, there's no law to keep them from riding the bus since it's privately owned. It's not a matter for the police, at least that's what they've told me. You know, Gettie, you mentioned something about testosterone a while back. Do you have some time when we can talk?"

"Why sure. Stop by after work one night? Oscar's working in the garage every night on the lawn mower that died two weeks ago trying to get the damn thing to work."

"How about tonight then? I can come over after I return the bus, like around six."

"Yes, wonderful. Whoops, here's my stop. Tonight then."

~~~~

Oscar Leary was a large man known for his bear hugs, *big enough to squeeze the gas right out of you*, Mildred thought every time she saw him. She braced herself for the worst. After parking the car in front she walked up the driveway to the house when he trudged toward her, leading with his shoulders as if pulling a tractor.

"Mildred, Mildred, how are you?" She held her breath but found it best to breathe during a hug from Oscar Leary.

"Ommph, ahh, I'm good Oscar and you?" she said an octave higher as he released her.

"I'm wrestling with this goddamn lawn mower. Can't get the damn thing to start. You don't know anything about Briggs and Stratton engines do you?"

"No."

"That's okay. I know Gettie Mae's looking forward to your visit. We haven't seen you around much. Be sure to holler before you leave."

If you hug me again I'm sure I will, she thought as she went inside.

Gettie Mae had set a ceramic tea set on the Duncan Phyfe table and was pouring black leaf tea into two cups. "Oh, sit down Mildred, please." Mildred sat as she slipped the jacket off her shoulders, and Gettie pushed the sugar bowl closer. An orange cat sat peacefully on a nearby stack of newspapers.

"How nice, Gettie Mae. You didn't have to go to all this trouble."

"Never trouble for you," she said while paying attention to the plate of biscuits, nudging them toward Mildred.

"Gettie, can I talk to you in confidence? I couldn't help thinking about your comment concerning those awful thugs on the bus and testosterone."

By the time they were on their second cup of tea, Mildred had told her everything.

"Oh, my word! I'm impressed, Mildred. You really have been plowing the field. My goodness! We all understand your frustration. I mean we see it, and believe me, we think you have more patience than any of us would have. Most of us would like to pick those boys up and toss them off the bus. We have a similar frustration with the cable company too . . . and everyone else who wants to control us, hurt us, or rip us off."

"Mmm, delicious," Mildred said holding a biscuit in her hand, her mouth half full. She checked her chest for falling crumbs, feeling her chin rippling in rows as she put her head down to look. "Gettie, do you think their behavior has to do with testosterone?" she said looking up.

"I definitely do but Oscar disagrees. He thinks it's just bad upbringing, but even kids with all the advantages and caring parents can grow up to have obnoxious behavior so it must be something else. I believe it's the testosterone taking charge, but what to do about it I don't know. You may be onto something with your licorice, but it seems like a flea on an elephant. Can't you step it up a bit?"

"Step it up?"

"I mean, really get on it . . . more licorice, more flax. And what about estrogen? Wouldn't that grind the testosterone to a halt?"

Mildred blinked and reared back, as if she was gunning the engine to pass a slow tractor.

"Oh! Well I thought I'd start slow. I think it's working though, because there was no graffiti the day I gave out the licorice. Real estrogen might be tampering with nature a bit too much, and I doubt if I could even get a prescription for it."

"Well, all the more reason to go full steam ahead with what you have then. Let's take care of this once and for all."

Mildred could now see why Gettie Mae was president of the League of Women Voters. They agreed to meet again soon.

Mildred left quietly by the front door instead of the driveway to avoid seeing Oscar again. After drinking two full cups of tea, she thought it best to be careful.

~~~~

That night Mildred changed into her lounging attire, as she liked to call her sweatpants with the elastic at the ankles, and the baggy shirt she bought at the thrift shop that said *Martin's Appliances* on the back. She spread her library books on the table before pouring her glass of *Chabliss*. Knowing Velda would be upset if she wrote in the books, she took notes on 3x5 cards she bought at the big box store and copied all of the snack recipes using the testosterone-reducing ingredients from the library books. She put the recipe cards into bunches based on the testosterone-lowering ingredients: soy, mint, licorice, flaxseed, and a host of other "remedies" as she liked to call them. On her weekly grocery list near the fridge she wrote at the top: *Special Purchases*. Dabbing the end of the pencil on her tongue, she wrote down the ingredients carefully. *Hmmm . . . soy beans? No, I'll buy soy flour instead so I can put it into cookies.*

Throwing her shoulders back she looked at the grocery list and raised her jelly glass of *Chabliss* into the air. "To progress and to 'stepping it up,' as Gettie Mae would say." She took a few steps and twirled in the kitchen.

"Tra la la, and scooby do," she kept singing, as she danced her way through the small house that night.

Nineteen

"WHAT'S THAT goddamn noise every time the bus stops?"

"Don't mind him Mildred, he just got new hearing aids. Be quiet Fred, so Mildred can get us on our way." Cora pushed him into a seat, and he sat with his cane on his lap.

Mildred chuckled and watched until Cora and Fred were settled. "The doors and the brakes are operated by air pressure, Fred." Mildred raised her voice while looking into the mirror to see if he could hear her. She noticed his hair was cut shorter, making his ears seem larger.

"I can hear you loud and clear, Mildred. A little too loud actually," he said.

She smiled and thought of all the hisses and groans in the bus that she took for granted like the hisses when she lowered the ramp so riders can board, and the noises when she operates the levers, doors, and brakes. When they all worked together it was a gentle hum, *a musical masterpiece*, she thought as she smiled.

"The leaves are turning," Mildred said to Bernice Johnson, as she waited for the door to open at her stop.

"Aren't they though." Bernice pushed the hair back from her face and pulled her jacket tight in front. "Mildred, you have a lovely day." She gave her a friendly wave as she stepped off the bus.

Mildred steered back into traffic and caught a glimpse of the sky full of white wispy clouds before coming to a row of shops near Baker and Fifth. Wilma Harrington waved from the hair salon as she was putting the *Closed for Lunch* sign in the window. At the next stop, an eddy of leaves swirled viciously against the curb as Mildred eased the bus carefully to the bus stop. That's when she spotted Gettie Mae standing by the curb wearing sensible shoes.

"Mildred, I need to talk to you," Gettie said as she bounded up the step. "I have something important to tell you." She sat in the seat across from Mildred and cracked her chewing gum before wiggling out of her jacket. Mildred noticed how round-shouldered she was.

"What's going on, Gettie?"

Gettie Mae leaned over the aisle. "Twang Yao."

"Who?"

"Oh goodness," Gettie said impatiently. "Can you meet me at the library tomorrow morning? I know you usually go there on Saturdays."

"Yes, I'm almost always there when it opens at nine."

Twang Yao, who is that? Mildred wondered as she continued on her route, noticing the fog laying low near the meadow and a slight dampness on the windshield. *Hmmm, weather changing. I suppose.*

~~~~

Velda was just unlocking the doors to the library when Mildred arrived and brushed the morning dew off her jacket before going in. A few minutes later when she saw Gettie Mae come through the front door, she was both surprised and relieved she came alone and not with Twang Yao. Velda joined them near the row of encyclopedias where they talked.

"What's that stuff called again?" Velda turned an ear toward Gettie Mae.

"Twang Yao. It's an herb that has estrogen-like effects and is used to treat female-related problems, and get this . . . including high testosterone levels!"

Velda gasped and put her hand over her mouth.

Mildred slapped her hand on the encyclopedia case in spite of the frown from Velda. "Hallelujah! I thought Twang Yao was a person. How in heaven did you find it Gettie Mae? It's not in the books I've been reading."

"Well," she whispered, scooting closer. "They sell it at Vitamin World mostly for menopause symptoms which is what I was looking for. But here's the important part." She looked around before whispering again. "The clerk said it's also used for a number of conditions, and . . . she happened to mention high testosterone levels."

"Good lord!" Mildred's eyes opened wide.

"You're not thinking . . ." Velda held her breath.

"Yes she is," Gettie Mae answered for Mildred.

"I wonder if it's safe," Mildred said. "I mean, I wouldn't want to hurt anyone, at least not seriously, if you know what I mean." She raised her brow. "I'd rather sell my tap shoes than . . . than kill anyone."

"It's sold in Vitamin World so it must be safe," Gettie whispered. "You can see what the instructions say, but I'm sure it's okay. I just wonder if it will work on men, but I don't know why not if you amp up the dosage."

Velda gulped. "Amp up the dosage?"

Mildred thought for a moment, ignoring Velda. "It has to work. I read this week that as teenagers, males have high levels of testosterone and low levels of estrogen, and as they age, testosterone levels decrease while their estrogen levels increase . . . so this would hurry the process along!"

Gettie Mae nodded. "Exactly, that's the point. Move them into the estrogen stage earlier, at least those with an over-abundance of testosterone. Mildred you seem to know the gang's habits. What are you thinking, spike the water with it?"

Mildred hesitated. "Yes, probably spike the water or cola or anything, in addition to the snacks I'm fixing. I'm dizzy just thinking about it."

Gettie Mae nodded.

"Thank you, Gettie Mae, I'll go over to Vitamin World when I leave here. I'll let you know what I find out."

Gettie Mae and Mildred left while Velda was still standing with her hand over her mouth. The line at the checkout desk wrapped almost out the door.

~~~~

Mildred parked in front of Vitamin World and tapped her finger on the steering wheel as she sat in the parking lot. Thoughts raced through her mind like an out-of-control train heading down the tracks. She had flashes of her frightened riders on the bus, and graffiti etched into the seats, and Albert rolling down the aisle in his wheelchair. She got out, slamming the car door so hard the hula dancer hanging from the rear view mirror danced frantically as Mildred headed toward the large supermarket of drugs.

The young man's face had a healthy glow and she wondered if that was required for employment, or if he'd been trying the samples left by venders on tables in the aisles. She approached him and asked, "Can you tell me where I can find Twang Yao or testosterone reducing products?

"Sure, over here," he said walking for several aisles as she trailed behind to keep up.

"Are these all vitamins, I didn't know there were so many?"

"Yeah, I know. We also carry food and health-related products so no, these are not all vitamins. Okay, you'll find the testosterone products here," he said, turning down aisle nine.

To her horror, she saw several shelves of products under the sign *Testosterone Boosters!* She stood in shock. "Oh my word, you mean people in town can actually buy testosterone? I mean, are all these bottles full of testosterone?"

She saw brands like *Macho Pride, Testoflex, Get It On, Big Moose, Mega Tough, Forever Young, RXLibido* . . . and the names went on. "Is this legal? Can someone really buy this stuff? Isn't there a law or something? If not there should be. I'm shocked!"

"Sure, lots of guys buy it, but we see mostly body builders, athletes, and some who just want to increase their . . . well I suppose, their manhood," he said, looking a little uncomfortable. She noticed him blushing.

She looked him over. He wasn't someone you'd notice on the street. She could see he had a slight build even beneath his argyle sweater vest. "Quite frankly, what do you think of these? I mean, are they really necessary?"

"What, to increase your manhood? I suppose if you think you're lacking. I haven't thought about it much. I don't lift weights or anything. My girlfriend likes me the way I am. But we sell lots of these products. In fact they're one of our biggest sellers. That's why there are so many brands. It's kind of weird isn't it?"

They sell lots of these products! Good lord, things are worse than I thought! She was momentarily at a loss for words.

"Is there anything else?" He smiled.

"Actually, I was looking for pills to reduce testosterone," she said, hoping he wouldn't escort her out of the store. "I think one product is Twang Yao."

"Oh, yeah, you did mention that didn't you? You'll find that in aisle twenty-seven with menopause products. Follow me . . ."

"No, that's okay, I can find it by myself. Thank you, young man."

Mildred bought three bottles of Twang Yao tablets and went directly to the checkout stand and then to the car. Turning on the engine, she put it in gear and the car shot out of the parking space squealing onto the road toward the big box store about three blocks up the street.

~~~~

"And can you cut off the tags please?" she said to the clerk at the big box checkout counter while looking at her watch. "I'm sort of in a hurry, thank you."

Once in the car she took out the new black nylon backpack that zipped open at the top, and gave it a shake before putting the car in gear and heading back in the opposite direction.

The young man she first encountered in Vitamin World was nowhere to be seen so she felt it safe to walk quickly to row nine, the one marked *Testosterone Boosters*. "How ridiculous!" she whispered to herself as she read the sign again. Scanning the aisle and seeing it empty, she unzipped the backpack and held it knee high while she walked slowly along the testosterone section sweeping the bottles into her unzipped backpack, all of them. When the shelves were totally empty, she zipped the bag, threw it over her shoulder and walked out of the store.

Sitting in the car, she stared straight ahead. *Good lord! Well I did it and that's that!* Her brief moment of guilt eased once her foot was on the pedal. Fifteen minutes later she was burning everything in her incinerator and disposing of the empty, charred bottles in the trash can. On her butcher paper list in the laundry room, she added Twang Yao to her list of "remedies," and underlined it until the lead in her pencil broke off.

Twenty

PURPLE ASTERS LINED the median along Main Street near the Myers Junction City Hall, their color brilliant against the deep green lumps of Midwestern grasses. Mildred slowed the bus to take a closer look before driving on. She remembered planting a row or two of Asters next to the wooden steps of her porch, and delighted in seeing them covered with frost in the fall and mist in the spring. But she'd all but let her garden go because of Angus Baumgartner's "beast of a dog." On occasion she tried sneaking out with her planting tools, but Buster was on her like fly paper. She suspected Angus of letting him out and then watching for his own amusement. "Pervert," she'd grumble before gathering her garden tools and running for cover.

~~~~~

It was Wednesday evening when she pulled her old blue Ford Fairlane into the driveway. As usual, her first sight was the plight of her garden, barren and empty of everything but weeds standing like corn stalks after a harvest. The washed-out hue of dried flowers and pale stalks was a stinging reminder of how she felt about everything at that moment. She didn't know which was worse, facing the destruction in front of her, or feeling the pain of remembering what it used to be; a glorious garden full of color and vigor. She changed her clothes and sat on the edge of the bed feeling the nausea and her sweaty palms, then walked quickly through the house, turning on every light and the television, letting it yell in to every room. Finally, she sat at the kitchen table in her baggy sweat pants, her loose socks down around her ankles.

Her melancholy came with a greater force of late. The fear of losing her job, the sight of the bus trashed at the end of the day, and her garden, dried up and gone, was defeating. The frustration of not being able to replant her garden dampened any prospect of joy. She let the screen door slam as she walked out and sat on the front porch watching shadows fall across her yard as the day was ending with night following close behind. *Eventide* is what she liked calling that time when the dim light let her see the remnants of the day. Her flower bed, pocked by dead plants and overgrown weeds, looked like the old Myers Junction cemetery up on the hill. She longed to rake it clean and plant Asters and ornamental grasses like she used to, and tend to it every day. She glared over at Angus Baumgartner's house before going in. "Creep," she shouted as loud as she could.

~~~~

On her way home the following evening she stopped by Dr. Carl Christensen's office, the local veterinarian next to the Bijou, the town's only movie theater.

"Your name?" The woman at the counter didn't look up. *She must be bored with her job,* Mildred thought, and she moved a little closer.

"Oh, I don't have an appointment. I just wanted to ask the vet a few questions." She noticed others waiting with their pets. "I don't mind waiting."

"Well, what kind of questions? Maybe I can help you." The receptionist had a chart on her desk, so Mildred thought she must know about veterinarian matters.

She hesitated before leaning over the counter. "I wanted to ask some general questions about getting . . ." her voice trailed to a whisper, ". . . you know, getting fixed."

"We only take animal patients here."

Good lord, what a nit! Mildred glanced over her shoulder. She noticed that every eye was on her. Her face reddened and she tweaked her neck.

By this time she was on her tip toes, leaning over the counter as far as she could and speaking in a whisper. "Oh no, I didn't mean to imply it was me getting fixed. You see, there's a dog that keeps . . . well, keeps mounting me, and I want to see what my options are." *Oh god, I'm going from bad to worse.* She wondered if people in the waiting room could hear. She inched even closer to the counter.

The receptionist swiveled her chair around toward the back and yelled, "Can we fit someone in? She has a humper."

Oh for god's sake! Mildred tried to lower her head away from those in the waiting room, and was grateful when the receptionist motioned her in through the doorway and down the hall. Dr. Christensen was sitting at a table in the treatment room looking at something in a vial.

"Sperm," he said looking up.

"What?" She waited for more, but he just sat looking at it in the light. She didn't want to dwell on the possibilities.

Carl Christensen came from a long line of veterinarians in the valley. His great grandfather was actually one of the settlers and had opened a business outside of Myers Junction where most of the customers were farmers with cattle. But with the demographic shift, Carl Christensen's clientele were now mostly townspeople bringing in their pets. She told him of her predicament.

He put the vial in a drawer. "Hmm . . . are you doing something to encourage his behavior?"

"What?" *Sweet Jesus!* "Well, it's not like I'm wearing a short skirt or playing dance music on the porch, if that's what you mean!"

"I mean why do you suppose the dog keeps coming after you? What do you suppose might be causing his inappropriate sexual behavior?"

I should keep his card in case I need a good therapist. She let go of a long sigh. "Well gosh, I was hoping you would tell me, Dr.

Christensen. I assume he has an overabundance of testosterone that needs to be curtailed. Is there some way to do that?"

"Well, normally we recommend de-sexing the female so the male has nothing to mate with."

She gulped. "Uh huh, well in this case . . ."

"Yes, I see your point."

"Isn't there something that will tamper down his whoopie . . . well, his urge? I know that with people, estrogen or certain herbs are used sometimes to lower testosterone levels."

"There is a suppository . . ."

"No, no, no," and she waved her hands frantically in front of him.

"Well, without examining him or running some tests, I don't know. Will the owner agree to castration?"

Mildred held her tongue. *If old Baumgartner would agree to castration, I'd be glad to cut the man's balls off myself!*

She realized Dr. Christensen was referring to Buster so she tried to stay on track. "I doubt it. I'm sure he thinks the dog is fine. Would there be any harm in trying a little estrogen or some of the estrogen-type herbs to see if they might lower the dog's urges; that is, if the owner agrees?" She knew full well old Baumgartner would never agree to anything, nor would she even in a million years ask him. But it seemed that what she did on her property was her business not his.

"No real harm I suppose with small doses. The dog might become a little lethargic, but then that's what might curb his sexual appetite."

"I see." Her mind was racing. "Well, thank you. Thank you very much."

The receptionist at the desk looked up. "No charge today," she said. "Need another appointment?"

"No, I'm all taken care of, thanks." *Hmm, I'm wondering if I*

Hazel Warlaumont

should have reworded that?

Mildred avoided eye contact as she walked briskly through the waiting room. On the way to the car she imagined herself skipping along like a schoolgirl playing hopscotch in the parking lot. She stopped at the big box store where she bought Buster his very own plastic water dish with cute paw prints. *Buster, meet Twang Yao!* She rolled the window down and whistled all the way home.

~~~~

The next morning with a devilish grin, Mildred pulled the sack of flax seed cookies from under the seat as the gang of thugs cavorted noisily at the bus stop, gyrating their hips and rubbing their crotches. The regular riders stood back until the gang boarded.

"Good afternoon, gentlemen," Mildred said to the gang of thugs as they stepped into the bus. She handed the brown paper bag to the first delinquent, the one with the greasy hair, wishing it was explosives instead of flax cookies. "Just a little something I baked this weekend."

"Hey, the mother fucker baked cookies for us. Yo, I'm thinking she likes us."

"Way to go mama bitch, now you startin' to treat us with respect," the one called Bruno said, twirling a chain from the waist of his baggy pants.

They chanted "bus bitch, bus bitch" all the way to the back where they turned up their boom box and Salvador, the one with the large black hoop earrings, stood on the seat and hung by the straps. The regular riders stood or sat close to the front as the thugs tore open the sack and crammed the cookies into their mouths.

"Hey, bossy bus mama, they so good," one shouted.

"Yeah, mother fucker bus bitch. More, more . . . we need to keep eat'n and we need to keep beat'n," they chanted.

At the next stop, Mildred saw Harriet Meckel waiting for the bus, her hair pulled up with combs, her clothes swank and neat.

According to the gossip on the bus, Harriet bought her clothes in the big city where her husband had an office.

"Good afternoon, Mildred," she said coming up the step in shoes that seemed too small. "Roger needed one of the cars today so I decided to ride the bus."

"Uh huh," Mildred said with a smile. "Well, good to see you, Harriet."

Walt Overland and Myrtle Perkins also waited patiently on the sidewalk, Myrtle fluffing her hair and glancing at her nails. Slim and with a small waist, she typically wore an apron everywhere, even outside her kitchen. Today it was a pink checkerboard with green trim.

Just then Mildred felt something hit the back of her head. Then a cookie slammed into the windshield. "Woo woo, these cookies got a life all their own," one of the thugs yelled from the back. Before long, flax cookies were being hurled everywhere. Harriet Meckel brushed some pieces from her skirt. "This is disgusting," she said, turning around.

"Whoa, you don't want to eat some of our cookies? Well, little neat bitch, maybe you want to eat some of this."

Mildred glanced over to see the one called Leon moving his hips back and forth as he stood over Harriet's seat thrusting his pelvis in her face. Mildred flinched and the bus weaved back and forth before she drove it into Miller's used car lot. Her voice was stressed as she gripped the fire extinguisher and got up out of her seat, her hands shaking.

"Enough!" she yelled, her eyes and voice unwavering as she walked toward him pointing the extinguisher.

"Aw, c'mon little motherfucker, we just havin' some fun," Leon said, and he backed up the aisle to his seat to join his noisy friends.

"Sorry, Harriet."

"No need to apologize, Mildred. It's enough to manage your own disgust let alone take care of ours."

100   Hazel Warlaumont

Mildred looked up at the card she kept above the dashboard. She winced at using the fire extinguisher. *Good grief, I could have hurt someone. What was I thinking?*

~~~~~

That night in the Bus Bay she and Spencer looked over the damage. Graffiti was etched everywhere, and cookie crumbs had been molded into dough and smeared on the windows and seats.

"So maybe I won't do the flax cookies again. Maybe they're not potent enough. Or maybe they are but will just take some tweaking. I know all of this will work."

Spencer just shook his head and put his hand on her shoulder. "Let me help you, Mildred. We can get this cleaned up in no time." But they worked late into the night.

~~~~~

Velda waited for Mildred in the History aisle at the library after getting a call the minute she unlocked the doors that morning.

"You sounded so upset on the phone, Mildred. You did the right thing."

"I blew it. I lost my temper. I could have hurt someone. We're to treat everyone the same, and I got mad, really mad."

"But who wouldn't? Those creeps are a danger to the riders and to you too. Can't the police arrest them?"

"They say it's a matter between the bus company and the vandals and even at that, Supervisor Studebaker has to file a police report and he refuses. Anyway, can we order these books?" Mildred handed her a list, her hand trembling.

"I think they might have some helpful information. I know my plan will work. It has to. It makes sense."

"Does it, Mildred?"

Twenty-One

THE YOUNG WOMAN behind the counter at Midwest Utilities took a bite of her jelly donut before speaking. "You again this month?" she mumbled not looking up.

"Yes, another incorrect bill," Mildred said with a showering of sarcasm.

"Take a number, please."

Mildred looked at the empty room with rows of vacant chairs.

"Take a number? I just need someone to look at my bill. It should only take a few minutes."

The young woman ignoring her, wore a jersey tank top that seemed out of season and unprofessional, Mildred thought as she waited. But then she knew young people had their own rules about things, like hair. Mildred couldn't stop staring. It wasn't just the rainbow colors but the texture, more like feathers. She decided not to ask her about it, and took a number instead.

Hmm, another Saturday afternoon sitting in the local Midwest Utilities office. She sat tapping her finger and toe at the same time. It was hard for her to think of cable television as part of progress, especially since they made everyone take the antennas off their roof, and then charged them for something they'd been getting for free.

"Miss Penniwink? I'm Mr. Calhoun, you know, from customer service."

Mildred recognized the man from the sales department and followed him to his desk where she sat down across from him. She looked around, sure her chair was lower than his. In fact, her chair was so low her knees almost met her chin. *This must be a child's chair. Ah! I get it! The old power play.* She strained to elevate herself.

"Miss Penniwink, I thought we'd solved your issue last month. We've raised our rates and yes, we did have a contract but the rates have changed and that's final."

In contrast to the scantily-clad receptionists, Mr. Calhoun, as he liked to be called even though his badge said *Fred,* wore a three-piece suit. He looked at his finger nails up close as she spoke.

"There seems to be an additional charge on my bill this month." She decided not to say "as usual." He took a nail file from the drawer and she continued. "I have the basic plan, but it seems I'm being charged for a higher-priced plan." She slid the bill across his desk and looked at him.

He didn't look at it. "What do you expect? The higher plan costs more because you get more."

She put her hand up on the desk. "But I didn't change plans. I don't want or need additional channels, and that's why I keep the basic plan."

He leaned way back in his chair. "You don't mean to tell me you don't want premium movies, nature shows, and porn?" He rocked back and forth in his chair and intertwined his fingers in front of him.

"I don't want them, nor did I request them, and I certainly don't want to be charged for them."

He stopped rocking and leaned over the desk, looking down at her. "No porn, Miss Penniwink?" he said with a smirk. His eyebrows almost met his hairline. "Really now," and he doubled his chin as he pulled his head in like a tortoise.

"I don't know what 'porn' is, but I don't want it or any additional channels no matter what."

"Oh, come now!" His grin showed wide spaces between his teeth. *Hmm, I wonder how that happened.* She leaned forward taking a closer look.

"Porn? It's pornography, Miss Penniwink."

She blew her nose.

"For god's sake, why don't they just call it that? To be clear," she said looking up over the desk, "I don't want that or any additional channels. Why am I being charged for these? Maybe I need to speak to a supervisor."

He coughed. "Now, now, that's not necessary. We are doing our customer's a big favor by letting them try something new. It's a special promotion. We increase your channels and you thank us for it."

"No, you increase our channels and make us pay for it. That doesn't seem like a big favor. Let's see what the supervisor says, please." She crossed her legs.

"Well, Miss Penniwink, since you are a loyal customer, let me talk to our promo department and we'll see what we can do."

"I need something more concrete than that. I work and can't be coming in here every time there are errors on my bill. Again, a supervisor?"

"No, no, not needed. As a special favor I'll see what I can do. Ask for me specifically next week and they will direct you to my desk. I'll make sure . . ."

"Please write down our agreement, that you will remove the charges and honor my contract, and I will bring the note with me next Saturday."

"You're a real negotiator, Miss Penniwink. Would you like to work for us? We're always looking for hard-driving sales people."

"Harrumph," she grumbled loudly.

While he reluctantly scribbled a note, she sat eyeing the employee's water cooler. Once she had the note in hand, she stood.

"Would you mind if I helped myself to a little cup of water from the cooler, FRED?"

"Of course not. Anything for a valued customer."

She dawdled near the cooler until he was wooing his next customer. *Perfect, the bottle is almost empty and the new one is sitting on the floor!* She looked around and then unscrewed the cap from the full bottle, dropped in four tablets of Twang Yao, and watched them dissolve.

"It's okay to try new things in life," she whispered to herself,

She waved at him as she headed for the door, and said, "scooby do, dear," to the receptionist while handing her the used tissue she'd used to blow her nose.

The following week the cable company relented by taking the extra charges off her bill. That night she waltzed around the house to the music of the Tommy Dorsey band. *Zippidy do da! The Twang Yao seems to be working!* Before bed she stuck a red star next to the cable company on her list in the laundry room. She looked at the entry for the Gang Intervention Center and decided that was next.

Twenty-Two

THE GANG INTERVENTION Center, housed in a building near the high school, was established to address a growing concern about neighborhood gangs. Myers Junction didn't have gangs but since the mayor was running for re-election he wanted a pet project. The irony was that once the Center was established, the town started seeing gang activity. Mildred was directed to an office down the hall with *Mary Louise Woodbead, Gang Intervention Center Supervisor* stenciled in black on the frosted glass pane in the door.

A softly-spoken "Come in," was the response when Mildred tapped lightly. "What is it?" the woman said without looking up as Mildred entered room.

"Ah, I'm Mildred Penniwink and I wanted to talk to you about a group of boys from the Center who ride my bus every afternoon. I've been having some problems . . ."

"Problems?" She looked up quickly. Mildred guessed her to be about forty. She was neatly dressed. Even her hair was perfectly in place like it had "teased" or "ratted" into a fixed position. Mildred knew because the hair dresser at Gloria's Salon once "teased" her hair with thick gel and it looked like that. It took her hours to finally get the snarls out, even using a wire brush.

"Yes, well you see the boys sit in seats reserved for senior and disabled riders and etch graffiti on the seats and windows. They also swear, smoke, and play loud music on their boom boxes, disturbing the other riders and defying regulations that prohibit such behavior. They regularly rip down the list of rider restrictions and . . ."

"That's enough Merryweather . . ."

"Mildred."

"What you obviously don't understand, and I wouldn't expect someone like you would, is that these young men need to express themselves. It's part of their rehabilitation. You see we take them off the streets and give them outlets in which to vent their frustrations in life, to make them feel a part of the community . . ."

Mildred blinked. *For god's sake, if that isn't horse nuts I don't know what is.* "Well, it seems you've taken them off the streets and put them on my bus, which is certainly not an appropriate venue for venting frustrations, as you can understand. And they certainly are not becoming part of the community. In fact they are offending the community of riders using public transportation in addition to vandalizing private property . . ."

"JUST . . . a minute. Who do you think you're talking to?" Mary Louise's pencil rolled off the desk and she reached for a cigarette. Mildred stared, hearing the scratch of a match being lit and watching as smoke curled up around Woodbead's face settling into a cloud before changing shape again. "I'm trained in crisis management and I run this program," she said while blowing a stream of smoke. Mildred fanned the smoke from her view.

"Then you are probably open to suggestions. Maybe we can all meet together, you and the gang of . . . well the boys, and find some solutions to this problem while at the same time discussing how the Intervention Center can help with this. Working with the community might help resolve some of the issues."

"Issues? Issues with the Center? Now they're issues? Look, I'm in charge here, and I decide what we do and don't do!" She slammed her hand on the desk, and papers fluttered before scattering.

Mildred shifted in her seat. *Oh jeepers creepers, is this a sign of dominance caused by an overgrowth of testosterone? So it's not always confined to men! Oh my gosh, I can't believe this!* Mildred stared, looking for signs of unwanted hair, a deepening of the voice.

"Ah, Miss Woodbead, I'm wondering . . . have you ever had your testosterone level checked ?"

The door slammed so hard Mildred could still hear the glass panel rattling as she walked down the hall to the exit.

~~~~

That night Mildred placed a call to Sgt. Patrick McCain. "Sorry to bother you at home Patrick. I didn't want this to be an official call. Do you have a minute to talk?"

"I'll be right over, Mildred."

"Patrick, no need to come all this way. I know you've worked all day. Let's talk on the phone. Do you have time right now?" Twenty minutes later, Mildred had spilled her anguish over the gang of thugs and her frustration with Supervisor Studebaker who refused to help or even file a report.

"Since this is an ongoing situation, Mildred, he should hire an armed guard to ride along for a while."

"I know, but I doubt if he'll do that. It would call attention to the situation and embarrass him in the eyes of the mayor and the community."

"Let's try something. Why don't I ride the bus in my uniform one day to see what happens. I'll check my schedule and you can tell me when and where they board the bus. Maybe one or two times might do the trick."

"Patrick, I think one has a switch blade knife."

"Okay, I'll bring a canon."

~~~~

Sgt. Patrick McCain, in full uniform, stepped up into the bus the following Thursday, two stops after the gang of thugs got on the bus and started their antics. Mildred held her breath and Patrick winked as he put his coins in the box. The immediate shuffle in the back was obvious. The gang separated and took different seats.

"What happened back here?" Patrick said, walking to the back and looking at the graffiti and torn seats.

Leon shrugged and spoke first. "Dunno, officer. The bus is falling apart, I guess."

"Yes, these buses are old and have seen some wear," Salvador said, stomping out a cigarette and sliding the butt under the seat before Patrick got close.

"Hmmm, where you boys from?"

"Oh, well we go to high school here," another volunteered. "Where's your patrol car. Don't the police here ride around in cars?"

Patrick shrugged. "No, not always. We like to see what's going on in town."

"Whoa, here's our stop," and they jumped off the minute the back door opened. Mildred watched them laughing as they ran down the street.

"Tomorrow will be the test, Mildred. Hopefully, they will be perfect gentlemen. I'll try to do this a couple more times to see if my visits have an impact."

"How can I thank you, Patrick? I know you are doing this on your free time."

"Chocolate chip cookies?"

The gang of thugs' behavior was predictable. When Patrick rode the bus they sat quietly but when not, they continued their obnoxious behavior. Mildred thanked Patrick with a box of his favorite cookies, realizing he can't ride the bus on a regular basis. She did, however, pose the idea of an armed guard to Supervisor Studebaker who proceeded to laugh hysterically.

~~~~

Mildred, Velda, and Gettie Mae decided it was time to meet

again, this again time in the library on a Saturday in the Poetry aisle. An autumn rain dampened the streets that morning reflecting the headlights of cars passing by. Mildred lingered at the kitchen table over a cup of coffee, listening to the never-ending drone of tires on the wet pavement and rain dripping from the eaves. She neither liked nor disliked the rain, but it put her in a mood. She poured herself another cup of coffee and brought her knitting basket to the table, touching the soft pastel-colored yarns layered neatly into skeins. She hadn't been to the hospital lately. *Too much going on*, she decided, but she did vow to knit more caps for the newborn after dinner that night.

They all huddled together near the collection of postmodern poetry while Mildred gave Velda and Gettie Mae an update on the dubious success of the licorice, and the dismal failure of the flax cookies she'd given to the gang of thugs.

"The good news is there's now *Twang Yao* in the water cooler at the cable company, and just this week I noticed the erroneous charges on my cable bill have been removed!"

"They took the charges off your bill?" Gettie Mae said in disbelief.

"Yes, just like that. I dissolved four pills the previous week, and the following week the charges were removed, of course also after I complained."

Velda stammered, then said, "I can't imagine the effects of the Twang Yao happening that fast, Mildred. I mean we're talking about changes in chemistry."

"Yes, but how long does it take to get a buzz after drinking a bottle of beer?" Mildred said. "Not very long. I think there's progress, but I'm disappointed I haven't seen results with the gang of thugs. I've tried the licorice, which seemed to work the first time, but the flax and soy flour cookies didn't seem to work at all."

Gettie Mae raised her hand. "Maybe the degree of testosterone makes a difference. You have to admit, the thugs' behavior is way out of the normal range so may be more flax is needed. Have you tried giving them the Twang Yao?"

"No, not yet. I'm not sure how to do that. Riders are not allowed beverages on the bus, and I'm already breaking every rule by giving them cookies and licorice. I've thought of putting some in plastic bottles of water hoping they don't give them away when they leave. What do you think?"

"Too bad they won't just swallow a capsule," Gettie Mae said, giggling a bit.

"Wait a minute," Velda said. "Can you embed a capsule in a piece of candy or something?" How big are the pills? Or, empty a capsule into a Twinkie?"

"Good idea, Velda. I like the Twinkie idea," Mildred said. "That way they won't detect a capsule since they'll wolf them down. It's just that, after the cookie mess, I'm not sure I want to give them more food on the bus."

"That reminds me," Velda added. "I had a few minutes the other day and looked through some of the books, and I noticed that spearmint also has the ability to lower testosterone levels. Do you have that on your list, Mildred?"

"No, but I do now. Very helpful, Velda."

Velda beamed and rushed back to the checkout counter, sashaying a bit on the way.

~~~~

Later that week Mildred stopped by the Gang Intervention Office after closing time, knowing Mary Louise Woodbead would have left for the day, at least she hoped. Peeking in the front door, she saw that Mary Louise Woodbead's office across the hall was closed, and the building was quiet except for a few group sessions being conducted in adjacent rooms. *Perfect! She's gone!* A tall, uniformed guard sat just inside the front door. She noticed a pistol in his holster.

Goodness, what's this world coming to!

"Excuse me, would you be so kind as to put this on supervisor

Woodbead's desk? It's just a little gift in return for a favor, that's all. I'm sorry I missed her."

"Yes ma'am," he said as he stood. "She left about an hour ago. I'll put this on her desk right now." She watched him unlock the door and put the box of nicely-wrapped spearmint candies on her desk with the note saying, *Thank you so much for all you do for our community.* She had scribbled an illegible signature at the bottom. He gave a slight salute and wave as he locked the office door, and Mildred left the building. *What a nice young man; normal testosterone no doubt. I'm sure HE doesn't tear up public property!*

Twenty-Three

MILDRED PLACED her coffee cup on the small table next to the front door, her broom close at hand but out of sight. The sun warmed the wooden porch making her feel warm and lazy. She waited, hoping Baumgartner's dog Buster might come bounding across the lawn although she usually had to be on all fours to attract the *mangy creature*, one of her terms of endearment for him. She checked the new plastic water bowl on the bottom step to make sure the Twang Yao was dissolved in the beef broth, and then walked down the steps and bent over her dried garden patch to pull some weeds. *This position ought 'a do it. . . it works every time.*

In only a matter of minutes she heard the snorting and turned fast to see Buster just inches away, his tongue wagging from side to side, his saliva and ears flying behind him. *Good grief!* She grabbed the bowl holding it in front of her and he skidded to a stop, dunking his head into the mixture and lapping with gusto.

*The beef broth! Of course he would love that! S*he quickly put the bowl on the step with Buster still slurping while she slipped into the house through the front door. From there she watched him empty the entire bowl before lifting his leg on the step.

Oh for god's sake, could he be any more obnoxious?

The following day she decided to test the Twang Yao again and stepped out onto the porch and into the garden. Within minutes Buster came galloping across the high grasses that separated the yards. Grabbing the broom for protection and planting her feet in the garden, she bent over but he ran right past her toward the bowl, licking and sliding it noisily across the walkway before running off. She wanted to shout with glee but stood up to see Burt Stillwell standing there.

"Mildred, are you alright? I don't mean to pry but I saw the goings on here this morning and wondered if everything is okay." He stood a distance away and unfolded his arms to scratch his head.

"Oh my, Burt, would you have time for a cup of coffee?"

Twenty minutes later she had told Burt Stillwell everything, even about the Twang Yao.

"Well no wonder you've had a bee in your bonnet, Mildred. It's not like you to let your garden go, and this morning it was as if you, well, you wanted Buster to . . ."

"No, no, no, good gracious no." Mildred put her cup down. "I was testing the Twang Yao again to see if it had the same effect as yesterday, and clearly it did. Burt, do you know Angus or have any problems with him? He's been unfriendly ever since he moved here. In the beginning I tried to have a word or two, but he'd just turn his back and go inside."

"Well, Baumgartner's dog used to do his business at the bottom of my steps every morning before I got up to get the newspaper." Burt's voice was gravely, befitting of his age. "Needless to say, he and I had some words. I told him I'd put a load of buckshot in the dog's behind if he did it again."

"What'd he say?"

"He just slammed the door in my face, so I put the sprinkler on a timer in the mornings and after the dog got soaked a few times he quit coming over." He shook his head. "Darndest thing."

They sat in silence for a while. "I just can't understand why Baumgartner can't be neighborly. He lets the dog out whenever he sees me working in the garden. He does it on purpose."

"Do you think that Twang stuff will work?"

"After today I'm convinced it will. The vet said it might calm him down, and I think he's right. He came flying over here earlier, and I put the bowl in his face and he lapped it up and ran off."

"Hmm . . ." Burt took his cap off and fit it back on giving it a little tug. "Maybe he was thirsty or would rather have the broth than give in to his urges. I wouldn't bet money on any of this, Mildred."

"Well, I'll soon find out. I'm buying some plants later this afternoon."

~~~~

The Plant and Feed store out on Miller's Turnpike was now more plant than feed, since it catered more to the people in town than farmers. Mildred went twice a year, spring and fall, after looking through her Midwestern Almanac that sat dog-eared on the table next to the television set. Mildred knew the Plant and Feed had an extensive selection of plants and the most experienced staff . . . unlike the big box store where no one seemed to know "a hibiscus from a hamburger," as Mildred was fond of saying. Also, she liked an excuse to ask for plants by their Latin names to show her own expertise, or actually the expertise of the Midwestern Almanac.

She liked the country feel out on Miller's Turnpike, and stood in the parking lot gazing at the beauty of farmland as far as she could see. A group of farmers in faded bib overalls stood in front of the Grange Hall across the road. One hitched up his jeans and straightened his crotch while another played with a stray dog throwing a stick. She wanted to wave because that's what people did in the country, but she went inside instead. Unfolding her list, she lingered, and then stepped up to the counter taking in the musty aroma of peat moss.

"How can we help you today?" The saleswoman wore a green bib apron with a pair of plant snippers in the front pocket, and *Nora* on her badge. "Doing some planting are we?"

"Ah, yes we are," Mildred said, sounding cheery. She didn't want to inform Nora that she'd be planting alone, so she let the

Mildred Penniwink   115

"we" comment pass. "I'd like some plants for a small garden." She glanced at her list. "Do you have *Helleboros orientalis* in white?"

"Lenten Rose, oh yes, of course. In a flat or quart size? We also have individual starters.

"Oh, I'm planting a row, so I'll take about six starters."

Nora pushed a button on her lapel and spoke into the small microphone attached to a battery pack she wore at her waist. "Six starters, *Helleboros orientalis.*" Mildred heard her order broadcast in the store and yard, and soon one of the yard workers arrived with her plants on a cart.

She smiled, pleased so far. "What about *Aster Oblougifolius*, about four of the quart sizes if you have them, Nora."

"I know we have Asters, but I'm not sure we have that variety." Nora spoke into her lapel mic again, "Does anyone know if we have *Aster Oblougifolius* in the quart size?" Mildred glanced around the store while waiting.

"Yes we do," the man's voice came over the loud speaker.

"Can you bring four please." Nora looked at Mildred and nodded.

"Okay! We're moving right along," Mildred said smiling at Nora. "How about two *Sequoia decentius*?"

Nora hesitated and took her finger off the microphone, her eyes fixed on Mildred. "Um, how big is your space? You said you had a small garden area. Do you have acreage? Also, I'm not sure those will grow in this climate."

"Really?"

"Yes, they're actually the giant Sequoia trees, the kind that grow along the mid-California coast. They're known to be one of the largest trees in North America."

Mildred raised her chin. "Ah, well I read about them in the almanac and . . . hmm, I didn't realize they got that big. I guess I'll pass on them."

Nora looked at her askance. "Yes, that's why we sometimes discourage the use of Latin names. They're not very descriptive unless of course you speak Latin, and many of us don't." She smiled painfully.

"Oh you're all so knowledgeable here. I just try to be helpful by jotting down the Latin names."

Nora smiled and waited.

"Well, let's see, do you have starters of *Clitoria Ternatea?"*

Nora flung her hands to her sides and turned away while sighing before looking up, her eyes almost disappearing into her head. Taking a deep breath, her face ashen, she said into her mic, *"Clitoria Ternatea?"*

After a long silence, the voice over the loud speaker said, "What?"

By that time people were gathering near the front desk, some standing back, but others moving in close.

Nora pronounced every syllable, *Cli-tor-i-a Ter-na-te-a."*

She waited for the reply over the loud speaker. The voice said, "Oh, yeah, the purple vine with the distinctive flower shape, if you know what I mean." There was laughter in the background. "We sell it as *Blue Pea* or *Butterfly Pea.* What size?" Again, more laughter.

Nora looked at Mildred. "Six starters, please," Mildred said. "And while he's at it, two quart- size containers of sage, any variety. Sorry, I don't have the Latin name," she said to Nora, who breathed a sigh of relief.

Nora put in the order and nodded to Mildred, "Anything else?"

"Do you know if it's too late to plant *Nipplewort?* I'm sorry again for not having the Latin name, but it's in the sunflower family."

Before the words were barely out of Mildred's mouth, Nora said, "Oh yes, way too late. Too very late. No need to ask the yard men. Definitely cannot be planted now."

"Oh Okay, well I guess that's all then. While I wait for the cart I'll just be looking around outside."

"Yes, take your time. Please stay outsi . . ."

In the yard, Mildred breathed in the fragrance of lilacs, red peonies, and verbena, and lingered at each one wishing her garden was larger. *I guess first things first. I need to see if that beast of a dog will let me have my garden back!* She spotted a six-pack of peonies and noticed that one plant was wilting a bit. She looked over her shoulder.

They'll never sell this, she thought, as she lifted the plant from the container and stuffed it into her coat pocket.

A young man was just wheeling her cart to the front, so she walked toward the counter to pay. By that time the crowd had disappeared.

"Not more plants, I hope . . . that is, I mean I hope you found everything you wanted." Nora looked helpless.

"Yes I did, now it's just a matter of Buster and Twang Yao."

"I see, but I don't think we carry either of those."

Twenty-Four

MILDRED DECIDED to skip church, a decision she made most Sunday mornings. She sorted her newly-bought plants according to placement, taller flowers in back and spreaders near the walkway. She put the lone peony, looking robust already, in front and stood back looking pleased.

"Ouch," she said aloud as she crammed her feet into her yellow rubber garden boots, evidently a width too narrow. *Oh hog's breath, dusty as sin.* She wiped the tops with the sleeve of her flannel shirt and adjusted the plastic garden apron she received as a birthday gift from her scrabble club. The can of Dog-Off sat close just in case. Stirring the concoction of broth and Twang Yao in Buster's new plastic water dish, she placed it strategically about ten feet away on the walkway where Buster usually ran full throttle toward her back side when she was in the garden.

Oh cripes this is a leap of faith. She took a long breath and leaned over on all fours, taking her spade to the first row in the back and keeping the can of Dog-Off next to each plant for quick retrieval.

She planted the Asters leaving plenty of room for growth, and then dug the second row eyeing the distance between holes to make sure they were even. It was when she was reaching for the *Butterfly Peas*, as Nora in the garden shop called them, that she heard the familiar gallop of Buster. She looked up to see him racing across the yard, ears back, tongue flapping back and forth, and legs flying in all directions.

Her instinct was to get off her knees and take cover, but she held her ground and her breath. Squeezing her eyes shut and bracing her arms, she waited for the dreaded mount. Instead, nothing happened.

She peeked over her shoulder and saw Buster's front legs spread wide and his face buried in his new doggie bowl lapping up the brew. She took a deep breath. *Now let's see if he wants his cake and eat it too.* She knew he liked the broth, but she wondered if the Twang Yao would kick in and render him platonic.

She leaned forward again and started on the third row, but her mind was not on planting. She waited a minute and then glanced over her shoulder again. The bowl was upside down and Buster was sprawled out on the lawn fast asleep!

~~~~

Later that morning, she found Velda at the check-out desk in the library. "Pssst!" Mildred motioned to Velda while standing near the card catalog shifting her weight from one foot to the other. Velda could only shrug since she was helping a long line of patrons. Mildred wandered through the library until Velda found her a few minutes later in the magazine section reading *Bowling Today.*

"Oh my word, Mildred!" she said, her eyes wide open. "He just fell asleep after drinking the Twang Yao?"

"Just like that. I planted my entire garden and not a peep from him. He was still sleeping when I cleaned up and put my garden clothes in the washer. Can you believe that?"

Velda stood motionless, her eyes wide. "He . . . he wasn't dead was he?" she whispered and looked around to make sure no one was listening.

"No, no, you ninny. He went home after his nap. And he didn't even glance back. Absolutely no interest! Just think, Velda, this could have important repercussions."

"Well, could it have been all that broth and not the Twang Yao? I mean, how do we know for sure his testosterone level dropped so suddenly? Maybe he didn't attack you because he was full. Sometimes my husband . . ."

"Velda!"

"Sorry, Mildred, it's just that . . ."

Mildred interrupted. "There has to be a connection between the Twang Yao and Buster's testosterone. How else can you explain that this is the first time he hasn't jumped me while I was bent over? The very first time," she repeated.

Velda's gaze wandered off and then back to Mildred. "But . . . well, if you say so, Mildred. You would know."

That evening Mildred checked her garden again, delighting in the beautiful colors next to her worn wooden steps. When nightfall appeared, she slipped into the slinky green silk robe she saved for special occasions and sipped a glass of *chabliss* while toasting her new garden and success with Buster. Twirling again and again and humming, she put on a vinyl Louis Prima record and with lights blazing bright and the music turned up loud, she danced the cha cha through every room.

"Yes! we have no bananas," she sang slightly off key with her arms swinging wide, "we have no bananas today."

~~~~~

The young man in Vitamin World was helping a customer so Mildred hurried down the last aisle, hoping to avoid him in case he made the connection between her last visit and the empty shelves in the *Testosterone Boosters* section. She needed more Twang Yao since her supply was getting low now that she was slipping it to Buster. She put three bottles in her shopping basket and peeked around until she noticed the young man was still with a customer. Her curiosity prompted her to inch along the back wall and turn down the *Testosterone Booster* aisle.

Oh my word! It had been three weeks and the shelves were still empty! *Holy cow!*

"I saved you the trouble of clearing the shelves again in case you returned."

Mildred Penniwink   121

She swung around to see the young man standing behind her. His skin was still dreadfully pale, but his eyes were bright and the slight smile seemed sincere.

"Oh my goodness!" She put her hand to her face.

"It's okay, really it is. I don't like what testosterone does to people either. I assumed that's why you took it all."

"I . . . I just, well I just . . ."

"No need to explain. Maybe you've also been hurt, or someone you know has, by someone revved up on this stuff. I understand totally. I'm the buyer for this section, and I told the manager the supplier is out right now. I'm not sure how long I can keep saying that, but I'll try."

She took a deep breath and relaxed her shoulders. "Thank you. I don't know what to say. I'm, I am totally at a loss for words."

She hurried to the counter to pay for the Twang Yao and then rushed from the store. *Golly, I must remember that young man at Christmas time with a small gift.*

The following morning she marked the date and Twang Yao next to the "Gang of Thugs" line on her chart in the laundry room, and then measured out the appropriate dose of Twang Yao after twisting off the caps of five small plastic water bottles, making sure not to mar the labels. *Ah ha! If it works for Buster it'll work for them.* She shook the bottles to make sure the Twang Yao was thoroughly dissolved and put them next to her lunch pail.

~~~~

"You're mighty chipper this morning, Mildred," Betsy Palmer said, as she took a seat up front. Betsy Palmer's hand-stitched quilts won first prize at the county fair last year and she is president of the Myers Junction Quilting Bee. Petite in size, she could wrestle her large quilts with ease. Bernice Lee had ordered one for her king-size bed and Betsy delivered it by herself in her station wagon. People talked about that for days.

"I certainly am chipper today Betsy, and just look at that sky.

It's going to be a beautiful day. Are you off to the senior center or shopping?"

"I'm playing bridge with the group at the center. You know most of them, Mildred, and they're all fun. Why don't you join us? We'd love to have you."

Argh, does she think driving a bus is volunteer work? "I'll give it some thought, Betsy."

That afternoon she worked up her courage for the gang of thugs. As she neared their stop, she reached under the seat and pulled out the paper bag with five plastic bottles of water. When the bus pulled to the curb, the rowdy thugs started kicking and pounding at the door.

"C'mon mama bitch, don't make us wait. Burp this thing and open the door." As they pushed the other riders aside, they stepped in one by one and she handed each one a bottle of water.

"It's dry today so I thought you might like something to drink."

"Motha fuckin' bitch is giving us water. The bus puss is finally catching on to treatin' us nice," Salvador said to the others.

She held her breath until they moved to the back and then greeted the few riders who were boarding the bus. With one or two exceptions, most of the others walked two blocks to the next stop to avoid the delinquents. "Best to stay near the front," she said to each one as they put their fare in the box. Traffic was light that day and she noticed Nancy Hensely's kindergarten class out for recess, and saw more cars than usual in front of the church. "It's not Sunday so there must be a funeral today," she said to Margaret Larson, who was sitting nearby.

"Old Jacob DeVries. Heart attack."

"Hmm."

When she could, she looked in the mirror and saw the usual pranks in the back. Two boys were on the seats trying to jump to the seat across the aisle without falling, and taking gulps of water in between jumps. The others were chanting, "Fall, fall, fall." Two others were taking some pills and washing them down with the water, and then shaking the bottle fiercely before squirting the water on the windows. Much to her disappointment, that caught on so they all starting shaking the water and squirting it at each other.

"Hey, mama bitch, you got more water?"

Mildred groaned. She stared at her hands gripping the steering wheel, watching her knuckles turn white.

"Do you, do you smell something, Mildred?" Mary Peppers whispered, leaning over the aisle.

"Not really, what?"

"Oh, it's probably nothing. I get nervous when those boys are on the bus, do you?"

"You don't know the half of it," Mildred said, scowling at the road ahead.

~~~~

That afternoon, Spencer waited with his bucket and squeegee at the Bus Bay. "How are you doing tonight, Miss Mildred? Busy day or slow day?"

"Oh, pretty normal, Spencer." She jumped off the bus and went looking for a bucket of soapy water.

When she returned, Spencer was just coming out of the bus. "You're not going to like this, Mildred."

"What? What, Spencer?" she said climbing up and walking to the back of the bus where she smelled the paint. The seats and walls had been spray painted with obscenities and graffiti. Mildred plopped down in one of the seats up front and put her face in her hands. The empty water bottles littered the floor, along with cigarette butts and two empty spray cans of paint.

"How can this be happening?" Her voice cracked as she stood and looked again.

"I've got something that will probably take this off since it's still fresh," Spencer said shaking his head. "It may not look really perfect but at least you won't be able to read it."

"Why, Spencer? Why is this happening?" She didn't tell him about her real disappointment; that she gave the Twang Yao to the thugs and it didn't work.

"I know you're trying everything, but nothing is working and it probably won't. I think you should go see Supervisor Studebaker again. I'll go with you. I'll take pictures of this and we'll show him."

"He'll fire me for sure, but actually I don't care anymore. I think Studebaker is just looking for a reason to fire me anyway. He wants to show that a woman can't handle the job. Maybe he's right."

Twenty-Five

SUPERVISOR STUDEBAKER leaned over his desk looking at each photograph in detail while Mildred and Spencer sat quietly.

"What? This mess is from the bus, one of our buses? The graffiti too?" Studebaker looked up. "How could you let this happen? Are you reading a book or something while the bus is being destroyed? I warned you Miss Perriwinkle . . ."

"Penniwink."

"I have no choice but to find a replacement for you. This bus is a mess, a disgrace . . ."

Spencer stood, towering over the desk and running his hand down his tie to make sure it was in place. Mildred had never seen Spencer wear a tie other than in some wedding photographs he showed her once. He always looked neat and clean, but today he looked spiffy, with a tie and regular shoes rather than work boots.

"I should mention Supervisor Studebaker, that if you fire Miss Penniwink for something beyond her control, it will be the talk of the town. She's very popular with her riders. And not only that, it will point out how dangerous it is to ride a city bus and that might trigger an investigation."

"Oh shit." Studebaker threw his hands up. "I want this bus cleaned up. I don't have time to sit around and look at pictures all day long. Let's all get back to work, and I warn you Perri . . . whatever . . ."

Mildred cleared her throat and leaned forward. "There's a bigger problem here and that's months of vandalism, obscenities, and dangerous behavior. It seems we have an obligation to our riders to provide a safe and pleasant experience . . ."

"I don't want to hear you both bellyaching about your jobs."

"It's more than that, sir." Spencer spoke softly. "There are some real safety issues with the physical abuse of the other riders and the disruptions to the driver when these boys throw items on the bus, play loud music, and smoke and do drugs, not to mention the obscene things they do on a public bus."

"Ah yes, yes I remember Miss Per . . . well, Mildred, saying something about a couple fornicating on the bus." He chuckled and shook his head. "That's one I haven't heard before," he said laughing. "Do I need to remind you that these are boys, and the Gang Intervention Center is a community effort? We all need to do our part, even if that means keeping this . . . this mess under our hats. These are childish pranks. Let's all turn our heads a little, for heaven's sake. I mean, what's a little graffiti?"

Mildred swallowed hard. "What is a little graffiti, sir? I'm wondering if you would consider letting one of your staff ride the bus one day just to see what's going on and to assess the danger? Or even you, if you have the time? Or better yet, an armed guard."

"Nonsense! Absolutely not! And as for my staff, do you actually think that's part of their job description? I mean, can't you see we are busy here?" He looked at his watch. "Miss Perri . . .you are about to get the boot. We expect our drivers to do more than just put their foot on the pedal. A driver should be able to handle all sorts of matters. Now I have nothing further to say and I think it best for all of us to get back to work." He looked at Mildred. "Your days are numbered here, so don't bother me again." He sat looking at them until they knew the conversation was over.

Spencer held the door and they walked out onto the street. "Sorry, Mildred, I see what you mean about him."

"It doesn't surprise me that he'd try to weasel his way out of this, the blithering mollycoddler. How can he possibly reduce this to a little graffiti?"

"Yeah, well he's far removed from it all and clearly doesn't want to get involved. If he could see what's going on, it might be different."

"Yes, like the gang of thugs hanging out in his office. Or, if the graffiti was outside his door?"

"Mildred? What are you thinking? I haven't seen this look before."

"Maybe it's not just the gang of thugs who need a jolt. Perhaps it's time for Studebaker to wake up and feel the pressure."

"Mildred?"

She dropped him off at the Bus Bay and he looked at her askance before getting out of the car. "Mildred? You're beginning to worry me. It's not worth what I think you are thinking."

"Thank you, Spencer, for coming with me today. Can I keep these photos?"

"Of course, but just to look at. Nothing else." Before she drove off, he tapped on the car window and she rolled it down. "Mildred, what's a mollycoddler?"

"It's a weak and cowardly person, Spencer. Just like the supervisor."

~~~~

On the way home she kept mulling over one of Studebaker's last remarks: "What's a little graffiti?" *What a jackass!* Her face flushed and she drew in a bottomless breath. When she got to her street she pulled over and sat in the car. The sun streamed through the windshield as she played the steering wheel like a piano and then turned the car around and headed back in the direction of the big box store.

The parking lot was full, but then it usually was ever since it opened two years ago after all the protests. The townspeople were adamant about supporting the small shops in town, arguing that the large one-stop one-shop store would put them out of business and change the nature of the town. Mildred put up flyers and took her turn standing in the rain with a picket sign, but in the end the store was built. The city fathers argued that the increased taxes from a large store would help to fund needed services for the citizens, and they had no choice but to approve the permit request by the big conglomerate. By the time the store opened the smaller shops had closed, and people were forced to shop there fueling the argument by the large chain that people actually preferred shopping in one-stop stores.

Hogwash, the local newspaper said in an editorial. *They have no choice now that you've put the other stores out of business.* In time, the issue finally died down but in a unified act of defiance, the people refused to call it by its name and it came to known only as the "big box store."

The sun felt good on her face that afternoon as she walked from her car to the main entrance. She relaxed her shoulders and stretched her arms. *So much frustration and anger after sitting across from Supervisor Studebaker. He sticks like a bone in the throat.* She found the jumbo chalk in the children's section and picked up several boxes in various colors, along with a drawing tablet. She stood staring at them in the shopping cart. *Holy cow, what am I doing?*

She looked away. Some children ran up and down the aisle while their mother tried to rein them in, and the loud speaker announced something about a special in the bakery aisle. She looked again at the items in her cart and walked away, leaving the cart in the middle of the aisle. At the exit, she hesitated, then turned around and walked back to where she had left her cart.

"Where would I find a black stocking cap?" she asked a clerk walking by.

Twenty-Six

MILDRED UNBUTTONED her jacket as she entered the library for her meeting with Velda and Gettie Mae in the automotive section that morning. Gettie Mae was already there waiting and Velda saw them and rushed over with a pencil stuck in her bun as usual. "Oh girls, I have the most exciting news."

The three moved in close while Velda's whisper was barely more than a private thought. "When I called about the usual overcharge on my cable bill this week, you'll never guess what happened?"

They all stood silent, waiting for Velda to continue. Evidently Velda wanted them to guess.

"WHAT Velda?" Mildred said impatiently.

"They took the erroneous charges off my bill even without excuses or arguments, and I didn't even need to ask to speak to one of the supervisors. I nearly fell through the floor."

"Ah ha!" Gettie Mae bellowed. "Could it be the Twang Yao is working? Didn't Mildred put some in the water cooler at the cable company office?"

"Shhh." Mildred looked around to make sure no one heard that, and drummed her fingers on the bookcase while leaning in close. The rest gathered around. "I'm sure it was the Twang Yao. It worked just like it worked with Baumgartner's beast of a dog, Buster."

"Have you tried it more than once on him?" Gettie Mae asked.

Hazel Warlaumont

"I've been out several times to water my plants and pull some weeds, and each time I put the bowl of Twang Yao and broth out, Buster goes right for it and then falls asleep. I can't tell you how excited I am to have my garden back!"

"I still think it's the broth," Velda mumbled quietly, as if thinking out loud.

Gettie Mae stood nodding. "And, what about the thugs on the bus? Any progress there? I was on the bus the day you gave out the Twang Yao in the water bottles. What a travesty! I heard from Clyde Mills they spray painted graffiti all over the back of the bus that day. Horrible, just horrible."

Mildred tapped her fingers on top of the book case. "No progress. I talked to our supervisor again. I even showed him pictures of the bus and the graffiti but he still wants to blame me, telling me my days are numbered. If the graffiti were in his face, he might think differently."

"So, what's next Mildred?" Velda asked, blinking more than usual.

"Yes, what is next" Gettie Mae said. "The regular riders are at their wits end, Mildred. Some are even thinking of quitting the senior center for a while because it's so intimidating to ride the bus these days."

"I'm doing what I can, Gettie Mae. I'm just running out of ideas."

"Well, Albert flatly refuses to ride after they unhooked his wheelchair and he rolled all the way to the back that day. I don't know how you put up with it, Mildred, I really don't. But something has to happen or no one will ride the bus."

Mildred shrugged and when she got home that night she left her nice robe in the closet and her recordings and player on the shelf.

~~~~

Later that week, Mildred garnered enough courage to spread

Spencer's photographs on the table, her new drawing tablet nearby. First she drew one word lightly with a pencil and then carefully drew circular bubble shapes around the lines. After looking at the photographs again, she drew the letters closer together so they overlapped just like the graffiti in the bus. She added colored chalk inside the lines and repeated it over and over until she thought it began to look like real graffiti. "Motha Fucker" and "We Rule" were terms the thugs used most often, but she decided to just use random initials.

After another hour of practice she stood back, her eyes fixed on the tablet. *Well sis-boom-bah, this isn't so hard! That's probably why these nincompoops do it; the vandals, the wimpy little vandals!*

She had an aching urge to scream through a bull horn or from the top floor of Hansen's Hardware:

ATTENTION: everyone has the right to ride the bus to the senior center or anywhere else without having to deal with a GANG OF THUGS!

From then on she read the weather report every day in the Myers Junction *Tribune,* making sure no rain was in sight. She rehearsed what she needed to do. *I hope the chalk looks close enough to the spray paint, It needs to look real; it definitely must look real! Then, maybe everyone will feel the indignation I do and get the thugs off my bus.*

~~~~

"Dark clothes," she mumbled as she searched her closet and drawers flinging several items of clothing on the bed. Finally she had what she wanted. She looked closely at the items on the bed and looked over her list again. "Dark jacket, black sweat pants, and . . . oh, yes, the black stocking cap and a black plastic bag." *Maybe I should start going to church, I really should.*

She chose late Sunday night and into the early hours of Monday morning . . . quiet times in town when everyone sleeps. *There's rarely crime in Myers Junction . . . no patrol cars at night,* she reasoned. She drew a map of the four locations and marked where she'd park her car at each location so it wouldn't be noticed. For the rest of the week her primary goal was to practice. Not to perfect her technique, but to practice working as fast as she could.

~~~~

Ah! No rain in sight! She was ready after one last check of the weather that night. Stuffing the plastic bag with supplies along with her stocking cap, she drove slowly out of her driveway a little past midnight without making a sound. Her first stop was the Gang Intervention Center on Mills Avenue; generally a busy street because of the high school nearby, but quiet that time of night. The Center was housed in the old Grange building that sat for years until the city fixed it up as a place for troubled youth. The newspaper questioned the renovation, but the mayor was running for re-election again.

The old Grange building was a wooden structure, and Mary Louise Woodbead's office was right inside the front door. Mildred knew for a fact that Mary Louise parked her car directly in front and entered from there.

She sat alone in the car looking in all directions feeling the perspiration forming on the back of her neck and her heart racing. *Oh good god!* She sat tapping her finger on the gear shift and looked at her watch and then over her shoulder again. *Chalk, my watch, and the small drawing.*

Pulling the stocking cap on and yanking it down to her eyebrows, she got out of the car and felt her legs wobble before walking slowly to the building where she stood alone in the dark until her eyes got used to the moonlight.

One by one, she took the boxes of chalk from her plastic bag, and choked for a second on her breath before starting to work. During her last visit to the library, she read that graffiti is not always intended to be readable, but most use letters have certain meanings like HOD to mean Hand of Doom, or MLS meaning My Life Sucks, or KWC to mean Kuz We Can. But generally, the assault from marring a space with graffiti was enough without it making sense, so she decided to just choose letters at random.

She started with some outlines, but when her arms got tired she filled in the bubbled letters with colored chalk, taking short breaks to rest, and looking over her shoulder with each stroke. "Ugh, this is hard work," she grunted under her breath. "No wonder it's done by young thugs and not by those of us over fifty."

She was slow, but picked up speed as she moved along until she was drawing graffiti with such artistry, her hands seemed to have perfected the skill without her knowledge.

By the time she finished chalking the front wall of the Gang Intervention Center, she had written ABC on both sides of the door in rounded letters with variations of color and design, and finished in just under eighteen minutes.

Yippidy do, not bad for a first try! She bent her head for a closer look. *A little too much orange but . . . hmm, not bad!*

She shivered and pulled her jacket tight at the neck as she rushed to her car and drove silently in the direction of the Brown Country Transit Authority and the office of Supervisor Roger F. Studebaker. The office was just about one mile from the Bus Bay and Mildred knew there was only one main entrance to the office.

She knew Supervisor Studebaker would be certain to see the graffiti when he arrived the next morning for work so she decided to use his initials, RFS. She drew rounded letters and several scrolls in green and yellow with red highlights, and decided to put it on both sides of the door.

Making giant arcs for her letters, she used bright colors in each section so the graffiti looked even larger than she expected on the BCTA building walls. It was illuminated slightly by the nearby street lamp. She put her whole body into it this time instead of just her arms, and she finished without taking a break. *Whoopdy do, now we're cookin'.* She stood admiring her work, and then noticed the time.

We'll see how Supervisor Studebakers feels about "just a little graffiti" now, the wagpastie! She brushed the chalk from her hands before moving on to the next stop. Feeling the night chill, she kept her stocking cap on in the car.

The Myers Junction Tribune and the City Hall were just a block apart, so she parked the car on the other side of the park and walked first to the newspaper office.

She put the graffiti on the walls in the front of both buildings with a tinge of regret. She had no ill feelings toward the newspaper or City Hall, but she hoped the graffiti might be mentioned on the editorial page, airing the problem in public, and perhaps putting pressure on Mary Louise Woodbead and Supervisor Studebaker to address the problem of gangs, especially on her bus. At least, that was her hope.

She knew the editor of the newspaper, Jim Cooper, to be a fine man who also wrote the editorials and stood on the side of the public. Same for City Hall. *Although the mayor could leave and no one would notice*, she thought. But looking at the vandalized buildings she felt both exhilarated and understandably shameful.

She was working faster now and had to be finished before daybreak. Ribbons of daylight were just beginning to push up over the hills and she had one more stop, so she headed quickly for the Bus Bay. Spencer was there waiting.

"Mildred, for the last time, I don't think you should do this," he whispered. "What if you get caught?"

"Too late now, Spencer. The bus is now the last, the others are finished. If I'm to lose my job at least I can say I tried." She looked at her watch and at him, and raised her eyebrows.

He shook his head but held the bag of chalk as she put graffiti on both sides of the bus using a step ladder to reach, with him standing by to make sure she didn't fall. She groaned every time she reached up high on the bus, but she kept moving along quickly as she made an attempt to cover as much as she could in the time she had left. She stopped once and sat on the ground.

"Mildred, let's stop now," he said quietly. "You've done enough to get the idea across."

She shot him a look and climbed up on the ladder again, starting on the other side. After an hour she stopped again and took a long breath.

"I didn't realize this bus was so darn big," she said, making an effort to laugh. At one point she leaned over and put her hands on her knees, letting her head fall forward.

"Let me help, Mildred, I can finish the rest."

"Best that this be my crime not yours, Spencer. I'm almost finished," she whispered, "and I need to go home to get dressed for work."

She kept looking at her watch, holding it up to whatever daylight was approaching up over the hills. Her urgency was driven by her need to put an end to the nightmare, to be rid of the gang of thugs and the helplessness she felt, so she kept moving as fast as she could.

She finished the last section of the bus just as a yellow ring of light came into view. She and Spencer put all the chalk back in the bag and she stood staring quietly in disbelief, feeling angry for vandalizing her own bus.

Spencer nodded and took a deep breath. He walked over and put his arm around her shoulder.

"As far as you know, Spencer, you came in this morning and the bus was already covered in this graffiti, Okay? And not a word to anyone."

He nodded. "Okay. I sure hope this works."

"Me too and thank you, Spencer." She walked to her car and he caught up with her.

"Miss Mildred," he whispered. "Well, . . you did a good thing tonight."

Twenty-Seven

GEORGE O'BANNON took his time but Mildred kept the door open. Slow to walk and stoop-shouldered, his one leg seemed to work better than the other but he got himself up the step and sat in the first seat. The riders usually kept that seat free for riders like George.

Mildred yawned but sat up straight. "How are you this morning, George? Did you get that leak fixed in your roof?"

"Sure did, and I'm good, Mildred. Damn good." His one leg bounced a little on its own and he put his hand on it to hold it still. "Say, looks like you're not the only one to get hit with that writing all over the bus."

"Oh, is that so?"

"Hell yes it is, take a look at this." His hands were as shaky as his voice, but he held up his newspaper so she could see the front page.

TOWN HIT BY GRAFFITI!

"Oh, my," she said, feigning her surprise. She couldn't believe it had only been a matter of hours, but she knew the newspaper staff started early.

That day, Mildred's bus passed back and forth through town as eyes turned, people stared, and jaws dropped. Mildred kept her eye on the road for the most part, but noticed people stopping all along the sidewalk, pointing as the graffiti-clad bus passed through town. A few drivers honked and pointed to the graffiti, as if to alert Mildred to the obvious, and she waved and nodded but kept the bus on schedule even with the disruptions and the myriad of questions and comments throughout the day. She could only shrug when it became the topic of conversation, saying "I don't know," more times than she cared to.

She stifled yet another yawn and fought to keep her eyes open. The gang of thugs normally boarded at the next stop. *Oh cripes, here we go!* She braced for the worst when she saw them, wondering if they'd read the newspaper that morning. *Probably not.* They waited alone, since most riders by then were waiting at other stops to avoid their antics. The door opened slowly and that's when she saw them bunched together talking. Leon, the tall one, walked over to the bus to take a closer look and then went back to the group. They stood like statues in the wax museum.

"Are you getting on or not?" she yelled from the bus.

The one they called Bruno stepped up on the first step and hesitated. Seeing him for the first time without his mouth going and his body gyrating, she noticed the color of his eyes and the pock marks on his face. He stepped up and leaned inside. "Is anyone else on the bus mama bitch, I mean, you know, guys like us?"

"I didn't know there were guys like you. Are you getting on or what?"

He turned to the others, and they stepped up cautiously and sat in the front row seats. Bruno leaned over the aisle. "Who tagged the bus mama bitch? Did you see 'em."

Oh great bats of brimstone! She stared at him. *Oh my god!* The unexpected became clear. She now realized the notorious gang of thugs feared another gang and a possible turf war! The entire bus in their minds had been claimed by a new gang. *Oh my word, the world is full of surprises!*

"I thought you boys did it."

They sat without talking, their faces frozen like in a blizzard.

Even their eyes blinked to ward off the imaginary ice hanging on their lashes. She rolled down her window as she neared the park and breathed deeply. She heard a warbler whistle from the Elm tree and she breathed in the fragrance of honeysuckle. She sat in the driver's seat not wanting to move, ever.

~~~~~

The weather was a gift all that week; clear skies and scant morning dew. She wondered what would happen with the first rain. *Would the chalk run and recreate itself on the streets and sidewalks?* The daily newspaper kept a running commentary on the graffiti, especially the editorial page. The debate over the necessity of the Gang Intervention Center came up again, and the title of one editorial was: *Are we wasting our money?* It was surely written by the editor, Jim Cooper, who took it upon himself to monitor City Hall's spending habits. *What's happening to Myers Junction?* appeared the following day, raising larger questions about the town's future. After that, the editorial titled: *Why isn't the Gang Intervention Center working?* pleased her more than any, and she hoped Mary Louise Woodbead was reading it that very minute and feeling miserable.

Mildred felt like a flea hiding in the fur after inflicting the bite. The graffiti gave the townspeople something to talk about in the Pastry Pantry over coffee and donuts, and again in the lines at Woolworths' five and dime; and, certainly on the bus. To see the town awaken to the issue validated her own indignation. At times she felt guilty for what she'd done, but she had pushed the issue out in the open. On the other hand, she knew for certain she was not about to come forward and admit it was her hand that set the town abuzz. The plan was to point the finger at the gang of thugs so someone would stop them from destroying her bus. As for now, the gang of thugs were lying low.

~~~~~

She shielded her eyes from the late-setting sun making its last hurrah before disappearing behind the old stand of Alders. Leaves fluttered and swirled into piles of gold and orange near her porch and she stopped to admire her flower bed, still flourishing, before going inside. She could never understand why the house at times seemed so barren.

Hmm, maybe just another throw rug? she thought, as she put her purse on the table.

The knock at the door surprised her. When she opened it, Velda and Gettie Mae stood on the porch looking lost and needing directions. "Sorry, Mildred," Gettie Mae said, "but we've been trying to reach you all day."

"Today was a work day but come in, don't just stand there." They stepped inside like intruders would, more or less on their toes. "I just got home. Let's have a glass of *Chabliss* want to?"

"Oh, yes," Velda responded with an almost verbal sigh. They dropped their coats on the couch, and Velda squeezed her eyes half shut as she examined Mildred's face.

Mildred knew why they were there and she dreaded that moment. She didn't want to implicate Spencer in the graffiti incident, and surely if anyone knew she did it, especially the graffiti on the bus, he surely would be seen as an accomplice. On the other hand, these were friends who'd offered support from the beginning and she didn't want to lie.

"Well," Gettie Mae said with firmness, "what on earth is happening with all this graffiti? Have the gang of thugs lost their minds?"

Mildred measured her words. "It's certainly the talk of town, at least on the bus."

"Indeed it is," Gettie Mae said, looking over the rim of her jelly glass of Chablis. "On one hand, won't this motivate those in charge to clamp down on these boys? I mean, won't this support our effort to get them off the bus so we can ride in peace? This seems like a hundred-dollar bill to me especially since nothing else has worked, don't you agree?"

"I would certainly hope so." Mildred poured more wine.

"I don't know if you've had a chance to read the newspaper

yet," Gettie Mae went on, "but they even marked up the office of Gang Intervention and that guy you work for, Studemarker."

"Studebaker. No, I just got home." She was aware Velda had not said a word while Gettie proceeded to summarize everything in the newspaper and from the grapevine. Their strained smiling and dancing around the issue made Mildred nervous. While Gettie Mae droned on, Mildred decided to sneak a peek at Velda.

It was Velda's eyes that had stopped her cold. They seemed enormous compared to the rest of the features on her face, which now seemed elongated because of the dropped jaw. Mildred's glance turned to a stare.

". . . and then Fred called to say he heard a work party was forming to scrub off the graffiti, and if anyone wanted to sign up they should call . . ."

"Gettie, Gettie Mae, I hate to interrupt, but it's been a long day. Let's get together at the library on Saturday and maybe we'll know more by then. Is that okay with you, Velda? Ah . . . Velda?"

~~~~

That night she nibbled on leftovers after rummaging through the fridge. Exhausted after missing last night's sleep, she felt a glimmer of excitement as she thought about the town's concern over the graffiti. But more than that, she was just beginning to realize the gang of thugs might stop riding a bus seemingly tagged by a rival gang. *Sweet Jesus!* A few minutes later she pulled out her Count Basie LP of *Chattanooga Choo Choo* and in her plaid flannel pajamas and worn slippers, she danced through the house until she fell into bed.

"Pardon me boy, is that the Chattanooga Choo Choo? Track twenty nine . . ." droned in and out and that was the last thing she remembered.

Twenty-Eight

THE NEXT MORNING Spencer's grin said it all. Neither said a word but they hugged when she walked up to the bus, and they laughed and nudged each other all morning while getting the bus ready. Spencer checked the graffiti and gave her a thumbs up. "So far so good, pray for sunshine," he said with a smile. "Oh, by the way, the office sent over this note for you." He handed her a slip of paper on the transit company stationary.

Ms. Penniwink, see me on your lunch break today without delay.

Supervisor Studebaker

She showed it to Spencer, raising her brow. "Maybe now he wants to talk? Or is he planning to fire me?"

"Let's hope he wants to talk. He'd have no way of knowing you were out so late the night of the caper."

~~~~

Mildred glanced around the room to keep from looking at him but as usual her eyes settled on the top of his head. Maybe it was because he had no other distinguishing features. His eyes were light brown like a hamster she once had; he always wore a blue tie; and on the few occasions he wore a jacket, the arms were too short. Usually she felt dismissed before she even sat down but this time was different.

"What the hell do you know about all this . . . this graffiti?"

Hazel Warlaumont

His effort to get the word out suggested his contempt. "It's on your bus, outside the front door, and all over town from what I'm told. Who's doing this? Christ!" He ran his hand over his head. "Does this have something to do with all your complaining about the young men who ride your bus? Huh? Does it?"

She brimmed, relishing his discomfort. *What a sapsucker. Now the shoe's on the other foot, you nincompoop.* "I don't really know, Supervisor Studebaker. I couldn't say."

He slapped his hand on the desk. "I'm getting calls from everyone, the mayor, the newspaper, the company president. Didn't you have some of this goddamn graffiti inside your bus a week or so ago? Whatever happened to those hoods who put it there?"

"Actually, nothing. In spite of my complaints to you and photographs of the damage, you basically said 'let's keep this quiet' and blamed me. So nothing happened to them. They've been vandalizing the bus for months. As a result we lost or disappointed many of our valued riders, sir. When Spencer and I were here to plead our case, I think your last words were, 'what's a little graffiti?'"

"Well . . . well I don't remember saying that," he said flustered. "Where are those boys now, where can we find them?"

"I don't know anything about them sir, other than they ride the bus and tear it apart. You told me once they might be from the new Gang Intervention Center, but I don't know for sure. You might want to talk with the woman who runs the program. I think her name is Mary Louise Woodbead , or Woodhead."

"Oh crap, if they ride the bus all the time don't you talk to them? Haven't you gotten to know them or exchanged names?"

She nodded. "Yes, but it's hard to know how to respond to *fuckin' bus bitch,* and *little motha fucker . . . sir."*

"Oh for god's sake, Mildred." He swiveled in his chair and faced the wall.

Hmm, completely bald in the back too. "I'm sorry I can't be of more help, Supervisor Studebaker. I should get back to my bus. My break is almost over and I don't like to keep the riders waiting." She practically skipped out of the office, humming a Broadway show tune under her breath.

~~~~~

The graffiti-covered bus created a sensation as it moved slowly through town. "My word!" Jeanie Whitehouse said from the front seat in the bus. "This is like being on a float in the Rose Parade with people starin' and lookin'.'I feel like we should be waving and smiling to all these people watching us drive down the street."

"Go ahead, Jeanie." Mildred said. "It won't hurt a bit."

The bus was an entertaining phenomenon on wheels the likes Myers Junction had never seen. The colorful graffiti held its shape as the dry weather continued and people still gawked as it passed. Mildred wondered what might happen when it washed off with the first rain, but she decided not to think about that for the time being. She was just glad her riders were happy at the moment and that she still had her job.

She braced herself as usual as she approached the Gang of Thugs stop. She pulled close to the curb wondering how they might behave now that graffiti was the talk of the town. She opened the door, lowered the ramp, and waited. She stepped off the bus and looked both ways, but no gang of thugs!

Could this be the dream of all dreams? Are they hanging up their foul mouths and rude behavior, at least where the bus is concerned, so as not to tangle with the anonymous taggers? Hubba dubba, is this my lucky day? Is this the end of the nightmare? She did a quick shuffle right there on the sidewalk and jumped back on the bus.

~~~~~

In the weeks to come, the City Hall passed an ordinance prohibiting graffiti or personal messages in public places without a permit, and instructed the Gang Intervention Center to teach a course in civic responsibility as a condition for public funding. The graffiti continued to be the talk of the town until Mildred woke one night as thunder rumbled and a storm came in with a vengeance. Not just sprinkles but a downpour. She dressed and grabbed her trench coat with the artificial fur-lined hood.

Standing there in the dimly-lit Bus Bay, Mildred watched her graffiti dripping from the bus in the pouring rain. Colorful little waterfalls created swirls of patterns on the pavement before settling into a brown and murky puddle.

"I thought you might be here."

She turned to see Spencer bundled in his red nylon jacket and baseball cap. "Oh, Spencer, what are you doing here in the middle of the night?"

"Same as you. Curious, I suppose." They stood there together looking as if watching a house burn, silent and with a horrifying awe.

"I didn't know what to expect," she said quietly. "I wasn't sure it would all wash off or leave streaks, or make an awful mess."

"I know. I came over prepared to clean off the left-over graffiti tonight but there it is in a puddle, and the bus clean as a whistle." He put his hands deep inside his jacket pockets to keep warm. "It's a little sad, Mildred, to see your beautiful art work gone."

She laughed. "I suppose. Let's hope it did some good. I think it did but not in the way I imagined."

"And thankfully the thugs still haven't come back."

"I haven't seen them since the day they saw the graffiti for the first time and were afraid to get on the bus." She thought for a moment. Spencer, do you suppose anyone knew it was chalk? And would that have made a difference?"

"I don't know. It looked like graffiti, so maybe it didn't matter. I suppose by morning it'll be gone from the buildings too."

"Hmmm . . . well, get some sleep Spencer. The morning is just around the corner."

"You too, Miss Mildred."

She hesitated and then turned to take one last look at her bus, the way it should look.

Twenty-Nine

THE SUDDEN disappearance of the graffiti during the night caused even more gossip as the town woke to see it gone. Leticia Crozier told her bridge group that she saw a mysterious gentleman the night the graffiti disappeared. Maribelle Swift, president of the Daughters of the American Revolution, said the government has a Seek and Destroy team that cleans graffiti off fences all across the nation as part of the Keep America Beautiful campaign. And, the editorial in the Myers Junction *Tribune* thanked the newspaper's loyal readers for their goodhearted work in "rolling up your sleeves" and cleaning the graffiti from the town.

Reverend Corbin Hayward, a regular rider on the bus, stood in the aisle of the bus that day and asked everyone in the bus to bow their heads in prayer. "We thank you dear Lord and hope the perpetrators of the graffiti can now confess their sins and purify us from all unrighteousness. We pray that . . ."

"Uh, pssst . . . Reverend Hayward, sorry to interrupt but the light has changed and I have to get to the next stop," she said with her head still bowed and speaking from under her arm.

"Oh, yes of course, Mildred. Go forth."

Go forth? What does that mean, that I should go with the light . . . or something more spiritual? The line of cars honking answered her question.

She stepped on the pedal with such gusto, Reverend Corbin lost his balance and fell forward in the aisle. When she glanced in the rear view mirror she saw him down on his knees.

"Boy oh boy, he really gets into this prayer thing," she said aloud to her riders sitting up front.

The stories proliferated throughout the day and Mildred heard them all as the town's bus driver. But then it was not unusual for her riders to get involved. Rather than rely on television or those little "hand-held gadgets," as Mildred called them, the townspeople relied on each other for better or for worse.

As for the disappearance of the graffiti, Alice Hawkins said on the bus that afternoon, "We'll get to the bottom of this graffiti business." Mildred winced.

The kind Reverend Corbin, perhaps the most engaging of them all, stayed on the bus all day standing rather than kneeling, and offering prayers of forgiveness for the perpetrators and prayers of gratitude for those who cleaned up the town.

Reverend Corbin was a tall and gracious man who had led the townspeople in prayer for as long as Mildred could remember. He wasn't married and used clear polish on his nails, but the townspeople accepted him as their own and at least one family invited him to Sunday supper each week. His white-steeple church was built after the rented room in the old A&P building got too small because his sermons were so popular. The parishioners raised the funds for the new church, and Hank's Deli moved into the old space offering a "Sunday Sermon" breakfast for those who forgot the services were now being held at the new church.

After leading the riders in prayer that day, he stayed and shared Mildred's sandwich and Oreo cookies in the park. They took a stroll and admired the jasmine and sweet alyssum in the garden, and listened to the different bird songs coming from the tall Elm. At the end of the day she offered to drop him off at his home, both of them knowing it was off her regular route, but he declined, saying the walk would do him good and please just to drop him at the church.

She stepped off the bus with him, and they stood on the sidewalk. "Thanks for offering prayers on the bus today Reverend

Corbin. I think it was helpful for those confused and a little mystified by the unknown."

His eyes stayed with hers. "I offer prayers mostly for you, Mildred, and have for quite some time. I know you've had some losses but you've never come in to talk. There's no greater pain than holding something in that could be told."

When she drove the bus by the church the next morning she noticed the message on the Church's marque.

"We all need to share our disappointments in life rather than harbor them until they fester."

~~~~

The setting sun reflected off the big windshield as she pulled the bus into the Bus Bay later that afternoon and looked up to see Spencer grinning, his hands jammed into the pockets of his dark green windbreaker.

"You look pretty happy," she yelled, as she stepped from the bus with her lunch pail.

"You will never guess what we just got Mildred," he said waving a white envelope in the air. "We've been invited to a party."

"A party? Someone's birthday? I always try to write them down but then I forget."

Spencer pulled the note from the envelope. Raising his eyebrows he read: "You are cordially invited to celebrate our two heroes, Spencer Matima and Mildred Penniwink, for cleaning off the graffiti from our office facade. As a result of their tireless work throughout the night, Spencer and Mildred have restored our beautiful building to its original condition. Join us at 5 p.m. in the office of Supervisor Roger Studebaker."

"What? Are you joking?"

He laughed. "Absolutely not. One of the drivers happened to be coming home from a party and saw us in the Bus Bay the other night while we watched it rain on your bus. He was in the office this morning when the staff was talking about the mysterious disappearance of graffiti from both your bus and the office wall, and he figured we removed it. I heard Studebaker was beside himself and suggested a party for us."

"Oh great balls of fire, he actually thought we scrubbed it off?"

"Evidently no one suspected it was chalk or even examined it closely. And certainly no one wanted to take on the job of scrubbing paint from a wall. By the way, where did you get the idea to use chalk?"

"Huh?" She was still taking this all in. "Oh tidily winks, I would never put real paint on someone's property. As children we drew in the street with chalk, all pretty colors, so it just seemed like a logical substitute to paint. I guess it worked."

~~~~

That night Supervisor Studebaker congratulated them while everyone enjoyed fruit cake and ginger ale "on him," he was proud to say. And everyone thanked Spencer and Mildred profusely for their fine work.

"Good job, my man," Supervisor Studebaker said when he cornered Spencer after the speech. He gripped his hand. "I know you're coming up for a review so let's look closely at that," he said, nodding several times. Mildred, who was standing nearby, noticed that with each nod his bald head caught the reflection of the overhead lights, creating a strobe effect.

Supervisor Studebaker then headed straight for her flashing a coy grin as if he had just caught someone with their hand in the cookie jar. "Mildred, you devil you, well done. Yes, well done," he repeated and then leaned in close.

Their foreheads almost touched as he lowered his voice, sliding it into a whisper. "The mayor is pleased that we've cleaned things up. I just may look into your provisional status here if everything continues to go well. I'm not making that decision yet but . . . well, good work in getting the bus and the building cleaned up. I'd like to see more of that kind of behavior."

She gave her best attempt at a smile and thanked him. When he went on to someone else, she rolled her eyes. Walking to the trash can, she slid the fruitcake from her paper plate and left with the crowd.

Thirty

THE GRAFFITI EPISODE finally became less newsworthy in Myers Junction, but speculation about the Good Samaritan continued as one might expect from a community relishing gossip. Whenever someone's name was mentioned in any context, it was often followed with, ". . . and he might have even been the one who removed the graffiti!" When young Thomas Turner hit two home runs one night during a high school playoff game, some were sure he was the one. And before elderly Walt Woodruff died at eighty-eight, word had it he scrubbed off the graffiti that night as his last act of kindness. But most assumed it was the mayor who was up for re-election.

Mildred's only real thought about the entire incident was that she was finally free from the gang of thugs. She liked to think the peppermint candies she left on Mary Louise Woodbead's desk at the Gang Intervention Center that night lowered her testosterone level and she forbade the gang of thugs from using the public bus system. But realistically, she thought that highly unlikely. She felt in her bones it was the graffiti and the fear of a turf war that drove them away. Whatever it was, she was just glad to get back to her regular routine and hoped she'd make it through her probationary period without any further incidents.

Her gardening now included a bowl for Buster with Twang Yao and broth, after which he slept like a baby on the lawn. And, her cable bill had been accurate for two months in a row, a first since they made her take down the antenna and pay for what she had been getting free. That evening she found peace sitting and knitting stocking caps for the newborn and she worked late that night sorting and packing them into a box. They were mostly pinks and blues, although she made some in creamy white. She lingered with the hats, keeping them in her lap feeling each one and on occasion holding one up to the light. When she was finished, she tied a ribbon around the box and put it by the door for the next morning.

~~~~

Nurse Eloise looked up from the nurse's station in the Neonatal ward at Mercy General.

"Well for goodness sakes, Mildred, I thought you'd forgotten about us. We've been wondering about you. I haven't seen you at bowling either. Was it all that graffiti business? I saw your bus on several occasions; was there any permanent damage?" She stood up and Mildred noticed how tall and slim she was, attractive in an interesting sort of way. Her features were uneven and her teeth not exactly straight, but she wasn't homely by any means, just more like a *healthy country woman,* Mildred thought. She guessed Eloise to be in her late thirties maybe, but she had no talent at guessing ages. To her there was young, middle aged, and old, and that's all.

Nurse Eloise's distinguishing feature was a severe limp that rocked her body from side to side when she walked and more so when she bowled. She told Mildred once her father had accidentally ran over her legs with a tractor when she was a child. The doctor was out of town and the father wanted to amputate what was left of her legs to save the girl, but her mother wouldn't let him. But after several operations she was able to walk with just a limp. Mildred passed Eloise's house on the bus, and on occasion saw her scooting across her property on her behind. She figured walking might be painful for her. The image always reminded her of a painting she saw once by Andrew Wyeth called *Christina's World,* depicting a woman crawling across a field. It wasn't sad, just different.

Nurse Eloise told Mildred once that she never married and still lived on the property out on Forks Road where the accident took place. It wasn't as rural anymore since the town stretched out that way long ago. In fact her house was not that far from the new Payless market. Her mother was still there and kept a few chickens. She had shot Eloise's father with a shotgun right after the accident. The newspaper reported that she claimed self-defense. The jury was too compassionate to find her guilty of murder, given that they wheeled the crippled child, Eloise, into the courtroom each day. The verdict wasn't too surprising, Mildred thought. Sometimes that's the way justice is done in Myers Junction.

"Well, how many today, Mildred?"

"Oh, I lost track. Mostly pinks and blues, I think, but a few in white for a change. Are there many babies right now?" she said peeking over at the observation window.

"About the same, but the good news is we have twins, born yesterday. That's the parents over there against the window.

The new parents babbled on about their twins, making important observations about whose nose he has and who she resembled most, his mother or her aunt. Mildred looked at the sea of bassinets, almost like a factory with the new models lined up waiting to replace the older ones. The newborns were all in the front few rows where they could be readily seen, and Mildred watched tiny toes and stretched little hands waving out of control. Some needed tubes, but all helplessly waiting to grow up.

"Is one your grandchild?" the father asked.

"Oh, no, none are mine. I'm just dropping off some hats."

"Mildred knits the little warming hats for newborns," Nurse Eloise told the happy parents.

The woman turned to Mildred. "Oh, ours are both wearing pink; that's all they had. Did you happen to bring a blue one?"

"We have one of each," the father said with the usual pride.

"Mildred brought both. I'll bring them over and you can pick what you like."

Mildred let her hand slide down the viewing window and then followed behind Nurse Eloise.

"They'll be gone in a few minutes. Stay for while Mildred. No need to rush off," Nurse Eloise said as she went behind the nurse's station for the box of hats. But by that time Mildred was leaving through the revolving doors.

"Well, she stayed longer than usual," an aide said.

"Hmm, I suppose, but not by much," Nurse Eloise said, pausing with the box of hats in her hand.

~~~~~

The night seemed darker than usual. Mildred filled the tea kettle. Darkness was no stranger as she frequently walked through the house after waking in the small hours from a dream. Leaning over the sink, she let the water run on her wrists, and then turned them over staring at the sun spots on her hands looking like specks of oatmeal. The white lightbulb seemed brighter, too bright, and looking into the mirror she saw the way she expected to look in years, decades even. *Skin, so much skin and sagging breasts.* She splashed water on her face, letting it drip into the porcelain bowl and listened to it struggle down the drain. She thought about the life she wasn't living. . . flashes of the expectation of a baby's cry, and then a mysterious silence; nurses and doctors rushing around the room and then feeling nothing, nothing at all except that force that comes and goes and cannot be controlled or predicted, but felt full of emptiness.

She poured her tea and walked through the house, scattered rugs on bare floors, some books on the table. The house seemed bigger at night, or maybe just emptier. She imagined a light rain but didn't hear it, only the hissing from the old wall furnace as she watched a nearby curtain flutter in its draft. She turned the lights on in every room, watching the shadows dance like strangers on the walls. She woke again when the morning sun made muted patterns on the floor, shifting slowly as if someone was in the room. She began the quiet ritual of the morning because there was no place else to turn.

Thirty-One

THE PILE OF LEAVES and bare branches at Pott's Corner near the library was typical of fall. Mildred stopped to look at several wet maple leaves pressed into the concrete walkway. She spotted Gettie Mae's car in the parking lot and Velda's little Plymouth in the staff lot. A tangle of weeds and pilgrim's ivy covered an unkempt garden nearby, with its wild but sweet smell. She scurried inside. The library smelled damp like it did after the carpets were cleaned and Mildred could see the light streaming in from the east window illuminating tiny dust particles dancing in the air. Velda was behind the check-out counter and waved. Mildred found Gettie Mae in the cookbook section.

"Mildred, do you know how to make baked apples?" Gettie Mae asked, looking up and then back at the Betty Crocker cookbook.

"I'm afraid not, Gettie. I've never made them."

"Well, why would you? I mean, you don't have apple trees do you?"

"No, barely a garden, and just flowers at that."

Gettie Mae lowered the book. "Well, who do think did it?"

"Did it?"

"You know, removed the graffiti."

"Ah, I couldn't say," Mildred said, avoiding a lie.

Velda soon joined in, a bit out of breath. "It's been busy this morning. Cool weather is when people turn to reading. How are you Mildred?" She reached over and touched her arm. "I suppose there's lots of speculation about the bus these days."

"Speculation?"

"You know, about who removed the graffiti." Velda looked directly at Mildred. "I'm wondering who put it there in the first place, let alone who removed it."

"Well the thugs on Mildred's bus, of course," Gettie Mae said as if she knew for certain. "That's what they do you know, mark everything up. Did you see what they did to the inside of Mildred's bus?"

"Doesn't mean they did the outside," Velda mumbled.

"I'd like to think this is all history," Mildred said. "It's been stressful, and the important thing is that the gang of thugs are not riding the bus after seeing it covered in graffiti. They evidently think there's another gang in town and they're afraid of a turf war. I'm just glad my life is getting back to normal." She took a deep breath and let her shoulders relax.

Gettie Mae cleared her throat. "I never understood why you didn't raise your voice or hit them with a broom or something, Mildred. Shouldn't you have been a little harder on them?"

"I couldn't physically overpower them and they knew that of course. Besides, we're to treat all riders with respect, That's part of the oath we take, Gettie. I did talk to them, even followed them off the bus one day to explain the rules. After the Albert incident, I told them to get off the bus and they just laughed."

"Hmm, well in the big picture, Mildred, do you think all that Twang Yao and licorice you've been spreading around has helped at all?"

"Sure, look at Buster the beast of a dog, and the people at the cable company, even possibly the woman at the Gang Intervention Center . . . but then again probably not her. Things are better now than they were weeks ago. I don't know how else to explain it."

Velda fiddled with her bun. "I'm still not sure about any of this, it's just too mysterious like the graffiti appearing one night and then disappearing later," she said, looking directly at Mildred.

"Well, what difference does it make? Things are better. What more can we ask?" Mildred gave a final nod and pulled her grocery list from her pocket. "Gotta go. My neighbor, Alphie, is coming to rake leaves and I need chocolate chips."

As Velda headed for the counter, Mildred caught up with her. "Velda, your birthday is coming up in two weeks. How about we go out for cocktails like we usually do on our birthdays?"

Velda's hesitation came as no surprise. "I don't know. We've been friends for a long time, but I don't think you've been entirely honest these past few weeks. I sense you know more about the graffiti than you are saying. There's . . . well, a certain trust that has to be there between friends."

Mildred took a deep breath. Velda had been her best friend for years and Mildred understood her feelings of betrayal. She didn't want to implicate herself by admitting she did the graffiti, but she suspected Velda already knew. And she also didn't want to implicate Spencer and put him at risk. A dozen other reasons rolled from her mind, but the bottom line was that she could not tell Velda or anyone else.

"Velda, you are my best friend and have been for a long time. I agree with you, there has to be trust between friends so I need to ask you to trust me. Not everything needs to be told or should be told. I'd really like to help you celebrate your birthday, so let me know."

When she got home there was a message from Velda on the answering machine. Her voice sounded even smaller when it was recorded, almost squeaky. "Hi Mildred, I'd love to go out for cocktails with you on my birthday. Just don't trust me to tell my exact age." Mildred could hear her soft giggling in the background.

~~~~

She glanced at her watch. Alphie was coming at one o'clock to rake leaves, and she wanted to get started on the chocolate chip cookies. Just as they came out of the oven she spotted him sitting on the front porch. His eyes revealed his own private hell and his hair looked awful, cut unevenly and sticking out in all directions. She sat down beside him.

"Ready to rake some leaves today?"

"Sure, whatever you want me to do, Miss Penniwink."

"What kind of project are you saving up for this week?"

"A hat."

She laughed hysterically and then he laughed with her.

"That's pretty funny, Alphie. Just a hat, no science project? I'll remember that when I need a little cheering up. C'mon, come with me." They traipsed around to the back porch where a decades-old honeysuckle vine draped the wall and shaded a rickety lounge chair. She said, "Wait here, I'll be right back."

She returned with a pair of scissors, and about ten minutes later had trimmed his hair, making it even on both sides and much better on the top. "It's not perfect, but it looks pretty darn good. Here, take a look," and she handed him a mirror. "Hair always grows back in just a few weeks anyway, so not to worry."

She didn't want to ask him who tried to cut his hair. She suspected one of his parents; both drinkers from what she'd heard in the neighborhood, and from the many bottles of liquor in their trash can each week. When Alphie started coming over with bruises, she filed a complaint with the police department. His parents in response got a court order to keep her from interfering, but the court did agree to assign his case to Juvenile Services but it takes months for them to act, according to the police.

He held the mirror close. "Yeah, that looks like hair is supposed to, right?"

"Right. Bring the mirror and come with me." Mildred opened the back door to the garage and flipped on the light. Against the wall were two hats hanging on hooks, one was her garden hat and the other, a man's baseball cap, blue with some kind of insignia. She took it down. "This looks adjustable, so try it on."

"Really? You'll let me wear this today? Wow!"

"No, I'm giving it to you to wear forever if you want."

"Forever? You mean, for always? This is so cool, and it's my favorite color. Really, Miss Penniwink, you're giving this to me?"

"Absolutely, but we have to have a little agreement, okay?"

"Okay, what is it?"

"Well, sometimes parents don't want other people to give their kids things. So, I'll pay you what I always do, but if your parents ask where you got the hat, you can say I gave it to you as payment for doing some extra work here today like bagging up the leaves once they're raked, Okay? I think your parents are fine with you working for me doing chores, but just not taking you in when things are not going so good at home, right?"

"Yeah, right." He kept taking the hat off and putting it on for a closer look in the mirror.

"How come you have a man's hat in the garage, Miss Penniwink? Does a man live here too?"

She felt the question pierce her chest. "No, no. One did for a short time, Alphie. I met him at the bowling alley. That was three or four years ago."

She could see he was curious, waiting for her to say more.

"You see, Alphie, sometimes people live together for a while, and then they don't . . . for some reason."

"Why? Didn't he like it here?"

She rubbed her fingers, each one. "It seems he was just passing through town, Alphie."

"And he left his hat?"

"Yes, he left his hat."

Alphie raked the leaves wearing his new hat and a smile while

160   Hazel Warlaumont

Mildred brought out several large plastic bags. She held them open while he stuffed them full with multicolored leaves from the yard. Later, they sat on the porch nibbling chocolate chip cookies with milk while Alphie took his hat off at least a dozen times for a closer look.

"Miss Penniwink?

"Yes, Alphie."

"Will the man be coming back for the hat?"

She watched the few remaining leaves skip across the walkway and settle on the closely-cut grass on the other side. "No, Alphie, he won't be coming back. The hat is yours to keep, forever."

Thirty-Two

NEWS SPREAD QUICKLY in Myers Junction. Riders flocked back to the Crosstown #2 once they heard the thugs were no longer riding the bus. Mildred was thrilled to see her riders once again waiting by the bus stops, huddled together in one single silhouette of friends. Some had umbrellas, some their daily newspaper, but nearly all gave her warm greetings or a light touch on the shoulder before dropping their fares in the box.

She felt their presence as each of them boarded the bus looking for seats . . . the familiar but faint trace of perfume, the smell of an extinguished pipe, the rustle of paper bags, and a mumbled *hello*. Once seated, they chatted as usual, and at each stop she'd hear the tapping of a cane or a wife saying, "watch your step dear," or "goodbye Mildred, see you tomorrow."

Even Albert Parks started riding the bus again one morning. Mildred and the others rolled his wheelchair up the ramp and attached the restraining hooks to hold him in place. She waited until he was settled in. A car honked from behind and she rolled down the window flashing the peace sign while muttering, "damn jackass," under her breath.

After calling first, Mildred had made a point earlier in the week to drive out to the Parks' house on Pritchard Road to tell Albert about the gang's disappearance, and to say she'd like to see him back on the bus again. It was a modest house in need of some repair, but adequate for a younger couple. The lawn needed mowing, and what didn't had withered to dust.

Hazel Warlaumont

Albert and Ruby Parks were fairly new in town and quite a bit younger than most of the riders on the bus. Mildred guessed they were probably in their late thirties or early forties. She had never met Ruby, and only knew Albert from the bus. He told her once he was a vet and had lost both legs in one of those countries Mildred could never remember let alone pronounce. He said he and Ruby moved around with the military, but when he was injured and discharged they settled in Myers Junction after seeing an ad promising a free down payment on houses for young families settling there. It was true. There had been a youth drain, and the town's population kept getting older each year. The mayor was fond of saying that before long the only property being used would be the cemetery. Without industry and jobs, small Midwestern towns did not have young people clambering to live in them.

Albert rolled his wheelchair out onto the front porch and let the screen door slam shut just as Mildred got out of the car. They spoke for a few minutes and then went inside. Albert's wife, Ruby, came into the living room with peach scones and a pot of tea. She was plain, with pale skin and light brown hair, and looked slim, Mildred thought, in her cotton house dress. Mildred thought she might almost be pretty with a little make up.

"Oh my, I didn't expect this, Ruby. Thank you. I just wanted to come over to let Albert know things have changed on the bus."

Ruby smiled modestly as she poured steaming tea into stained cups.

"How do you two like living in Myers Junction?" Mildred asked, trying to get the attention off herself while she brushed scone crumbs from her skirt and into her hand.

"I'd like it better if I could find work," Albert said, glancing at Ruby. "We were so anxious to have our own home, we didn't think much about jobs. Ruby's applied at the big box store, so we're hoping that might work out but there's little prospect for me. I mean, who needs a legless bomb detonation expert in a town like this?" The room was silent except for a shutter banging against the window out front and the clicking of an old clock on the mantle.

Albert was well built, at least what was left of him. Mildred suspected he'd been working out with weights because his arms were muscular and his jaw square. He had a *US Marine Corp* sticker on the back of his wheelchair, but his long stringy hair belied the typical clean-cut Marine Corp look. But despite his muscular upper body, he seemed a broken man. Mildred noticed that his piercing blue eyes were troubled, moving rapidly and never quite settling in one place.

"Can you get retrained Albert? Is that possible?" Mildred felt uncomfortable holding the crumbs in her hand, which by now were squeezed into a ball. She looked around to see if they had a dog but didn't see one.

"There are no vocational schools or colleges out here, and the nearest base is a couple of hundred miles away."

"There are other options, honey," Ruby said to him almost as a question. He didn't respond and Mildred glanced down to make sure she hadn't dropped the crumb ball. She hadn't. She sensed the job predicament was an issue with them, and Ruby added, "Albert gets disability, of course, and that helps immensely."

"That's not the point," Albert said irritated. "Do you think I like sitting around in this wheelchair all day?"

The silence felt like a long slow freight train. Minutes passed, and Mildred reshaped the crumb ball many times over to take her mind off the tension. She thought she should just leave when Ruby broke the silence.

"We hope to have children." Ruby blurted out. Mildred glanced over to see her shoulders slumped, her hands limp and thrown in her lap.

"Oh no, not this crap again." Albert swiped a hand across his face and gazed out the window.

Mildred felt a pressing urge to fix the situation, to bring some remedy so they would perk up and be happy. Yet she knew it was their problem to fix, their cross to bear. When she left, Ruby followed her to the car.

Rubbing her hands together, Ruby said, "thanks for coming. We don't get many visitors here." She stood toying with her fingers, touching each one nervously, her body leaning slightly forward. Mildred could see she wanted to say more, maybe to chat or have some girl talk, anything so Mildred wouldn't go.

"Thank you, Ruby. I'm glad I came by also. I hope Albert will start riding the bus again now that those thugs are gone. It's probably good for him to get out." She walked toward her car and then turned. Ruby looked like the only stock of corn standing after the harvest. Mildred walked back toward her.

"You know, Ruby, there's a quilting bee here in Myers Junction, and some very nice women attend, mostly to be social."

"Oh, I don't know anything about quilting."

"That's the good part. You don't have to. It's a good way to meet other women in town. We can go together the first time."

"Oh, well that would be nice, if it's no trouble."

"No trouble at all."

~~~~

The driver in the car behind the bus honked again while Mildred was attaching Albert's wheelchair to the hooks. He put his hands on the arms of the chair. "You're sure those damned hoodlums won't be on the bus today?"

"They seem to be gone, Albert. Where are you off to today?"

"The Senior Center has pool tables and, believe it or not, they let me play even though I'm not a senior. I guess I might as well be."

"Well scooby do, maybe they'd let me play too. It's just that my arms are not long enough to reach over the table." He smiled. She was glad to see him back on the bus, but wondered how playing pool all day might affect his self-esteem.

Thirty-Three

WHILE SUPERVISOR Studebaker was in a good mood now that the graffiti had been removed from the building, he agreed to repair the back of the bus but only after some convincing. Mildred and Spencer warned him the entire operation could be cited for safety issues unless the bus was repaired; plus, the mayor would not be pleased to hear the town's bus had been cited. So, the senior and disabled seats were replaced with new ones, and the walls were refinished. Even the windows where graffiti messages had been scratched were replaced. Betsy Palmer and her husband Glen donated four acrylic blankets for the bus, brand new ones. Not like the used ones Mildred bought at the thrift store that were later ruined by the gang of thugs. The new throws were much nicer, warmer, and even pretty.

The Palmers lived at the end of Colby Road in a large house sitting upon a gentle rise in the land shadowed by willow trees and coarse grasses, and overlooking a vista of farm land that seemed to stretch on forever. Mildred never knew if it they owned all that land, but they did drive a big car and Betsy's face always looked lifted. Rumor had it Glen Palmer's grandfather, who built the house during prohibition, had been one of the biggest bootleggers in the region and had ties with the mafia.

Glen inherited the house, and rumor had it he was still making booze with stills hidden on the property, probably in the garage.

Mildred wondered about that. *Why make liquor when you can buy it at the big box store? A half-gallon of Chabliss costs no more than a half-gallon of milk! Oh, well.*

While Glen's pastime was questionable, Betsy Palmer was respected as a quilter in town. Mildred had been to quilting bees at her house, but preferred to knit rather than sew little of pieces of fabric together in odd patterns. That evening however, she picked up Albert's wife, Ruby, to introduce her to the group. She could see Ruby was nervous.

"You can just watch the quilting Ruby, you don't have to join in if you don't want. I'm not really a quilter myself, but I do like to have a social evening out once in a while." She saw Ruby's shoulders relax a little.

Betsy liked to show off her house and always took the women on a tour of the mansion and yard, except for the large old barn that always remained locked. Unlike most country properties, the Palmer's yard was manicured and devoid of the usual piles of dirt, errant shovels, and rusty wheelbarrows.

"We'd love to see the barn Betsy, can we take a peek inside?" Marilee Marks asked.

"No, actually it's locked right now," Betsy said, leading the group back inside.

Mildred did notice the large padlock on the barn door, but it was the air strip next to the barn that puzzled her even more. *Could they really be making and selling whiskey? I can't even imagine!*

Betsy's quilting bee was reminiscent of rural gatherings of the past to bring women together and overcome the loneliness that so many country women experienced. Often times the women sang and cooked and even exchanged recipes or gave child-rearing tips. Mildred heard that next to church going, quilting bees were the primary contact for women living in the country.

But Betsy's quilting bees didn't always fit the country image. That night the women sat around on shag carpet drinking mimosas and nibbling on hors d'oeuvres while taking turns at the frame working on a large quilt and talking about movies. The quilt was to be a gift donated by the women of Myers Junction to hang on the wall in the reception lounge at Mercy General. Mildred liked the idea, even if the Palmers were making whiskey in the barn.

"I had a real nice time, Mildred. Everyone was so nice," Ruby said at the end of the evening.

"They meet each month Ruby so plan to go. It's good to huddle with friends once in a while."

~~~~~

Albert Parks had been playing pool at the senior center on Thursdays, but when Mildred pulled up to his stop that day she felt a surge of adrenaline and something gripping her chest. It had been a couple of weeks since she'd seen Ruby at the quilting bee or Albert on the bus, but that morning Ruby's hair was uncombed and her gray cloth coat was pulled tight and misbuttoned, causing a small bulge in front. Her arms hung lifeless at her sides. It was not the face of a random person on the street, but not the face of Ruby Parks either, at least not how Mildred remembered her.

Mildred opened the door of the bus before turning off the ignition and stepped down to the sidewalk.

"I . . .well, I wanted to let you know," Ruby said. Mildred watched her chin quiver, her eyes never settling.

It was the last time Mildred would see Ruby Parks, except at Albert's funeral.

The newspaper reported that Albert Parks shot himself in the head with a shotgun propped between his thighs, as he sat in his wheelchair in the back yard of his home. The blast woke his wife, and the wheel of his tipped wheelchair was still spinning when the police arrived. Albert's body, what was left of it, was sprawled on the lawn and then moved to the mortuary.

On her lunch break after leaving Ruby Parks standing at the curb, Mildred parked the bus at the edge of town near the park where she often ate her sandwich and took short walks. But that day she sat on a bench and dropped her head in her hands. The tears ran down her arms, and she was okay with that. *Albert deserves our tears*, she thought. *They all do. If they don't die on the battlefield they die in their wheelchairs. Is dying the trophy for wars where men fight for turf, or oil or greed and beat their chests*

168   Hazel Warlaumont

to show they're the biggest, bravest, and strongest? Or is the reward the house you can't tend because your limbs are gone, and you can't find work to pay the mortgage, or for the family you can't have, or for the self-esteem you left on the battlefield? She stood and wiped her face on her sleeve. *Oh cripes, this moaning doesn't serve any purpose.* She started walking back to the bus. *But maybe the enlistment posters should show men in wheelchairs under the slogan, "The Military Builds Men . . . One Replacement Limb at a Time."*

~~~~

Ribbons of blue and lavender clouds with dashes of white streaked across the sly that Saturday afternoon in Myers Junction. A northeasterly blew through a row of Elm trees, and leaves swirled and fell settling where they could. Next to the steps leading to the church sanctuary, a tangled web of dried wisteria vines sprawled motionless. Reverend Corbin Hayward moved the patriotic standing wreath just inside the church door to keep it from blowing away, and he fussed with the red, white, and blue arrangement as people filed into the church.

"I wouldn't have done this service, but the military offered a small amount toward it and the nice pastor said there would be no charge. I need the money," she said shrugging as she sat with her hands in her lap toying with her finger tips. Ruby had asked Mildred if she would sit with her and her sister at the funeral service. Her sister Charlotte drove over from the city since Ruby hardly knew anyone in Myers Junction other than the few women she'd met at the quilting bee and some neighbors across the road, and, of course, Mildred.

Ruby looked around. "Who are all these people, Mildred? We didn't know anyone here. We didn't even attend services at this church."

"These people are from here Ruby, Myers Junction."

"Oh my, how nice. He had said many times over that he didn't want a military funeral. He was stubborn. Just like in the military, he took on the toughest job just to prove his strength, driven by testosterone I suppose."

"What was that?"

"The military is all about beating your chest trying to be the strongest and the bravest.

"No, I mean about testosterone."

"It's what drives them, Mildred. All of them."

Mildred sat in silence, shocked this word was coming from Ruby in this context.

"After all was said and done, he just wanted to be cremated, that's all." She no longer looked distraught, Mildred thought, just broken. "He died a long time ago, Mildred. Look at what war did to him. Look at what was left of him in the end. Just a midsection. No legs, and he blew everything above his chest off . . . just a midsection, that's all that was left."

Mildred watched her fidgeting with her hands and a button on her coat, but she couldn't get the thought of testosterone out of her head. "What will you do Ruby?"

"Oh, I'll go back with my sister. We've called a realtor and he'll take care of selling the house and the estate sale, but we didn't have much, hardly anything really."

"Ruby I don't want to pry . . . but I guess I am. Did Albert leave a note?"

"No, he wouldn't have done that. He was past that." She thought for a minute. "I'd hoped we could have had a child. That might have given him some purpose but he wouldn't even try, and we weren't even sure he could, given the extent of his injuries. He was a broken man, Mildred, ashamed of how he looked and how incomplete he felt. He had wanted to be a macho Marine and just couldn't accept being 'a half man,' as he put it."

" Doesn't the military offer counseling to returning vets?"

"Well, not way out here, and this is the only place we could afford to live."

"My, something just doesn't seem right with all of this."

"You know, Mildred, I'm sure there would have been help but Albert was depressed and I have no business sense. We didn't have what it took to use the resources available to us. We just got the disability check every month and that was that."

Bits of sunlight edged in through the front door and fell on her face, yet there was nothing there, just a blank stare.

The townspeople filed into the church that day. That's what they did in Myers Junction. You didn't decide which funeral you'll attend, you went to them all whether you knew the deceased or not. Reverend Hayward put the urn of ashes on a table in front and played some recorded music, but solemn marches not popular tunes. When the last cough and throat clearing was heard, Reverend Hayward spoke from the written notes provided by Ruby's sister, Charlotte. The chapel was silent but for the occasional wind pushing through the slightly open door.

"This is a story of a young high school athlete, Albert Parks, and a pretty gymnast, Ruby Baker, and their first dance at the high school prom. The young man wanted to marry this girl at first sight but at the dance he kept stepping on her toes and he knew he'd be lucky to even see her again." Some chuckles were heard in the chapel. "But she invited him to her parents' house for dinner the following week and they married a year later before he entered college for his engineering degree. Ruby worked at the local department store to help pay expenses during those years." Reverend Hayward stopped to drink from a plastic water bottle and cleared this throat before continuing. "Albert was recruited into the military after graduation as an officer and worked as a bomb detonation expert." Reverend Hayward turned the piece of notepaper over a couple of times and looked over at Charlotte. "Is there more?" he said. She shook her head.

He hesitated and then pulled a loose-leaf notebook from under the pulpit. Turning the pages for a few minutes, he reached in his breast pocket fumbling for his glasses, and put them on just before looking up.

"This short piece is called *Eulogy for a Veteran.*" He cleared his throat. "'Do not stand at my grave and weep. I am not there, I do not sleep. I am a thousand winds that blow. I am the diamond glints on snow. . . .'"

Mildred glanced at Ruby who sat stoically, although Mildred could see her squeezing her hands. There were no whacking sobs or signs of grief. Mildred assumed those had happened long ago.

Reverend Hayward looked at those in the chapel. "The author, I'm sad to say, is anonymous, though this quote by General George Patton is not: 'It is foolish and wrong to mourn the men who died. Rather we should thank God that such men lived.' May our hearts and minds be with Albert Parks and his loved ones."

There was a little shuffling of feet and the wooden pews creaked as people shifted their weight and looked around wondering if the service was over. Reverend Hayward glanced at Charlotte, who then whispered something to Ruby who shook her head. The reverend nodded and walked to the door, thanking everyone for coming as they left, one by one.

Mildred sat with Ruby, who chose not to stand at the door. Mildred thought about the moment. *No one knows the deceased and no one knows the survivor*, she decided. *It doesn't really matter who died, funerals are for everyone who needs to mourn something*, thinking that the people did not come in vain to the short service.

After everyone left the chapel, Ruby took the small urn with Albert's ashes and a white carnation from the wreath and clutched it gently on the way out, leaving Mildred sitting there thinking about testosterone.

Thirty-Four

ANGUS BAUMGARTNER fumed. Feet apart and hands on his hips, he watched as Buster slept soundly while Mildred dead-headed her marigolds a few feet away. He kicked at Buster's backside and the sleepy dog whimpered but then rolled to the other side and went back to sleep.

"I don't think you're allowed to mistreat your pets, Angus. There are some pretty stringent guidelines about animal cruelty," Mildred said, standing up and brushing the soil from her knees. She walked toward him with her plant snips in her hand.

She was reminded that Angus Baumgartner always looked like he just woke up from a very long sleep. His pale face had no color or expression and every limb, every muscle in his body appeared unhinged.

"Do you have a problem with him taking a nap on my lawn, Angus?"

He stared at her, but didn't answer.

"Angus, I don't think what happens on my property is any of your business. I've asked you several times . . . oh never mind, I need to get back to my plants."

"Your plants?" He stood there looking as if at a loss of what else to say, and then walked over and stomped his foot in the middle of her multicolored Asters.

"Why you . . . you creep!" She picked up the hose, turned the nozzle on full blast, and charged toward him aiming it right in his face. She fantasized about putting the nozzle down his throat and threading it down to his bowels, but she held it at his face as his hair flew up and he squeezed his eyes shut. He dodged the stream and went for her just as Burt Stillwell caught him by the arm.

"Whoa, that's enough Angus. That's quite enough," he said, still gripping the sleeve of Angus's shirt. "Now get the hell out of here, and if I ever see you on her property again, I'll call the police. The police, you hear?"

Baumgartner stumbled toward his house batting at his drenched clothes before going in. Burt Stillwell turned to Mildred, "You okay? What got into him? I saw him over here mouthing off and kicking the dog. Next thing I knew he was in your flower bed. The guy's nuts, really nuts."

"Good grief! Thank you Burt, that was scary." She stopped to take a deep breath. "He seemed wound tighter than a bed spring right on the edge of snapping. Well I guess he did snap, didn't he? Whew! He was upset that Buster was sleeping while I worked in the garden, probably depriving him of his morbid satisfaction of seeing the dog jump me."

"Sit on the porch, Mildred. You need to catch your breath." Maybe you should call the police just to get it on record," Burt said, rubbing his chin. "Baumgartner has gone over the edge, beyond a neighborly spat. He was going right for you."

"Well I did turn the hose on him, so that's probably just as bad. I didn't want a confrontation but he was stomping on my plants." She looked over at her flower bed. "Good lord, look what he's done! I know one of the police officers and I'll mention it to him just in case something happens again, just to be safe."

"Tell him about the problem I had with him, too, so he won't think it's just you. I hope you'll do that soon, Mildred. "

"I will. I'll call him this afternoon. Thanks again, Burt."

~~~~

Sgt. Patrick McCain was still in his softball uniform that

Hazel Warlaumont

afternoon. He'd finished his Sunday afternoon game and rushed right over after getting Mildred's call on his cell phone.

"And you were standing here on your own property?"

"Yes, I was here in front of my garden. I don't want any problems Patrick, and I did turn the hose on him . . ."

"Yes, but after he damaged your property. You have a reasonable right to protect what's yours. I'm more concerned about him going after you. What was that all about?"

"I have no idea. We've never been . . . well, what you'd call neighborly. I've talked to him about his dog coming over, but then another neighbor had problems with the dog as well. Baumgartner wasn't very responsive to him either. I just wanted someone to know about this, Patrick. I don't want to file charges or anything. Who knows what he's going through? I'll just go inside if I see him again."

"Well in the meantime I'll do a little checking and file a confidential report so the incident is at least noted." He stood to leave. "You wouldn't by any chance have any of those chocolate chip cookies would you?"

"I have 'em wrapped and ready to go."

~~~~~

It was early Monday morning when she noticed the milkman down the street as she pulled out of the driveway. She waited at the corner and watched as the driver stopped in front of Angus Baumgartner's house and appeared to take two glass quarts of milk in a metal carrier up to his porch.

Oh my god, Bingo! She thumped her hand on the steering wheel.

On the way to the Bus Bay that morning, she planned her caper. *Unscrew the bottle caps, and put the Twang Yao in his milk! Hubba dubba, easy as that! But what if he's an early riser . . . and what if Buster barks while I'm on the porch? Cripes, back to the drawing board.*

Thirty-Five

STEWART WAS SPRAWLED on the sofa reading the newspaper when Mildred stopped by to get Velda for her birthday.

"C'mon in, Mildred. I'm just fixing his dinner and it's about to come out of the oven. I got home a little late but I'm almost finished."

Stewart Vanderhoff moved into Velda's house when they married four years ago. Twice divorced, he'd been living alone in a small apartment so living in Velda's home was a bonus. It was close to work and had a yard for his dog, Rumpus. Mildred met him on several occasions and liked his sense of humor. He did seem to belittle Velda at times even though she confessed to Mildred that she had finally found the "right man." Mildred said to go for it. Stuart did have a problem with their "girls' night out" for cocktails, so they agreed to go out on their birthdays only. Even then Stewart said he'd rather she stay home and cook for him. Velda insisted that twice a year was reasonable and she'd try to arrange it on his poker night if possible.

"Hi Stewart," Mildred said quietly so as not to disturb him.

"Yeah, yeah." He dropped his newspaper below eye level. "Don't you think this is a little stupid? I mean two women your age going out for cocktails?"

"Stewart! What's wrong with you? This is my friend Mildred and we're going out to celebrate my birthday."

"What, the card I got you wasn't enough? You have to go whoring out to bars?"

Mildred straightened her shoulders and blinked. "Jeeze Velda, maybe I should go."

"Absolutely not," Velda said, shaking her head and glaring over at Stewart. She took a casserole from the oven, sat in on the stove top, and threw the oven mitts on the counter.

"Your dinner is done and on the stove when you're ready," she said to Stewart and grabbed the coat she'd put on the chair.

"Set the table and dish it out for me, and then tell me my dinner is ready," he said, still looking at the newspaper.

Mildred watched aghast. She wanted to pull him off the couch by his feet and push his face into the casserole and say: *How's that, Jackass?*

"Let's go, Mildred."

They both sat in the car for a few minutes until their breathing returned to normal.

"Cripes, Velda, was that my fault?"

"No, not at all Mildred. It's the way he is. It's the way marriage is, actually."

Mildred drove on in silence. *Note to self: never get married.*

~~~~

On their second or third drink they laughed hysterically at the Karaoke singer who couldn't have been more off key. When it was Velda's turn Mildred winced, wondering how Velda would ever get up in front of people and sing Karaoke. When Velda belted out "Hey Jude," leaning into the microphone sounding wild and gritty, Mildred sat wide-eyed and the audience clapped and joined in with the *Na Na Na Na* part. Velda's hair hung over her face, and although she slurred her words, she got them right. Mildred chose "Who Let the Dogs Out" when it was her turn, and had the whole bar clapping loud and singing along. She even included a little improvised tap dance at the end. When the lights dimmed and the music ended, they made their way out to the car still singing "Hey Jude."

"Velda, maybe you'd better stay at my place tonight. You can call Stewart to tell him we had car trouble or something like that."

"Oh, he'll be alright. Probably sound asleep by now."

They drove in silence. "Does he ever hit you?"

"Not much. It will be fine Mildred."

"Well, that does it."

Mildred drove straight home and made up the sofa bed, while Velda called Stewart to tell him she was staying over at Mildred's because it was so late. She was still pretty tipsy. "No, we're late because we had bar trouble."

"Bar trouble?" Mildred looked up, laughing uncontrollably. Velda hung up quickly before doubling over in hysterics. Every time she tried to call him back, they were both laughing so hard she knew she'd never get the words out.

Finally Velda composed herself and called him back, speaking slowly as if talking to a small child. "No, we had a bad connection. I said we had *car* trouble. I'll stay at Mildred's and be home in the morning," and she hung up abruptly, looking pleased. "I smoke slowly this time, did you see?"

"Smoke slowly?"

They were still laughing an hour later.

~~~~

Mildred dropped Velda at her house the next morning after Stewart left for work, and then drove to the Bus Bay still feeling woozy and prone to fits of laughter.

"Coffee," is all she said as she walked toward the bus.

Spencer looked at her askance. "You never drink my coffee. Now you want some coffee? You always say the old coffee pot looks like something from under the hood of a truck. In fact, you don't even drink coffee. You told me you prefer Chablis," and he chuckled.

Mildred giggled and put her hand over her mouth.

"Ah, I see," he said with a curious smile. "Mildred?" He walked around and looked her in the eye. "What exactly did you and Velda do last night to celebrate her birthday?"

She tried to hide a giggle. "Karaoke," she squeaked out, and then succumbed to uproarious laughter.

Spencer shook his head and came back carrying the largest mug he could find. Handing her the hearty brew, he raised an eyebrow. "You will drink it all before you step into the bus, Miss Mildred."

He also had the box of Girl Scout cookies she usually ordered from his daughter and shared with her riders, after temporarily removing the sign: *Passengers will refrain from eating on the bus.*

"Well, I need to get going," she said glancing at her watch.

"Uh, just a minute Mildred. Let's see the finger to the nose first."

She did and he gave her a thumbs up, so she climbed up into the bus and pushed her lunch pail under the seat. Spencer stepped up briefly and poked his head in.

"Hey, Mildred, good to see you laugh."

"Oh get out of here. And that truly was the worst cup of coffee I've ever had," she said laughing as she drove off

At the end of the day she had an empty Girl Scout cookie box for the trash but then thought twice and took it home.

~~~~

The message light blinked impatiently. She put her lunch pail on the table and pushed the play button. "Couldn't have asked for a more perfect birthday celebration, Mildred, so thank you. Loved the evening, especially the *bar trouble* we had." Mildred could hear her giggling in the background and she smiled at the thought of their silliness the night before.

She knew when she saw Velda again in the library her hair would be pulled tight in a bun, her face small and tight, and her lips pursed. Not the good-time woman yelling *Hey Jude* into the Karaoke mic ala Janice Joplin with her raspy voice while a crowd clapped and stomped their feet. Mildred made a point to stop by the library for a minute later that week to say hello, and to make sure Velda didn't have any bruises.

Thirty-Six

THE EMPTY GIRL SCOUT cookie box sat on the drain board in Mildred's kitchen, and her wine glass was almost empty that evening by the time the flax-seed cookies were cool enough to pack for the next morning. She printed the note carefully: THANK YOU FOR YOUR ORDER, and then stuck it to the box with a little smiley face for a personal touch. She planned to get up early the following morning and leave the box on Baumgartner's porch right after the milkman delivered his two quarts of milk.

Hmmm . . . milk and cookies. He'll soon be sleeping on the lawn with Buster!

The alarm woke her fifteen minutes early and she watched for the milk truck, the one with a picture of a full-uddered cow on the side. She dressed in black – the same outfit she wore for the graffiti caper. When she heard the milkman drive on up the street, she grabbed the box of cookies and stepped quietly across the lawn to Baumgartner's house, tip-toeing up the steps. She laid the box of cookies down and looked at the glass quarts of milk. *Swell! How can he resist milk and cookies? Cripes, better still, how can he resist milk also laced with Twang Yao!*

The lawn shimmered with dew in the last of the moonlight as she sprinted back to her house and opened the quart of milk she'd grabbed from Baumgartner's porch. In one swift move she emptied a capsule of Twang Yao into the milk and screwed the lid back on before prancing on her toes back across the lawn. *Lord to goodness, I am busy this morning!*

Once back inside her own house, she closed the door quietly and turned the lock. *What, what, what could possibly be more perfect? A double whammy . . . the milk and the cookies!* She rushed into the shower while singing Broadway show tunes, *". . . tra la la . . . don't cry for me Argentina . . ."* A few minutes later she smoothed out her uniform on the bed and dressed. She could be heard humming her way out the door to her car.

~~~~

As expected, Velda was back in character when Mildred entered the library on her break. Velda's Queen Victoria outfit was in character, and if her hair had been pulled any tighter it would have been sheared from the scalp. Her long, black skirt almost touched the black and white saddle oxfords she wore with white socks. She was covered with pencils everywhere: two in her hair, one in her blouse pocket, and two in her hand. Moreover, her rimless glasses were so far down her nose Mildred expected them fall any minute. *Funny, I can't remember Velda even wearing glasses. Oh well, this is just her library persona.* She wondered, especially after seeing Velda at karaoke, which one was actually the real Velda? Seeing no sign of bruises, Mildred told her about Angus Baumgartner's cookies and milk.

Velda gasped. "You didn't!"

She dragged Mildred by the arm into the Gothic Horror aisle of the fiction section. "You gave him both the testosterone-lowering cookies AND the Twang Yao in the milk? Oh, my goodness, Mildred! What if he dies?"

"Well, then, that would solve the problem wouldn't it?"

Velda's jaw dropped and one of the pencils slipped from her hair.

"I'm only kidding, Velda. He won't die, he'll just mellow."

"Mildred, I'm not sure it really works that way. The Food and Drug Administration would investigate if these things were that potent."

"But how do you explain the effect of Twang Yao on Buster

and the jerks at the cable company?"

"I can't, but with Buster it's probably just the meat broth and a whole bowl of it. He lost his sex drive because he had a full stomach. Stewart's that way a lot. In fact he . . ."

"Velda, please!"

"Oh well, sorry Mildred. It just doesn't seem plausible that it would work so fast and have such results. Do you actually believe it works, Mildred, I mean really?"

Mildred stared out the window at the vast expanse beyond the over-arching trees and took a deep breath. "I have to believe it works, Velda." Mildred didn't want to explain any more than that.

~~~~

Supervisor Studebaker lived up to his word to fix the back of the bus, although the loss of Albert still put a damper on the joy of a newly repaired bus. But once she heard the hum of people coming and going with friendly greetings and newsy chatter she felt better. She loved that part of the morning, seeing the shops open and the town come alive. At Olive and Third, she opened the door and watched the Millers get off and wave before crossing the street on their way to the butcher shop. She waited for Margaret Olsen coming out of the beauty parlor and rushing toward the bus holding her hair so it didn't blow flat. While she waited, she noticed Alice Murray and Marge Sweeney seated near the window in the salon, chatting while in the grips of huge metal hair blowers.

Old Man Thompson stood to get off at the next stop. He leaned over Mildred's shoulder. "Maybe that graffiti was not such a bad thing after all Mildred, if it scared those skunks away," he said stepping closer to the door.

"Hmm . . . yes perhaps. Say, why does everyone call you Old Man Thompson? Don't you have a first name?"

"Mildred, they've been calling me that for so long it . . . well, it just stuck. You can just call me Old Man if you want, lots do."

She was still smiling when she pulled the bus over to the stop adjacent to the Big Apple market where Gettie Mae was brushing the wrinkles from her already perfect dress. Mildred sighed and thought about her own wardrobe, if one could call it that. *I do wear a hat well*, she thought.

"It's wonderful to have the bus to ourselves again Mildred. And such beautiful new seats back there in the senior section near the back door. I see you have some new throws."

"Yes, donated by the Palmers. How are you Gettie Mae? I haven't seen you lately? We must have a library rendezvous soon."

"Back door please, Mildred."

"Oh, sorry Jake, I didn't see you back there."

Mildred passed City Hall and flower beds of violet and umber, and watched the wind stir the leaves in front of the barbershop before slowing for the next stop. Bob Talmadge, the president of the Myers Junction Gun Club, walked to the front of the bus to exit. "You know, Mildred, if those young hoodlums ever come back, well the gun club would be happy to use 'em for target practice. You just let us know. It sure is nice to be able to ride the bus again, believe you me."

"Thanks, Bob. I agree." *Target practice? Is he serious?*

Polly Becker waited until Bob Talmadge stepped off, and then came up the step waving the latest pictures of her grandchildren.

"Oh, swell," Mildred said under her breath. Polly wore a turquoise pantsuit and explained each picture before taking a seat.

After her, two young men waited below, and once they were on the bus fidgeted in their pockets to find the exact change.

"Just put in what you have fellas. You can put more in next time, if you like."

"Oh, thank you, ma'am."

"Yeah, thanks a lot."

Hmm . . . normal amount of testosterone. How refreshing!

Thirty-Seven

THE SUN WARMED the porch as Mildred watered her purple fuchsias next to the railing. Buster slept peacefully on her lawn nearby. When she turned she noticed Angus Baumgartner out the corner of her eye as he was stepping over the tall grasses separating their properties. He walked toward her. Her heart thumped a couple of times, but rather than have a confrontation, she turned the hose off and went inside.

A few seconds later he pounded on the door, sending a shudder that bolted to her toes. Peeking out the window, she looked to see if Burt Stillwell might be working in his yard but no sign of him. Baumgartner banged again, this time even louder. She waited a minute and then relaxed her shoulders and took in a deep breath. *Of course, it's the milk and cookies! I should have known. He's coming to say he's sorry for the other day and to invite me to tea.* She put on her best smile and opened the door.

"Well, good afternoo . . ."

Before she got the words out, he thrust Buster's new dog bowl in her face. "Are you feeding my dog?"

She gulped. "Feeding him? No, no of course not."

"Then what's this?"

Heavens! "Oh that? It's just a water bowl. He spends so much time over here when I'm in my garden, I just give him a little water. Yes, just something to drink."

He lacked any expression, but that wasn't unusual for him. "Is there a problem, Angus?"

She looked for at least a slight smile or frown but saw nothing as if he was in some type of stupor or unresponsive state. She grabbed hold of the bowl and stepped back far enough to close the door and turn the lock. She waited with her heart doing the jitterbug.

A minute later she heard, "Git, git home. Goddammit, git home." She opened the door slowly and went out to the yard in time to see Buster running back home.

"That's no way for you to talk to your dog," she yelled, but Baumgartner didn't look back. When she turned to go back in the house, she noticed her fuchsias had been stomped into the ground. Her first thought was to call Patrick again but what could he do? *Maybe the Twang Yao isn't working after all. Maybe Velda was right. How could it change behavior?* That thought was more sobering than seeing her fuchsias crushed beyond recognition.

~~~~

Later that week she stopped for more plants, this time Allium and Bluebells. She also bought a small piece of wire fencing to protect them from Baumgartner's heavy foot. The musty aroma of plants and soil drifted through the car. She couldn't wait to plant on Sunday, the day she liked being in the yard instead of church. It wasn't that she didn't enjoy a good sermon, or singing hymns with the congregation, but she reminded herself that sitting in church was a bit like sitting on the bus. It was reverent and shared with a group of people, but she sometimes felt the need for a different experience.

At ten o'clock she put out Buster's brew in case he came around. She also kept a close eye on any activity next door. It had been almost a week since she'd left the batch of cookies and spiked the milk. She assumed Angus Baumgartner had been treating himself to them all week. She hoped for a peaceful morning since that would confirm the testosterone-lowering ingredients were finally working. She planted the Allium alongside the steps and the Bluebells in front, and was patting the ground around the last row of Bluebells as Buster came running across the lawn. He went right for the bowl of broth and Twang Yao, lapping it up and making his usual mess.

As she stood back admiring the newly planted flowers, Angus Baumgartner appeared out of nowhere staring. He had the same glazed look he had the other day and he stood like a zombie, his arms hanging at his sides.

"Oh, hello, Angus. Did you come over to get Buster?" She tried to hide her nervousness by sounding sing-songish.

He didn't answer and for the first time she wondered if he might be impaired in some way. They rarely spoke over the years, and typically he just stared without saying much. She decided to ignore him and swept off the walk way. But when he walked over to the flowers and looked as if he might step on them, she went toward him.

"Don't step on the flowers, Angus," she said, as if speaking to a child. He didn't respond. Instead he turned and walked back across the lawn.

~~~~

Mildred remembered seeing a small red car at Angus' house about once a week and assumed it was a cleaning lady. But later that week when the car appeared again, she walked over just as a dark-haired woman got out carrying a large three-ring binder.

"Excuse me, do you have a minute," Mildred said, as the woman was locking her car door.

"Sure," the woman said looking up. She was young, maybe twenty-five or thirty, and wore a navy blue coat and large plastic-rimmed glasses that filled her face. She wasn't dressed for cleaning, that was for sure.

"I'm a neighbor of Angus Baumgartner, and while I don't know him very well, I've observed some . . . well, some strange behavior lately. Do you know him well? Are you a friend?"

"I'm Rose Newland, his case worker. What kind of behavior?"

"Case worker?"

"As his neighbor you probably know he had a head injury while serving in the military. What type of behavior are you seeing, and is this something new? If so we really should talk."

Forty minutes later Mildred understood all about Angus Baumgartner. He had been on disability for years because of his injury and had a plate in his head. Since there was no VA hospital nearby, he was assigned a case worker who helped him manage his life so he could continue to live at home.

"Well, horse feathers, I had no idea! I seldom see him out, and he's never made an effort to talk or be friendly. In fact, he keeps destroying my flowers and that seems deliberate . . . and quite honestly, I've been afraid of him, especially lately when he's been coming over here."

"I don't think he would hurt anyone," the woman said. "He's always friendly with me. In fact he just offered me some Girl Scout cookies, so he can be social at times."

Mildred gasped. "Cookies? How many did you have?"

"Oh, just a couple. It's hard to predict behavior when the brain has been damaged. There's not much logic to it, or pattern. He probably equates your garden with the anger you expressed that time when his dog was jumping on you. He may see the garden as the cause of the friction rather than the dog, and he probably wants to eliminate the friction. That's how their minds can work at times, but there's really no way to tell. I can talk to him about the dog if you want me to. Maybe he can keep it in the yard or get it neutered. He may not be able to remember to keep the dog in the yard though. The neutering would probably be the best bet."

An hour later, Rose knocked on her door. Mildred was curious to see if she was any different after the cookies took hold, but she wasn't. She was still nice. "He's agreed to the neutering but he's on a limited income so it may have to wait. He's also confused about the whole process."

"Well I can take the dog to the vet, that's not a problem. I've already talked to one about the dog a few months ago. I'm happy to take him and pay for it just to save my garden, if that's what it takes."

"Really? That's very generous of you. I'll try to explain all of this to him. Hopefully, this will eliminate the friction and you both can get back to your lives."

Thirty-Eight

THE FOLLOWING Saturday, Angus waited on his porch with Buster as Mildred pulled up in front. She left the car door open and walked up the stone pathway.

"Angus, do you have a leash for Buster?"

He reached behind his back and brought one out that still had the price tag.

She nodded and hooked the leash to Buster's collar, and led him down the steps and then paused and turned before putting Buster in the car. "It will be okay. Buster will be back in a day or two." She waited to make sure he understood, but his lack of expression left some doubt.

~~~~

She still remembered the receptionist at the desk in the veterinarian's office the day of her embarrassing consultation with Dr. Christensen. The receptionist didn't look up so Mildred moved a little closer.

"Excuse me, I have an appointment for neutering."

The receptionist uncrossed her legs and rolled her eyes. She reached for an office form and searched for a pencil while shaking her head.

"Name?"

"Buster."

"What's your last name, Buster?"

"Oh, no, my name is Mildred, Mildred Penniwink. That's Penniwink with two 'n's.'"

The receptionist took a deep breath and blinked several times. "Dog's name?" she said louder.

"That would be Buster."

"Type?"

"Actually, I had to drop out of business school because my fingers were too stubby to type, so I'd have to say no."

The receptionist dropped her forehead into her hand and dropped her pencil at the same time. "What type of dog is it?" she said, looking up and enunciating each syllable.

"Gosh, I don't know. Maybe a hound of some sort. Yes, I would say a hound dog."

"Age?"

"Fifty-three."

The receptionist removed her glasses, letting them fall to her chest on their chain, and looked at Mildred as if waiting for an earthquake.

"The dog is fifty-three? I'm assuming that is in dog years?"

"Oh no, I'm fifty-three. I don't know how old the dog is. Can't the vet tell by looking at him? You know, they can tell the age of a tree by the number of circles or something like that."

The receptionist cleared her throat. "I don't think dogs have circles, but I'll certainly mention it to the doctor." Even her face shrieked of sarcasm.

A few minutes later, the door to the waiting room opened and Mildred was surprised to see a woman standing there in a lime-green outfit resembling summer pajamas. *Hmmm, that's odd; it's so informal here,* Mildred thought. The woman motioned for her to follow with Buster, but once through the door Buster put out both paws and stopped short in his tracks. He started to tremble.

"Oh, no." Mildred stooped and patted his head.

"He's just scared," the helper said. "How would you feel going into new surroundings for surgery?"

"Well, if I had those things swinging from my backside, I'd feel grateful, that's how I'd feel."

"Ah, yes, well . . ."

"He'll be alright won't he? I mean no pain or anything?"

"No, we take very good care of them. You can pick him up tomorrow any time after noon."

Mildred hesitated, and then reached down and rubbed Buster behind his ear.

She sighed walking out to the car. *All of this unpleasantness is my fault, just because of my garden, my insensitivity, and misreading Baumgartner's behavior, and now his fear and confusion seeing his dog being taken away, and poor Buster trembling as he's about to lose his manhood in some strange clinic. Oh god, what's the matter with me? How could I have let all of this happen?*

~~~~

That night the rain battered against the window pane and she felt the familiar monkeys stirring in her chest. She walked through the house turning the lights on in every room, and went to the closet and reached for the box with her tap shoes. She looked at each one then carefully put them back in the box and slid it up onto the shelf. In the kitchen she watched the clock above the stove and stared at the dishes in the sink while listening to the drip-drip-drip from the rain on the roof. In the living room, she spread the knitted hats onto a table and then put them back neatly into the box between soft sheets of tissue paper, and walked through the house again. On every table, every shelf, she looked at the hordes of items from the thrift store: vases, teacups, saucers, and bowls, all designed to hold something but sit empty.

She shook her head and ran her fingers through her hair and

Hazel Warlaumont

then again, leaving some of it in bunches, and spun around and around feeling sick. She went to the spare bedroom and started to open the door but didn't. The night dragged on and on and finally there was nothing left to do but acknowledge the grief. Walking down the hall, she opened the door to the spare bedroom and stared at the boxes of furniture, baby furniture that was never unpacked.

~~~~

Shortly after noon on Sunday she picked up Buster at the clinic. She was apprehensive not knowing what to expect, so she got to the clinic early and parked in front.

"He did fine, just let him rest when you get home. Maybe a short walk but nothing strenuous," the assistant said.

Buster leaned against her leg while she stood writing a check at the receptionist's counter, and then she walked him slowly out to the car, strapping the seat belt around him before driving home. Instead of parking on the street, she backed the car into Angus Baumgartner's driveway and saw him rush out onto the porch. She unhooked Buster, and he jumped out wagging his tail and turning in circles. Baumgartner hugged him, looking a little awkward and then embarrassed.

Mildred spoke slowly. "It's best to keep him quiet today, maybe a short walk on the leash and then tomorrow he should be back to normal. Here's a sheet of instructions and the doctor's phone number if you need to call him."

She watched them play gently on the lawn and Angus stopped to look at her. Hints of words, bits and pieces of them, seemed on the tip of his tongue, but she knew they would probably never fall into place. She didn't know what to say, so she just said, "Buster did fine, just fine," and she nodded.

In the weeks to come, Buster still came over when she was in the yard. She had his bowl filled with water now, just water, but what he really liked was sleeping on the lawn while she worked in her garden.

Thirty-Nine

GETTIE MAE waited near the curb and lowered her umbrella just as Mildred opened the door to the bus. "C'mon, Gettie, get out of the rain. A little wet out there this morning?"

"Yes it is, but good for my petunias so I won't complain," she said, boarding the bus and bringing the cold in with her. It lingered until she settled in her seat.

"Grab one of the throws in the box. You don't want a chill," Mildred said.

"I think I'll just sit up here, Mildred. I wanted to talk to you and maybe Velda. Can you meet at the library Saturday morning around ten?"

"Sure, what's going on, anything important?"

"Let's talk on Saturday," she said, pulling her umbrella out of the aisle.

~~~~

Velda was just signing for a shipment of books when Mildred came in and Gettie Mae followed close behind. Velda wore boots, a floor-length paisley skirt, and a long knitted sweater. Her hair was piled high on her head.

When she came toward them, Mildred looked her over. "Will you be breaking out in a Joanie Mitchell song this morning, Velda?"

"What do you mean, Mildred. Joanie Mitchell?"

"Oh never mind, it's just that you're dressed like . . ."

Getty Mae interrupted. "And take that damn pencil out of your hair," she said, while situating herself on one of the old sofas near the travel section. "I don't know why you store them in your hair, anyway."

Mildred and Velda giggled while Velda removed the pencil. Velda whispered, "As president of the League of Women Voters, Gettie Mae sometimes gets bossy but no one really seems to mind since she has such an important job."

Gettie Mae got up and stood close. "There's trouble at the Palmer place."

They waited for more, but Gettie Mae just stood looking at them.

"Tell us more, Gettie Mae. What kind of trouble?" Mildred coaxed.

"Well, it seems Glen Palmer's grandfather was a famous bootlegger with ties to the mafia, and get this. The whiskey-making equipment is still on the property, hidden in Glen and Betsy's barn. If they're making booze without a license, it's a federal offense in this state. A neighbor said some investigators were snooping around this week and discovered a bunch of equipment."

Mildred remembered that big lock on the barn door when she was there last. *No wonder Betsy didn't want the quilting bee ladies to see inside the barn. And then there was that small airfield.*

She didn't like talking about her riders, so she sat tight lipped.

Velda gasped. "What will happen if they've been making whisky illegally?"

Gettie Mae raised an eyebrow. "Ah, that is what's interesting. It's not what will happen to them, but what will happen to Betsy. Evidently, Glen transferred ownership of the property to her a while back, so it's in her name."

Velda squinted. "I don't get it. Why would she be in trouble?"

"Because technically she's the one breaking the law since the gin still and all of the equipment are on property that's now in her name. Something about taxes, I guess. If you make and sell your own whiskey, the state or city loses out on the taxes. Liquor is taxed higher than other things."

Velda's face reddened. "Oh no, I sold three loaves of my apple nut cake to neighbors last Christmas. Will I get in trouble?"

"Good lord, Velda!" Gettie Mae rolled her eyes and shook her head at the same time. "Sometimes I think you must have been raised by a pair of salt and pepper shakers."

Mildred took an interest in the conversation because the Palmers may have broken the law. That thought resurrected her guilt for putting graffiti all over town.

News about the Palmers became the most talked-about topic on the bus that week. Everyone had an opinion but no one had any facts. By Friday afternoon, word had it the Palmers were not only making liquor, but were also running a gambling hall in the barn. Prissy Wiggins even suggested they might be harboring a brothel in some of the upstairs bedrooms, and some rumors had it there was a history of madness in the family. The gossip stirred enough interest to keep people riding the bus just to get the updates.

News passed back and forth on the bus probably more than any other place except Hank's Barbershop, where on any given day seven or eight men might be embroiled in some animated discussion. Mildred listened to the gossip on the bus, but as the driver she felt it her duty to be impartial. On some days there was so much discussion that she had to remind riders their stop was coming up. The bus company, as a matter of policy, posted a sign in all its buses that read: *Do not speak to or distract the driver or passengers with conversation while the bus is in motion,* but Mildred taped the peace symbol over that sign some months ago when she first starting driving the bus.

Forty

ALPHIE WAITED on the front porch early, tossing his rubber ball against the house and catching it on the rebound with one hand. The neighborhood buzzed with activity as usual for a sunny day in Meyers Junction. Across the street, Burt Stillwell was replacing a broken brick in his walkway, and Angus Baumgartner washed his car in the driveway, while distant lawn mowers created a familiar chorus throughout the neighborhood.

"I didn't see your bike, Alphie, so I didn't know you were here. How's your week and school, and where is your bike, by the way?" Mildred stood in the doorway wiping her hands on a kitchen towel.

"Oh, well I don't have it anymore, and I'm not supposed to do any work for you now unless you pay me a lot of money."

Mildred came out the door and sat next to him on the porch.

"Well, let's start with the bike. What the heck happened?"

"My dad took it to the palm shop."

"The palm shop?"

"Yeah, they had a bunch of stuff there, and they gave my dad some money for it."

Mildred felt the anger creep into her jaw. "Oh, that's the pawn shop. They buy things from people and then sell them to other people." She squeezed her fingers blue and took a long, deep breath.

"Alphie, why did your dad sell your bike, do you know?"

"For medicine."

"Medicine? For you?"

"No, the medicine in those big bottles they drink, I guess. He just said for medicine."

"I see, and what about not working for me. What's going on there?"

"My dad said you are just using me, and that you should pay me more money."

"Did he say how much more, Alphie?"

"No." He thought for a minute. "To just to get as much as I could."

"How do you feel about all of this? Do you think I pay you a fair amount of money for your help."

"Oh, yeah. I mean, I bought all that stuff for my science project and some streamers for my handle bars . . . yeah, you pay me a lot. Plus you're nice."

"I think you're nice too, Alphie. I don't quite know what to do. What if I pay you a little more, and then you can tell your dad I paid you as much as I could. Do you think that would work?"

"I think so." He tied his shoe lace.

"Alphie, was it the . . . the palm shop over in Grover's Mill? You know, out where the cows are?"

"Yeah, I didn't see the cows though. I was sort of . . . I was crying until my dad said to stop it."

Mildred tapped her finger on the wooden porch. "Well, let's get started on chores and then we can relax on the porch with some milk and cookies. Is that okay?"

"Sure. Are they chocolate chip cookies?"

"Is there any other kind?"

~~~~~

The dust swirled in spirals and settled on her shoes. "It must be here. It has streamers on the handle bars and a playing card in the spokes." The aroma of dairy farms was unmistakable so she knew she was at the right pawn shop.

"Lady, we have a whole yard full of bikes. You're welcome to look, but we haven't had a lady's bike in here for a couple of weeks."

"No, it's not a lady's bike."

"Well, whatever. Why do you keep cards in the spokes? You can get a wire basket that hooks on the front."

"Well, the playing card is not my idea, and it's not being stored in the spokes exactly."

"And the streamers in the handlebars? It's none of my business how you folks decorate your bikes, but it just seems, well different. A bike is just transportation for getting from one place to another, same as a car . . ."

"Look, can you just direct me to the bicycle section? I'd very much appreciate that."

~~~~~

The following week Mildred was taking cookies out of the oven when Alphie came up on the porch after finishing his chores. She tossed her oven mitts on the counter and stuck her head out the door.

"Grab a seat, Alphie, I'll be right out."

By the time she brought out the tray of milk and cookies he was sitting at the table and had slipped off his shoes like she usually did. She smiled. His face was young but bewildered. His hair was growing out and looked funny, but better than before. His clothes were mismatched and needed washing. But it was his eyes, showing all the pain and disappointment one shouldn't have to deal with at such a young age.

He pointed to her mouth and she wiped the chocolate off while they both laughed. Usually she was the one to notice chocolate on his face. She asked about school and he sat up straight and leaned forward, telling her about an exciting experiment his teacher did in class, and that he wanted to be a scientist one day when he grew up.

"Oh my, how exciting, Alphie! You will be such a wonderful scientist."

He smiled for the first time that day. "Alphie, we need to talk about something serious, are you okay with that?"

"Sure, is it about my dad?"

"Yes, and your mother. I know they must love you very much but . . ."

"But they drink that medicine all the time."

"Yes, and that requires an understanding on your part and probably some changes on their part, right?" He nodded and Mildred wondered if he could even fathom what all that meant. She leaned forward a little. "I'm your friend, and I'd like to help in some small way, but I don't always know how." She watched his eyes. "For now, I hope you will just trust that I want to help, and if I can think of some way to help I will. I don't think it's a good idea to keep secrets from parents, but in this case I'd like to talk to you about something sort of private."

"Okay," he said, picking at cookie crumbs on his napkin.

"Well, slip on your shoes. I want to show you something." They walked around to the back and into the garage.

"Hey, that's where my hat was," he said looking at the hooks on the wall. He turned to look at her and then saw his bike leaning against the wall. His parade of expressions seemed to change with each blink. He buried his head in her waist and hugged her with all his might, and then walked slowly to his bike, touching the seat and adjusting the playing card in the spoke.

"Where did you . . . how did you . . .?"

"So here's the deal, Alphie. I think your bike needs to stay here until things get fixed at home because . . ."

"Because he will just sell it to the palm shop again," and he nodded while looking at her. This he seemed to understand on his own and she felt some relief he said it and not her.

"I will leave this door unlocked for you and you can visit your bike anytime you want. But Alphie, I'm not supposed to interfere with your life other than paying you to do chores. There's such a thing as a court order that prevents other people from interfering with how parents raise their children. I know how confusing that must be, but it is what it is."

"I heard my parents talking about that with someone who came to the house once, but they want me to earn money so they might not care."

"But then again they might."

"Will you get in trouble?"

"Probably not up to now, but if they knew I bought your bike back, and that you can come here to see it, I'm not sure."

His eyes got big. "You bought the bike? You mean it can stay here. It's yours now?"

"No, it's yours Alphie. You're just keeping it here for the time being."

"Whoa, cool, Miss Penniwink!" He climbed on the bike and revved the handlebars. "Why are you doing this?"

"Oh, heavens." Her smile faded quickly. "Because, I don't want you to grow up to be like the boys who ride my bus."

Forty-One

THE OLD BROWN COUNTY Court House in Barstow Creek resembled a big mansion from the past, but without the circular driveway or a herd cattle nearby. Impressively, it sat on a hill surrounded by acres of green grass and groves of poplar trees just in bloom. Built in the 1800s, the halls still had that echo often found in old buildings with high ceilings, transom windows, and hardwood floors. Each office had a bubble-glass window in the door with the department name painted in black. Mildred walked past three before coming to the one marked Child Protective Services. She took a deep breath and opened the door.

After talking to three clerks and waiting for an hour, she was finally ushered into the office of Harold Wilkinson, a case worker for the agency. His sleeves were rolled and his tie loose. It was after seeing his eyes that she knew he might help.

"I can understand your frustration, Miss Penniwink, but unfortunately we have critical cases waiting to be investigated. From what you tell me, and from what some of the initial complaints have described, this is not considered a critical case."

"Wouldn't the scratches and bruises and the liquor bottles in the trash can and that the father sold the boy's bike for booze money make this critical? What could be more critical?"

He leaned back in his swivel chair and put his hand on the desk drumming his fingers.

"Unfortunately, it would take more than that. It's sad, and the

Hazel Warlaumont

boy is being damaged both physically and emotionally, but he still has a home and food and no one has killed him yet. I'm sorry to be so crude but we see cases like this every day. They're abusive but not dangerous. No one is raping a child, or chaining them in the cellar, nor is this a drug house."

"But his parents do drink, both of them."

"That alone doesn't count; it's what they do that counts. There are no laws being broken here so it's basically out of our hands. The most we can do is pay a visit, but our critical cases are piled up. There's just no time."

"What if there were laws being broken? What then?"

"Then we step in along with the police department and try to change the pattern that's causing the problem. If the parent has committed a crime, then the children might be put in foster homes depending on their age."

"If there was a crime committed and the people involved were alcoholics, then what?"

He leaned forward and smiled. "It depends on the crime. If they don't need to serve jail time, we do get people into rehab to straighten them out, and that's done by a court order. Either they go to rehab or they go to jail."

"And in this case, there's no way you can intervene and make the parents go to rehab?"

"If there's no crime, then it's out of our hands. You obviously care a lot about this boy and what happens to him. Have you approached the parents and suggested Alcoholics Anonymous?"

"No, and quite frankly they have a court order keeping me from interfering in their business. They say I'm turning their son against them by letting him come to my house when things get rough at home. Actually, it's true. I'm offering a safe haven for him. Any decent person would do that. I'm appalled they were able to get the court order. There's something terribly wrong with the system if we can't take in a child who is being traumatized."

He looked at her for a long time. "I couldn't agree with you more, Miss Penniwink." He tapped a finger on the desk, and stared out the window for a moment and then back at her. "I'd like to end our conversation here in my office, but I'd like to walk with you to your car and we can talk more there. Is that okay with you?"

She shielded her eyes from the sun, but the air felt fresh as they walked across the parking lot. He stopped at one point and turned to her. "I wish we could recruit you; we need people who don't give up when it comes to child abuse. Unfortunately, case workers often become desensitized after seeing it every day. Let me ask you a question. Do you still spend time with the boy even with the court order?"

She hesitated and looked at him askance.

"Well let me put it this way," he said. "I have no obligation or authority to report you, nor would I under any circumstance. I appreciate what you are trying to do, and our conversation out here is private, off the record."

"Yes, I still see him. He comes every Saturday morning to do chores for me, and I pay him. So far that seems to be alright with his parents since they often take the money. He has on occasion come at other times with scratches and bruises. I take him in, and it's at those times the parents object and the reason for the court order. They call the police, who then come take the boy back home."

"It's hard to understand the insanity of this," he said shaking his head. "Personally, if I were in your shoes, I would continue doing what you're doing for the boy's sake. But there could be consequences. After all, it is a court order." He shrugged.

"Can't you intervene? I mean, you see what's happening here."

"It's not a critical case by definition, Miss Penniwink. There's no crime, no major physical injuries to the child. The agency doesn't assess emotional injuries."

"You have children." She remembered seeing some family

Hazel Warlaumont

photos on his desk.

"Three sons." They both stood silent watching the traffic on the street below. The grounds were perfectly landscaped and she admired the new blooms on the azaleas, unusual for that time of year.

"You're sure they're not selling drugs?" he said abruptly. "So many alcoholics do in order to get money. I'm just going to say this and I'll deny I ever said it, but in many communities there's very little proof needed to label a place as a drug house in the eyes of the law. No one goes to jail, but if there's a minor in the house, the parents must go to rehab under certain circumstances. It's just a thought, Miss Penniwink. I see it happen on occasion and when it does, we intervene along with the police when there's a child involved." They stood looking at each other without saying another word.

A drug house? She tapped her finger on the steering wheel all the way home.

Forty-Two

BETSY PALMER was almost unrecognizable behind a large pair of sun glasses as she waited for Mildred to pull the bus to the curb.

"Oh my, hello Mildred." She dropped her coins in the box. "Glen had to take the car today, so I'm back riding the bus."

"It's good to see you, Betsy. Here, sit up front." Mildred took the *Reserved for Handicap* sign from the seat across the aisle.

"Oh my," she repeated, taking a deep breath and brushing something off the seat. "I suppose you've been hearing all the talk about our place out on Colby Road?"

"Well Betsy, when haven't we all heard talk of each other? It's part of country living. Otherwise, we'd live in the city with smog and traffic and houses so close we can hear each other's toilets flush."

Betsy chuckled. "You're right Mildred. Just a small cloud over the garden, I suppose."

Small cloud? Mildred hoped that would be the case. She liked Betsy and didn't want to see her get in trouble with the law. *Actually, neither do I.* She winced thinking about the graffiti.

At the next stop, she waited for Reverend Corbin who rushed across the street from the church. He wore the clerical collar and robe he wore for pastoral visits. But today he had on a pair of Converse high top sneakers, black and white of course to match his collar and robe.

Hazel Warlaumont

"You're not wearing your collar because you knew you'd be seeing me today, are you, Reverend Corbin?"

"No, no, you're beyond saving Mildred," he said laughing. "Actually, you are one of my favorite misbehaving angels so I give you a lot of leeway. Are you still doing good deeds in the world?" he said coyly, as he counted out his change.

She wasn't quite sure what he was referring to, so she let it pass. She always suspected he knew everything in the community, more than he let on . . . *maybe through some divine message from above, or something like that.* A few minutes later, when he walked back up front for his stop at Third and Washington, she hesitated and then said, "Reverend Corbin, will you be in your office this afternoon by any chance?"

"As a matter of fact, yes I will be."

~~~~

After returning the bus that afternoon, she drove over to the church and found Reverend Corbin in the chapel. They sat in the first row of pews.

"You want to what? Sell drugs?" He thought for a moment. "How has the Lord failed you, Mildred?"

"No, no, no, it's nothing like that."

Mildred spilled out her story of Alphie and her visit to Child Protective Services. "I just don't see any other way. Something has to happen. This boy is becoming even more detached and any self-esteem he might have had has diminished. The father is now taking the money Alphie earns, and just recently sold his bike, which was Alphie's only joy. They chop off his hair so he's embarrassed to be seen, and he shows up with signs of physical abuse and torn clothes. I'm afraid he's going to end up like those thugs on my bus if someone doesn't intervene"

"So, what exactly are you thinking?" Reverend Corbin said, straightening his collar.

She let out a long sigh. "Make it seem like his parents are

selling drugs, and that Alphie lives in a drug house," she blurted out.

"The police and Child Protective Services can then intervene and require the parents to seek rehab or go to jail, at least I think that's how it works."

"Won't that be traumatic for the boy? I mean what boy wants to be associated with living in a drug house?"

"I've thought about that and it's the one drawback, but I can't think of any other solution. It's a long shot, I know. And, I'm sure in your eyes it's a bad thing to do."

"Hmm, tell me Mildred, do you think it's a bad thing to do?"

"No, no I don't. If it works it may help Alphie, and his parents. I wish you could see his face, Reverend Corbin. It's sweet and innocent and kind."

"Well, the scriptures say, 'So whoever knows the right thing to do and fails to do it, for him it is a sin.' We can't have you sinning any more than you already have, Mildred," he said smiling. "So what's your plan? We should get started."

"We?"

"Yes, I think it's the right thing to do, too."

~~~~

Velda stumbled toward Mildred with an armload of books, and pencils sticking from every part of her hair. "I was just thinking of you, Mildred. I haven't seen you in here for a while and wondered if you were okay."

"I know, I've been busy and I don't remember the last time I was in . . . I guess it was when we talked with Gettie Mae about Betsy Palmer."

"Poor Betsy, have you heard anything new? I'm sure the investigation will take a while. What brings you in today? Looking for a good murder mystery?"

"Actually I'm looking for something about current events, you know, current trends and that sort of thing. Just head me in the right directions and I'll browse."

"Okay, well let's try the section on sociology, and maybe history, since it can be current, and then . . ."

"Wait, you're going too fast," Mildred said, taking a piece of scrap paper from the table and grabbing a pencil from Velda's bun. She didn't want to tell Velda of her plan to help Alphie, so she said, "I'll check out these sections, Velda, and I'll holler goodbye before I leave." But by that time Velda had wandered off to find a place for her armload of books.

An hour later, Mildred was elated to find several articles on drug dealers and drug houses. *Yabba dabba do, just the stuff I need!* She dabbed the end of the pencil to her tongue and took notes at one of the tables in the back. She thought it particularly clever that a pair of sneakers tossed over a telephone line signaled a drug house directly below. *Goodness, all this time I thought shoe tossing was just kids having fun not drug dealing! Golly, what a person can learn!*

She also discovered that blinking a pocket-sized flashlight to oncoming cars signaled drugs for sale. That particular article described the color codes, and that a blue light meant cocaine for sale. "Hmm, we'll go for the blue light." she mumbled to herself while underlining *blue light* in her notes.

She was reading an article in one of the crime magazines but stopped cold when she read the next sentence. "The most obvious way of identifying a drug house is from the graffiti visible from the street." *Oh my word,* and she slapped her hand on the table. Velda appeared out of the blue.

"Are you alright, Mildred? You're acting a little weird, looking over your shoulder every few minutes and mumbling to yourself. Everyone looked when you slapped your hand on the table like you were having some kind of a fit or something. And why are you sitting way back here?"

"I'm doing important work and I don't want anyone to see me back here," Mildred said, looking over her shoulder.

Velda stared and narrowed her eyes. "Mildred, the whole library knows you're back here." She leaned over the table and whispered, "Is this more research about, you know, testosterone?"

"Can I trust you, Velda?"

"Well duh, what do you think?"

"Well okay, it's not about testosterone, it's about Alphie, the boy who lives down the street. Can you sit for a few minutes?"

Velda sat wide-eyed and slack jawed for the next fifteen minutes. "Oh, my gosh!" she finally said. "You're going to turn it into a drug house? Mildred, you can end up in prison . . . or worse yet, a convicted drug dealer."

"I won't be selling drugs, you Ninny. But if the police think it's a drug house, they and Child Protection Services will step in and make the parents go to rehab for their drinking because Alphie is a minor living in the house."

"Oh my goodness!" Velda had both hands on her cheeks and her mouth open.

"Velda don't look so shocked, you're drawing attention. I just hope it works. Something has to happen or Alphie will end up like the gang of thugs."

"Oh, no, really? So what are all these books?"

"I'm getting instructions on how to spot a drug house. There are certain clues."

"My goodness, you sure are learning a lot of new things, Mildred."

Mildred tapped her pencil on the desk and thumped her finger on the other hand at the same time. She whispered, "I'm going to need help with this Velda. This is a one-night operation. We need to get the sneakers up on the telephone wire, put graffiti on the front of the house, and flash a blue light that can be seen by the police when they arrive based on an anonymous tip."

"We?" she said in a *high* quavering voice. "You mean you

want me to help you with this . . . this crime?" She sat down and stared at Mildred. "And an anonymous tip? From who?"

"It's not really a true crime, Velda, just a mischievous . . . well, prank of sorts, but a serious one."

"Serious? Are you kidding? I don't want to end up in jail, I don't look good in stripes and . . . I'd rather live with my husband than with someone named Bubba. For god's sake, Mildred, get a grip and think this over!"

"Look Velda, at least think about it. Reverend Corbin is helping too. We can all work together . . ."

"What? Reverend Corbin Hayward is in on this too? Good lord! Oh, I didn't mean to say that, it's just that . . ." Velda's body convulsed like she had just sucked a lemon. She ran off, shaking her head with pencils falling from her hair all the way to the counter.

Forty-Three

REVEREND CORBIN opened the side door of the sanctuary and led Mildred and Velda to the dimly-lit section at the foot of the altar. Velda wore a heavy coat with a hood in spite of the warm evening, and slipped it off once she was sure no one else was in the church. She sat in the chair facing the statue of Christ at the altar. She whispered something to Mildred and they changed seats.

"I want to thank you both for your offer to help," Mildred said.

"As I mentioned before, the key is to coordinate our efforts so this will fall in place a week from today and probably around ten o'clock at night. We need to toss the shoes over the telephone wire, place an ad for free firewood in order to draw lots of cars to the neighborhood to make it look like they're looking for drugs, put graffiti on the house, stand at the corner and flash a blue light, and call the police department tipping them off to a drug house. And, we need to do all of this without disturbing the parents. What do you think?"

Reverend Corbin sat thinking. "If the blue flashing light is to be seen by the police, won't they arrest the . . . the flasher? That would be one of us."

"Yes, good point, Mildred said. That person should probably be at the corner and able to make a quick get-away once the patrol car turns down the street looking for the drug house. From what I've read, typically the flasher would not stand in front of the house but on a nearby street."

Velda raised her hand. "I can do that since it's not against the law to flash a blue light, and I can run pretty fast."

"Great, Velda. I think we can do the shoes ahead of time, since it's not unusual to see sneakers over the telephone wires in neighborhoods. We just need to find a time to do it when we can't be seen, like one evening this week."

"Why don't I call the police to report the drug house?" Reverend Corbin said. "I can do that around nine or nine-thirty that night. I can also place an ad for the free firewood, but I'm wondering if we shouldn't say free furniture for curbside pickup any time after nine-thirty instead?"

"Perfect." Mildred jotted that down on her list. "By the way, here's the house address since you'll need that. And Velda, we can get together this week, and I'll show you where to stand to flash your light. I'll get a blue flashlight bulb if you can bring the flashlight."

"And that leaves the most difficult of all, the graffiti," Velda said. "Who on earth will you find to do that?" The sanctuary became silent, and then Reverend Corbin and Velda looked at Mildred in a knowing way.

"I'll . . . well, I'll find someone. The house has to be tagged quickly and quietly, and before cars come for the furniture. Oh, and neither of you should be at the house that night. If this doesn't go as planned . . . well, Reverend Corbin, you can make your call from home and Velda, you should park your car nearby, and once you see the police car you should leave."

Reverend Corbin cleared his throat. "And what about you, Mildred?"

"Well, since I live up the street, it wouldn't be unusual for me to be in the neighborhood. So, no problem there."

Velda stood and then sat again. "This just sounds too farfetched to work. There must be an easier way to help the boy."

Reverend Corbin glanced at Mildred and then patted Velda's hand. "There may very well be, but I told Mildred the scriptures say, 'So whoever knows the right thing to do and fails to do it, for him it is sin.'"

Velda blinked.

"I'm behind her one hundred percent. If there's just one small chance it will save one of God's children, then we must."

"Oh, okay," Velda said in a flat tone of voice, and then looked down and blinked rapidly.

~~~~

The thrift shop was just closing as Mildred hurried in and rushed to the shoe section. Thelma stood at the counter while Mildred put a pair of white converse high-top sneakers down and opened her pocket book.

"Now you know these are too small for your big clumsy feet, girl."

"Well I've seen you squeeze your rump into some pretty small tights, Thelma, so don't talk to me about things that don't fit."

"Alright, alright, but you must have some dire need for these old shoes. How about a dollar?"

"Too much." Mildred leaned over the counter and smiled. "I think seventy-five cents is more like it."

"You drive a hard bargain, Mildred, but I would have given them to you for a quarter."

"And I would have paid five dollars." They laughed and made a little small talk about the weather. Mildred left having crossed one thing off her list of things to do that day. She was meeting Reverend Corbin and Velda that night after dark to toss the shoes over the telephone wire, so she had to hurry.

Dressed in dark clothing, Velda and Reverend Corbin parked their cars in front of Mildred's house at eleven o'clock that night, and walked up the street to Alphie's with the pair of sneakers tied together by their laces. Relieved to see the lights off inside, they decided to take turns tossing the shoes. Reverend Corbin would go first because he was the tallest. His first toss barely reached the telephone wire. Velda's try was puny and the shoes came back to hit her in the head loosening her bun. They waited until she secured it back in place and then Mildred tried, but with her short arms and stubby fingers she barely got the shoes out of her hands They all took another turn.

After several tries, they sat on the curb to rest their arms. "I never dreamed it would be this hard," Mildred whispered. "How do the kids do it?"

"How do kids do anything," Velda said. "Since I'm the smallest, maybe I should get on your shoulders and . . ."

"Too dangerous," Reverend Corbin whispered.

Mildred kept looking up at the wire. "If I had the bus here we could climb on top with a step ladder and throw from there, but the bus on a residential street would cause too much attention." They tried again. Reverend Corbin took his white collar off this time and put it in his pocket. Velda and Mildred hoped that might make a difference, but it didn't. After several more tries they decided to abandon the idea of the shoes and focus more on the flashing blue light and the graffiti.

"I'll make one last try," Reverend Corbin said, but missed miserably again.

"Oh, oh," Velda said, as she looked up the street. A man walking a dog was coming toward them.

"Great balls of fire, just what we don't need," Mildred said. "Wait a minute, that's Buster and that must be my neighbor, Angus Baumgartner. Hide the shoes. We'll wait until he passes and then leave."

Buster wagged his tail when he saw Mildred and pulled on his leash so hard Angus let go. Buster sprinted toward Mildred, running in circles and making little whining noises. Angus nodded at Reverend Corbin and put his hand out for the shoes. They looked at each other and Mildred shrugged, so Reverend Corbin handed them over. Angus walked around eyeing the wire and then gave the shoes one mighty fling. They flew high in the air, well beyond the wire and came down straddling the wire, swinging back and forth before dangling securely with one shoe on each side.

The Reverend, Velda, and Mildred all hugged and quietly rejoiced in the street. Angus just stood smiling before taking the leash and continuing on his walk.

"Sometimes prayers are answered in the most unexpected ways," Reverend Corbin said before they ended the evening.

Forty-Four

THE NIGHT OF THE caper Mildred dressed in dark clothing, the same outfit she wore during her graffiti incident. She gathered her chalk before walking swiftly up the street with the night chill creeping through her black jacket. She straightened her shoulders. The lights were on at Alphie's house and she heard the television as she got close. She felt her heart pounding and her knees wobbling. It was the one night she hoped Alphie's parents had emptied one of those large bottles of gin she'd seen in the trash. She also hoped Alphie was fast asleep in bed. *I hope this doesn't go bad for his sake.*

She focused mostly on the garage door. It was dimly lit and easy to hose off. She worked fast, knowing cars would be driving by looking for furniture. Soon after applying the last bit of color, she stepped back into the shadows and nodded. In the distance toward the main road, she saw the faint flashing of blue light. *Velda is at her post, hopefully not traumatized.* At that moment her heart ached for Alphie, hoping he wouldn't see any of this, hoping the police wouldn't arrest his parents, and hoping he would wake up in the morning knowing his life as a child might now begin.

~~~~

Mildred had never seen a crime scene before. Actually no one had in Myers Junction. But within the hour three patrol cars flashed yellow lights, one of them parked on the lawn as the neighborhood swarmed with cars obviously looking for free furniture. Alphie's parents sat on the curb in front with their hands cuffed behind their backs, and someone from Child Protective

Services had just arrived and rushed in to the house. Mildred spotted Patrick in his uniform at the same time he saw her.

Mildred grabbed his sleeve. "Alphie?"

"He's asleep in the back bedroom. The parents are drunk as hell. How did this all come about, Mildred?"

She wiped her tears and her nose at the same time.

"Mildred, Mildred, Mildred," he sighed. "The flashing blue light, the graffiti, even the shoes over the telephone wires? Really?"

She pushed him gently and then again. "What would you have done, Patrick? Let this boy's life end in ruin?" she said, wiping her face again. "Just what would you have done, let him grow up to be a hoodlum, like that gang on my bus?"

He put his arm around her shoulder and they just stood there together. "I'll tell you what I would have done, Mildred. I would have done the exact same thing, but probably not as well." He turned her around and put his hands on her shoulders, leaning in close. "I'd do the same damn thing Mildred, do you hear? You got Alphie's case in the system and nobody got hurt. Now go home and let it be."

"Can you tell me what's happening inside? I hope the parents won't be arrested, and is Alphie still asleep?"

"Go home, Mildred. I'll call you tomorrow and fill you in."

"Tonight, Patrick. Call tonight."

~~~~

Alphie's parents spent the night in jail to sleep off their lack of sobriety. They weren't officially arrested, but were warned that they would be for endangering a minor if they didn't enter a substance abuse program immediately, or if any alcohol was ever found in the home. The case worker from Child Protective Services stayed at the house all that night, and the parents were released the following morning. She informed the parents that she planned to visit daily until she was sure they were fit to have custody of their child. Patrick washed off the graffiti that night at Mildred's request, so Alphie wouldn't see it the next morning.

It was two weeks before Alphie showed up on Saturday morning for his chores. When he finished, they slipped their shoes off and lounged lazily on the porch; idle, quiet, full to the cusp of everything that makes an afternoon special in spring: the scent of jasmine, the heat rippling in waves, the sound of buzzing insects, a distant hum of lawn mowers, and the rare joy when things go as planned. After milk and chocolate chip cookies, Mildred watched Alphie ride his bike home, the playing card flapping in the spokes.

~~~~

"This is my treat tonight," Mildred said when she picked up Velda, even though Stewart objected to her going out again. He stood at the door yelling something, as Velda slammed the door to Mildred's old blue Ford and they drove off. Reverend Corbin was waiting on his porch when they picked him up. He squeezed himself into the back seat. He had on dark pants, and his clergy shirt with a white clerical collar.

"Ditch the collar," Velda said, already a little high from the glass of wine she had at home before leaving. He took it off and left it on the car seat.

Once inside the karaoke bar, the strobe lights kept pace with the music as they took a table in front of the stage.

Reverend Corbin fiddled with the collar that wasn't there and looked around. "You two come here often?" he said with eyes wide open.

"No, only on special occasions," Mildred said, just as an almost topless waitperson came to take their drink orders.

"We want those drinks with the little umbrellas," Velda said, clearly excited and already tapping her toe to the music. "Don't we, Mildred?" she added, hoping Mildred would agree.

Mildred nodded and smiled. She looked at Reverend Corbin, who shrugged, looking a little awestruck by the surroundings but still happy to be there.

"I want to thank you both from my heart for the amazing thing you did for Alphie," Mildred said, raising her voice over the music. "Someday I'd like you to meet him. I think he's well on his way, and he has you two to thank."

Reverend Corbin struggled with his little umbrella, trying to move it aside while he raised his glass. "To you Mildred. This was your doing and it looks like it worked."

"Hooray, Mildred," Velda said, raising what was now an almost empty glass.

By the time the karaoke started they were all wearing the little umbrellas in their hair and on their third drink. Velda was first up and chose *Stayin' Alive* by the Bee Gees. Feet wide apart and arms in the air, she let the pins out of her bun and shook her head until her hair wrapped around her face swishing back and forth as she belted out the words to the song.

"You're stayin' alive, stayin' alive. Feel the city breakin', and everybody shakin', we're stayin' alive, stayin' alive." The audience roared and clapped in rhythm, and sang along with the chorus.

Reverend Corbin stood and shouted "stayin' alive, stayin' alive," even after the song had ended. When it was his turn, he went with Michael Jackson's *Billie Jean*. Mildred and Velda looked at each other and raised their eyebrows.

"I would have expected a hymn, or at least *Onward Christian Soldiers*," Velda said, slurring her words.

"I don't think those are karaoke songs, Velda."

"Oh, yeah, I guess not."

Just then a beat started and Reverend Corbin appeared, moving across the stage trying to do the moonwalk like Michael Jackson.

"Oh, my god," Velda said. People were on their feet cheering, even when Reverend Corbin kept getting his feet jumbled up. But then he sang, ". . . beauty queen from a movie scene . . . her name was *Billie Jean*." When he hunched up his shoulder to imitate

220   Hazel Warlaumont

Jackson tipping his hat, the crowd went wild.

"Where did he learn to do that?" Velda screamed above the crowd.

"I don't know. Maybe some divine inspiration, I suppose," Mildred yelled, still clapping to *Billie Jean.*

When it was Mildred's turn, she took a tablecloth from an empty table and wrapped it around her waist to imitate an evening dress, and belted out Dinah Washington's *What a Difference a Day Makes* in a sultry voice. "Twenty-four little hours . . . scoobie do . . . scoobie do." The audience leaped to their feet and raised their glasses, shouting "more, more." When the clanking of dishes in the kitchen signaled the bar was getting ready to close, they walked arm in arm to the car, still humming their songs and trying to do the moonwalk.

Forty-Five

"MILDRED, DID YOU HEAR all the commotion the other night? I've never seen so many cars on our street . . . and the flashing lights of patrol cars, what a mess." Burt Stillwell called from his mail box just as Mildred was walking out to hers. She crossed the street and they talked at the curb.

"I think there were some goings on at the corner but it turned out to be a mistake. By the way I've been meaning to tell you that Angus Baumgartner agreed to have his dog fixed. His case worker convinced him."

"Case worker?"

"It seems he had a brain injury in the military, Burt. I should have told you about that sooner, but I've been so busy."

"Well, I'll be damned." Burt took off his hat and scratched his head. "I guess you really never know who your neighbors are. I knew something wasn't right but I thought he was just an old curmudgeon."

"I think we all did. Anyway, he's on a limited income so I agreed to pay for the procedure and took Buster myself."

"Make a difference?" Burt said with a sly smile.

"Oh my yes. The romance has now turned into a friendship." They laughed. "You know Burt, Buster really is a sweet dog, and Angus is not such a bad old guy once he thinks you're not out to hurt him. In fact, there's a kindness to him."

"Hmm, well I'm glad that whole thing worked out. I know how frustrated you were with him and that dog of his."

"Yes, I'm glad, too. It feels more peaceful here."

Mildred walked back across the street to her mail box and pulled out several envelopes. *Oh, that mail carrier, jeeze!* She sorted everything in her box: the mail addressed to her and the mail addressed to someone else that she'd steam open later.

~~~~

An orange sun was just rising in the East as she arrived for work and saw Spencer waiting next to her bus with a broad grin. He was a tall, handsome man with a kind face and an angular jaw. His dark eyes sparkled even when he wasn't jubilant about something, which was almost never the case. He liked life and it showed.

"Have I got news for you, Miss Mildred." He reached for her lunch pail while she grabbed her sweater and bag and got out of the car.

"Okay, but it better be good news," she said with a smile as they walked toward the bus.

"Well, climb on in," he said. When she did she stopped cold. The advertising spaces above the windows which were rarely used were now filled with the works of famous artist and poets.

"Oh my gosh!" Mildred walked the length of the bus looking at the art, and reading the lines of poetry out loud. She stared at the works of Van Gogh, Picasso, and Michelangelo.

"I wanted you to have the beautiful bus you deserve, Miss Mildred. We had some rainy-day funds, so I ordered these posters for you and put them in last night."

She put her face in her hands and then looked up. "I'm speechless . . . I just don't know what to say . . . except thank you. I've never seen anything more beautiful, Spencer."

"You'd better get on your way," he said a little embarrassed. You don't want to be late."

She listened happily to the *oohs* and *ahhs* all day as her riders discovered the beautiful new inserts. In fact, they changed seats at every stop just see each panel, and Mildred had to remind everyone to please sit while the bus was in motion. There was so much enthusiasm for the art that Mildred asked Superintendent Studebaker if they could have an "open bus" one day, so the residents of Myers Junction could see how beautiful a bus can be.

He agreed, and the newspaper publicized the event. Mildred parked the bus in front of City Hall on a Sunday afternoon and offered home-made cookies and punch at tables set up in the parking lot. People walked through the bus going in the front door and leaving from the back in order to see each panel, and Mildred stood by introducing Spencer as the curator of the exhibit. Spencer wore a tie and brought his family.

~~~~

The headline in the Myers Junction *Tribune* later that week read, *Betsy Palmer to Stand Trial,* but the news spread faster on Mildred's bus. According to the newspaper, Betsy Palmer would stand trial for making moonshine and selling it without paying taxes to the government. It seemed everyone had an opinion now that the word was out. The town knew Betsy and Glen Palmer had been upstanding citizens in the community, contributing to local causes and excelling in civic duty.

According to the gossip on the bus, Glen fell out of favor when he threw Betsy to the wolves by putting the property in her name when he suspected trouble coming his way. Betsy, being a quilter, had the staunch support from the women in Myers Junction, especially after it was disclosed that the transfer of title would let Glen off the hook. There were whispers in the past couple of months of an indictment, but the newspaper now made it official: Betsy Palmer would indeed stand trial for the crime.

Mildred's bus was full of chatter again. Clyde Patel and Henry Booth were in a heated discussion in the back as others joined in.

"I don't see the difference in brewing up a little wine or beer without penalty, but make some hooch and you go to jail?" Clyde said. "It doesn't make a bit of sense to me."

"Well, the paper said this morning that liquor is worth more to the government than beer or wine because it's taxed more," Henry said. "Evidently Uncle Sam takes an excise tax of about two dollars for each 750-milliliter bottle of 80-proof spirits, compared to a few cents for a bottle of wine or a can of beer."

"I doubt if anyone knows exactly how much money changes hands in the moonshine business," Bill Bentley chimed in. "It sure as hell must be enough to bring the Feds all the way out here. I wonder how they even knew where to look."

"Ah, easy," Henry said. "Glen's grandpa was one of the biggest bootleggers in the county in his heyday. Glen inherited that property. I'll bet the Feds have had their eye on it for years."

Winnie Pepper had been listening in. "All I know is that it was pretty lousy of Glen to put that property in Betsy's name. After all, it had been in his family for generations. He's the one who should be going to jail. "

Mildred listened to the gossip every day and didn't mind. The bus was a good venue to find out what her neighbors knew and thought about things. The talk about the Palmers continued for a few weeks until everyone had their say . . . and then the bombshell hit! The large headline that morning in the newspaper read:

Illegal Search, Palmer Case Dropped!

It seemed the federal agents had an out-of-date search warrant to search the Palmer's barn. When Betsy Palmer was informed by her attorney, she quickly had everything in the barn hauled away during the night including, as word had it, Glen's underwear in spite of his pleas that the title transfer was just meant to be temporary. Betsy now owned the house, barn and acreage free and clear, and Glen was out looking for an apartment.

Mildred was invited to Betsy's next quilting bee and decided to go because she heard the champagne would be flowing from buckets.

Forty-Six

A SLIGHT SHOWER put a fresh face on the town and brightened the sky once the clouds drifted to the west. Mildred watched it all from the bus. As she passed the hardware store she waved to Louise, who was putting a "Spring Sale" sign in the window of her fashion boutique. Mildred knew Louise from bowling, but didn't shop at her boutique because Louise told her, "the sizes are too small for your stout figure." So Mildred continued to buy her clothes at Thelma's Thrift Shop. She drove on to the next stop and then pulled to the curb and opened the door, making a quick note of the time in her log.

"Hey it's the mother-fuckin' bus bitch."

"Yo, the sorry-ass little fucker's still driving the bus?"

Mildred sat in a trance and her log fell to the floor. Like a nightmare, everything seemed to be spinning. It took her a few seconds to realize what was happening and she tightened her grip on the wheel, turning away to face the window trying to catch her breath.

"Coins into the slot please," she said, without looking at them.

She could feel the heat on the back of her neck. It wasn't just the sight of them piling onto her bus once again, or the stench, or breath that reeked of stale beer, it was the fact that they were back.

"Now look bitch, don't go telling us what to do. We ain't paying to ride this bus. Hey, what happened to those other guys, you know, the ones who painted the graffiti on the bus? They still around?"

She sat motionless without responding.

"Well look little bitch, we got some muscle now. This here's Dreamer, and this is Creeper."

Two men, bigger and older than the gang of thugs, were just coming up the step onto the bus.

A voice from the back of the bus yelled, "Hey dudes, check it out back here. Whoa, like some fuckin' art museum. Oh look at this, ain't this cute."

"Well, well, well, look at all this here fucking art! And looky here, brand new seats?" In the rear-view mirror Mildred watched two of them jumping from one seat to another while one of the others hung from the overhead strap. Annabelle Drake and Emma Barns who had been sitting in the senior seats, were huddled way in the back.

Mildred put the brake on and walked down the aisle. "These seats are reserved for the disabled and senior citizens. There are seats in front or in back, you can take your pick." She motioned for Annabelle and Emma to go up front, and she waited until they rushed to sit with the others.

"Please find other seats," she said to the gang of thugs with more force.

They sat laughing and turned up their music.

"If you don't find other seats, I'll need to ask you to leave the bus, all of you," she said, raising her voice.

The big one, the one they called Dreamer, glared and lunged. She stumbled backwards, catching herself on one of the seat backs. She kept backing up until she turned and hurried up the aisle. She started to grab the fire extinguisher, but thought twice. *This is useless. Why am I doing this?* When the door finally closed, the bus became a war zone. She took the brake off and drove to the next stop trying not to listen to what was going on in the back.

At the Bus Bay that evening, Mildred sat with her head down. Spencer waited and then walked toward her, his eyes straining to see through the window. He banged on the door, and she opened it enough for him to step in.

"Oh for Christ's sake. Goddamn it." He put his hand on Mildred's shoulder and helped her up.

"You don't want to look, Mildred." But she did.

The stuffing from the new seats littered the floor like small clouds fallen from the sky, and the art posters were defaced with colored markers. Graffiti covered most of the windows, some etched in with a knife. The smell of urine hung in the air, and cigarette butts were strewn about, leaving the putrid odor of tobacco.

"I can't do this anymore, Spencer. I just can't."

Spencer took a deep breath. "I'm going to call Supervisor Studebaker right now to see if he's still in his office. Don't go anywhere, Mildred. I'll be right back."

~~~~

An hour later, Supervisor Studebaker stood with Spencer looking at the carnage, his shoulders hunched, his hands in his pockets. Mildred waited in her car. She glanced up once to see them arguing, and then Spencer motioned her over.

"I just don't see how you can let this happen, Mildred. We put in new seats and replaced the damaged windows, but we can't keep doing this. Do you know how much it cost to fix this bus the last time?"

Spencer paced and huffed before glaring at him. "Supervisor Studebaker, how can anyone possibly stand up to six vandals, including two adults now, not just kids? One of them physically accosted Mildred almost causing her to fall. The bus needs an armed guard, and she needs to be protected, along with the bus and the riders."

"That's absurd. We don't do that here. We're not some fancy, big city bus company with a lot of money. The drivers need to take responsibility for a smooth-running operation. Mildred obviously can't handle her job and she needs to look for another. We took a chance hiring a damn woman for this job. That was obviously a mistake."

"Now wait a minute . . ."

Mildred put her hand on Spencer's arm. "It's okay, Spencer. Look, Supervisor Studebaker, the bus is not suitable for use right now. It smells of urine and the Health Department probably wouldn't let us operate it anyway. And the damage, well the seats are not safe and need to be fixed, and visibility is impaired by graffiti on the windows creating a safety hazard. You could be cited for all of those infractions. I'd like to suggest you take the bus out of circulation until it's ready to go again. At least do it for the riders' safety. That will give you time to look for another driver."

"Mildred don't do this," Spencer said.

"It's alright Spencer. I just can't do it anymore."

Studebaker glanced at Spencer. "Is it true we can be cited?"

"Absolutely, and possibly the entire operation could be shut down."

"It's your entire fault, Mildred." He bit a nail. "If you'd have done your job . . ."

Spencer pounded his fist on the side of the bus and looked at Studebaker. "No, if you had done *your* job! Just imagine how this will sound once word gets out there are vandals riding the bus again, and the bus is now a war zone and unsafe. And, a popular driver is being fired because you think it is her fault? Do you realize she could sue you for hazardous working conditions? I wonder what the mayor would say to that, or the newspaper? And what about Mildred's riders? I can just see them picketing in front of your office, and in town, and everywhere. They won't let you get away with this. Mildred is their favorite. How do you think they will react if you fire her?"

"He's not firing me. I'm quitting. My probation is almost up and I can't work for a company with such a lack of respect for their own drivers and their riders. And, it's just too dangerous now with Dreamer and Creeper."

"You're quitting?" Studebaker said.

"Yes."

"Ah, well, let's not make rash decisions here." He walked back and forth in front of the bus. "Let's get this bus fixed this week. Spencer, I'll put you in charge. You did a decent job last time. And then Mildred, we can talk about this." He turned and rushed off without looking at either of them.

Spencer put his hands deep inside his pockets. Mildred stared at the cracks in the concrete driveway. "What are you thinking, Mildred?"

"I'm thinking I need time to think, that's what I'm thinking." She smiled, but her color was gone. "I feel like I'm sitting on a limb wondering if and when it will break. I don't know who I am anymore."

Forty-Seven

"No bus? What do you mean no bus, Mildred?" Claire Connolly, a regular rider on the Crosstown #2 had the same reaction as the others. "What is it this time? We just thought we had our bus back, and now this?"

"I know Claire, but it's just some maintenance issues. It should be ready by next week, and they'll post signs at the different stops so you'll know."

"They'll post signs? Won't you be doing it, Mildred? You usually let us know what's going on."

"We'll see, Claire. Someone will post a sign, not to worry."

Mildred called as many riders as she could and made sure the office sent someone out to post signs at each stop and place a notice in the newspaper. She hung her uniform in the closet, at the far end where she couldn't see it, and pushed her work shoes with the thick rubber soles to the back as well.

Her black regulation lunch pail sat on the drain board. She finally had the heart to open it. A crumpled Oreo wrapper, the dried rind of an orange, and some seeds for the birds in the park fell out as she held it over the trash can. *Somehow that seems like eons ago*, she thought, as she scrubbed and dried it well before putting it on the bottom shelf in the pantry. She studied the butcher paper chart in the laundry room labeled *The Plan*, looking closely at the intricately drawn lines and the names. She took it down and read the names on the list and nodded, feeling some degree of success: *The cable company, Buster the dog, Angus Baumgartner.*

Well whoopdy-do, not bad, not bad . . . except for the Gang of Thugs, and perhaps Woodbead. She shrugged and threw the list in the trash can.

The following morning she woke with a start. Sitting up quickly, she looked at the clock and then fell back on the pillow. *Hmm, I could probably get used to this.* She rolled over and slept for another hour before having a leisurely breakfast outside once the sun warmed the porch. She brought out the newspaper and scanned the classified section, then read Dick Tracy in the funny pages before getting dressed.

As she was getting ready to leave, she stood in front of the closed door to the spare bedroom. She rarely opened the door during the day, only at night after a bad dream. Yet, that morning she stood, hands on hips, looking at a room filled with boxes of baby furniture. She pulled the chintz curtains open, almost blinded by the stream of sunlight pouring through the east-facing window. She remembered why she liked that spare bedroom. *So light and airy, especially with the window open in the spring.* She sneezed from the dust and tugged at the window, opening it a couple of inches to air the room. After nodding she left, this time leaving the door open after loading the unopened boxes into her car.

~~~~

"Mildred, I've been thinking about you." Thelma greeted her with a hug. "What's happening with the job, made any decisions yet?" She paused to ring up a sale for a customer.

"Oh, everything is still up in the air, Thelma, Right now I'm taking one day at a time. The bus is out of commission. The gang of thugs have really done a number on it this time, so some safety issues need to be fixed."

Thelma shook her head. "It's hard to imagine how this can be happening here in Myers Junction. But I'm sure you're not here to talk about that. So you have some time off?"

"Yes, actually I'm here to make a donation."

"Ah, cleaning out some cupboards?"

"More than that, Thelma. Can you help me carry in some boxes?"

They hugged in the parking lot for a long time without saying a word; both teary, both still. Together, they carried in the boxes of baby furniture.

"I want to paint the room, Thelma. Can I borrow your ladder?" Mildred said, once they were inside.

"Of course, want some help?"

"Hmm, I think painting should be my therapy," Mildred said, knowing Thelma would understand.

A customer waited at the counter. "Go ahead, Thelma. I'll just look around."

A few minutes later, Mildred appeared with a large, framed poster in bright colors by the abstract artist, Mark Rothko.

"Mildred! Really? I thought you liked the old stuff."

"You're always telling me to rattle the cage, Thelma. Besides, I want to use that spare room as a reading room. The light is good, and once painted and with some interesting art on the wall, it should be nice . . . you know, part of the house again."

Mildred left after paying a quarter for the poster, along with some empty boxes to pack the vast number of trinkets, vases, saucers, and kitsch she'd bought from Thelma during the past few years. Thelma agreed to take them back, but only if Mildred agreed to stop by the thrift shop regularly to chat even if she didn't buy anything.

Mildred glanced at the classified section of the newspaper on the car seat next to her and stared straight ahead. *Hmmm, never thought I'd be looking for a job again so soon.* Several ads were circled and a few had big question marks. She drove first to the Woolworth's Five and Dime on Main and Fourth where she had worked for years before her position at the transit company. She knew it closed recently but curious just the same. *Not much of a job but no stress,* she thought as she drove further up Main Street.

The JC Penney store stayed open and hadn't changed much over the years except for fewer customers because of the big box store. It still had the same feel, the shiny linoleum floors, the soft green walls, and the familiar retail smell. The upstairs had an escalator now in addition to the stairs, and the lighting was brighter, but the cafeteria was gone. Mildred lingered in the jewelry department, looking over to see if Mrs. Blanchbury, the corset fitter was still there. She decided to ask.

"Corset fitter?" the young clerk asked. "What's that?"

When Mildred explained, the clerk laughed. "Are you serious? We don't put anyone into anything. It's all ready to wear. We do have a dressing room, and you're welcome to try something on if you like."

Mildred noticed a small jewel on the side of her nose. *Hmm, how'd that get there?* "No, that's okay, I won't be trying anything on today."

Mildred walked around the store and then stopped at another counter. *Another young woman? They must be hiring right out of junior high these days.* " Excuse me, do you know if they're hiring here in the store."

"I dunno, you can ask in Customer Service, but your kid should come in and ask . . . I mean we're all pretty young here, if you know what I mean, like you know, school age I suppose, so they might be looking for someone. But, like, you know, it doesn't hurt to ask, like they'd want to see your kid in person, you know."

"I know."

Mildred walked down the street to the hardware store since she'd seen an ad for a clerk in the tool rental section. *How hard could that be? No stress in renting tools.*

The young man had shoulders like an ox and the breath to match. Mildred took a step back. "I'm here about the position."

"What position?"

"You know, the job advertised in the newspaper."

"Oh the job, yeah, well we need someone here in the office who can also deliver tools when the customer wants a delivery." He gave Mildred the once over. " Ah, have you worked in a tool rental yard before. You don't really look like . . ."

"I know about tools, yes. I'm familiar with tools, of course."

"Well, right now we need someone with knowledge of pile drivers. They're starting a new commercial building out on Cobb's Road."

"What? Good lord, sounds like you should be looking for a proctologist."

Once out on the sidewalk, she regained her composure. *He didn't need to be so rude about it.* She unfolded her newspaper and looked at the classified section again. Her next stop was the Nail Boutique, but she realized they'd probably want someone with nails. She bit hers to the quick, so decided she'd better pass on that one.

Since she was near the library, she decided to stop by to see Velda, who was just leaving for lunch.

"Mildred what a surprise, are you on your lunch break?"

"Actually, the bus is out of commission for about a week, so I stopped by to say hello."

"Oh oh, I sense something's wrong. I didn't have time to make my lunch, so c'mon, let's go to the Moonlight Cafe where we can talk."

Velda listened intently. "Oh gosh, Mildred, that's awful. Are you really quitting? You won't be happy in those jobs in town. Besides, you love your job. What about Bishop's County, any bus jobs there?"

"I haven't really looked, Velda. I'm just letting it all settle. It helped to look at a few jobs today. At least I know what I don't want to do."

"Can't you just switch routes and take the one out to the steel mill?"

"No, I think the supervisor will fire me no matter which route I have. Besides, no one wants my route and I don't blame them. What can a man do against six angry and dangerous thugs intent on raising havoc?"

Velda looked at her watch. "Cripes Mildred, I'm off to the library. I don't want to be late."

"I know. I just wanted to say hello. It's always comforting to see a familiar face."

Velda hugged her tight. "We'll talk soon Mildred, real soon. I'll call you."

Mildred walked to the park since it was sunny and warm. Several sparrows were gathering twigs and fluttering in a panic, and a woman with a baby stroller walked in the shade next to a city gardener trimming a holly bush. She thought about her riders and hoped they were finding a way to the senior center and the barbershop. She tried not to think about the gang of thugs because when she did she felt the anger spreading to every limb. She sat on a bench and felt herself immersed in the sludge of despair.

At home, Mildred dropped her keys on the table and looked around the house, wondering what people do when they're not working. She dusted some tables, straightened the knickknacks on the mantle, and looked through her box of knit hats for the newborns. She counted seven blue and five pink, then looked at her watch. She picked up her keys and left for the hospital.

~~~~

Feeling a shiver she pulled her sweater tight at the neck as she walked through the hospital lobby. *Why are hospitals so cold, or is it just the sterile environment with the disinfectant halls and light green walls?* She noticed the change as she approached the Neonatal ward with the smell of scented diapers and colorful walls with striped curtains covering the windows. Nurse Eloise stood at the nurse's station as she walked in.

"Mildred, what a nice surprise! We were just talking about you this morning."

Hazel Warlaumont

"I've been busy and got behind in my knitting, Eloise, but here are twelve new hats. I can have more in a couple of days. I have some time off from work right now so I can knit more."

"Oh Mildred, how sweet. We always love getting your special little hats, and these are adorable. We still have a supply, but we never know how many we'll need, so it's good to have them. Bring as many as you can whenever you can. Do you want to take a look at the newborns?"

"Oh, perhaps just a peek. How many this week?"

"We have nine right now," Nurse Eloise said, as they walked over to the glass window of the nursery. We expected ten babies but a woman just gave birth to a stillborn. She's alone here. I don't know any more about her than that. She's distraught and wanted to leave the hospital, but the doctor wanted her to stay another couple of days because it was a difficult birth for her."

Mildred straightened her shoulders.

"The woman's name is Susan. We put her in Room Seven down the hall, away from the others celebrating their joyful events. It's . . . it's difficult, as you know."

Mildred stared at the seams in the tile floor. "I must go, Eloise."

Nurse Eloise was still holding the box of knit hats. "Mildred, thank you for bringing more hats. The parents love them for their newborns and look at these little designs you sewed on this time. You know, Mildred, doing things for others can give us comfort in the face of something lost . . . a heartache or a companion, or something that never was."

Mildred kept looking at the floor tiles. "Or, never had the chance to be."

"Mildred, why don't we sit down and talk. You don't need to bring hats. Just come in. It's good to talk. "

Mildred pulled her sweater tight again. "Perhaps. Maybe one of these days."

Eloise and the other nurses watched Mildred go out the double doors. She turned left to leave the building, but then they saw her walk past the door again, going slowly down the hall in the direction of Room Seven.

Nurse Eloise looked at the others. "Hmm, that's interesting. I'm not exactly surprised though. Sometimes, it takes another's tragedy to help us face our own."

Later that afternoon, Mildred called the Neonatal ward at Mercy General and asked to speak to Nurse Eloise. She was on hold for quite a while before Eloise came to the phone.

"Eloise, this is Mildred. I hope I'm not interrupting anything."

"Mildred, no. I was just taking some blankets to the nursery. It's so nice to hear from you, and thank you again for bringing in more baby hats. Parents love to have their pick of colors."

There was silence on the line. "Mildred?"

"Yes, Eloise, can you pass a message on to Susan in Room Seven? I invited her to Betsy Palmer's quilting bee but wasn't sure of the date. Can you tell her it's next Friday and I will pick her up, as we agreed?"

"Why, Mildred, how wonderful! I will tell her right now."

"Ah, also, I was wondering if we could find a time for that talk, Eloise. I think it's time."

~~~~~

The light on the answering machine blinked rapidly as she came in the door. This time it was Spencer. "Hey Miss Mildred, just thinking of you. I wanted to tell you the window glass was replaced today, and we have new seats coming the day after tomorrow. I also cleaned off all the graffiti and ordered new art posters and they're on their way. I'm also looking into something to gate off the senior section but haven't come up with anything yet. Mildred, Supervisor Studebaker has been here all week worrying you won't come back. I think his bark is worse than his bite. He really does want you to drive the bus. Well, I guess that's

Hazel Warlaumont

all. It sure is boring here without you."

She smiled and plopped herself down on the sofa just as the doorbell rang. Alphie stood there with a big grin and ran his fingers through his hair. "Well, what do you think of it, Miss Penniwink?" His new haircut was perfect, she thought. Just right for a boy his age.

Before she could answer, he said, "And, that's not all. My parents gave me some money to buy supplies for a science project we're doing in scouts."

"Wow, that's wonderful Alphie. How exciting!"

"Well, there's even more."

"Yeah, tell me, tell me. I can't wait to hear."

He teetered back and forth from one foot to the other talking faster than usual. "My parents wanted me to ask if you would help me with my science project, like on Saturday after I do my chores for you."

Mildred grasped her hand over her mouth and squeezed before taking a deep breath. "Well . . . well, only if we can have chocolate chip cookies while we're working on the project."

"Yay!" Alphie raised both arms in triumph, before turning his bike around and heading home.

Forty-Eight

AFTER THE LAST "Amen" and when people filed out of the church, Mildred caught Reverend Corbin walking back into the sanctuary after chatting with his parishioners on the lawn. He walked slowly with his shoulders stooped as if carrying a heavy load. Mildred thought he was perhaps lonely when his flock left much like she felt when the bus emptied of riders. She smiled when she thought of him singing *Billie Jean* in the karaoke bar. *I guess we all wear different hats at times when life demands.*

"Reverend Corbin, do you have a minute?"

"Mildred! How are you? I didn't see you in church, where were you sitting?"

"Now Reverend Corbin, are you trying to make me feel guilty for not going to church every Sunday?"

"No, Mildred. For never going to church every Sunday," he said laughing. "And by the way, can't you just call me Corbin instead of Reverend when we're not in church? After all, we've broken bread in the karaoke bar."

"Ah, well we've also sang hymns together so you're still my pastor."

"Alright then, come in and we can talk."

As the sun shifted, Mildred told him of her frustration and that she was thinking of quitting her job, but fearful she might not find another.

"Yes, well the problem with burning your bridges is that you still have to smell the smoke."

She looked askance. "I don't remember reading that in the scriptures."

He laughed. "Are you talking to me as a friend or a pastor?"

"Both, but mostly as a friend. You've always steered me in the right direction."

"Well Mildred, it's hard to separate the friend from the pastor in this case, but let me remind you of what I said before that last caper down the street from you. The scriptures say, 'So whoever knows the right thing to do and fails to do it, for him it is sin.' What's the right thing to do here, Mildred? Is it running out on your flock, or is there some other solution?"

"Ah, that seems to be the dilemma. I just don't know. I feel as though I've hit the wall and don't know where to turn next."

He thought for a minute. "Whatever you decide, the scriptures also say, 'Be strong and courageous. Do not fear or be in dread of them.'" He smiled. "I think only you can decide what to do, but I hope if you err, it will be on the side of action and not desertion." He put his hand on her shoulder before she left.

Mildred walked to a park nearby and thought about what Reverend Corbin said. *Holy moly, how can I be strong if I don't know what to do?*

She thought about the difference between action and desertion, and imagined how her riders might be without her; their empty faces as they sit on the bus, quiet, stoic, just going from one place to another with nothing in between.

~~~~

Monday morning came and she laid out her uniform on the bed as usual, a ritual she'd been doing for almost six months. She looked in the mirror. *Maybe they won't even show up today . . . or any day for that matter. Maybe they've moved on now that they've ruined the bus, on to something new to destroy, even some other encounter to fill their own void to compensate for some harm that came to them at some time in their life. Maybe I'm getting upset over nothing . . .just nothing.*

Spencer waited by the bus standing on one foot, then the other. The bus was sparkling; totally repaired and cleaned throughout.

He gave her a big hug. "It's not the same when you're not here, Miss Mildred. There's nothing to look forward to at the end of the day."

"Oh Spencer, thank you . . . and the bus looks wonderful, so clean and new once again. What a great job you've done to bring it back to life."

"We will have a good day, you'll see."

"We?" She looked surprised.

"I'm going with you today, Miss Mildred. You know, just to make sure it all goes well. Just today, and maybe even tomorrow. I'm taking some vacation time and I don't have anything better to do."

She shook her head. "Spencer, the last thing I will let you do is go on that bus. Those thugs will . . . well, you're not going with me on the bus. You can't out-number them, and there's no telling what they might do to a tall black man who tries to interfere with their antics."

"I can take care of my . . ."

"No, no you can't. You haven't seen them. I know at least one of them has a switchblade knife and together they can be ruthless. I have a feeling they won't even show up today. The bus has been out of service all week."

"Mildred, the newspaper said service will resume today for the Crosstown #2."

She sighed. "Yes, yes I know, Spencer. And, you don't have vacation time by the way. I know that for a fact. I can't have you losing your job for not showing up. Thank you anyway and for making the bus beautiful again and for wanting to protect it. It will be what it will be."

"It's not the bus I want to protect, Mildred. I'm worried about you."

She eyed the scraggly brown grass near the curb and thought it needed trimming, and then looked back at Spencer, putting her hand on his arm and squeezing it gently.

"I've come back to drive the bus because that is what I do." She glanced at her watch. "Gotta go, Spencer. I'll see you later. Oh, and the bus looks beautiful, really beautiful," she said over her shoulder as she climbed on board.

He leaned inside before she closed the door. "It always amazed me that with your short arms you can turn that big steering wheel let alone see over the top of it. I think it's your will power that drives this bus, not your short arms." He stepped back off the bus but stood there looking at her "You're a natural Mildred, but I see a hint of anxiety in your eyes this morning. Just remember, this is your bus not theirs."

Forty-Nine

"ALRIGHT, MILDRED! I see we're back in operation!" Ted Thomas and his wife Dora climbed on board and dropped their coins in the box. He squeezed her shoulder as he walked by. Penny Pringle followed them up the step and dropped in her coins.

"We're glad to see you back Mildred. Say, did you hear that old Walt Thornton had a knee operation and that Phyllis had to run the shop while he was laid up last week?"

"No, I didn't hear that," Mildred said smiling as she closed the door and pulled the bus back onto the street. She noticed young Iris Simpson pushing her baby carriage near the fruit stand, and in the next block Thornton Sparks was putting out a sign in front of his hardware store, *Knives sharpened, never a dull moment.* There was some heated discussion outside the barbershop and Mildred wondered what they were arguing about now. *It must be about politics or baseball scores, since either one gets them riled up.*

At the next bus stop, Mildred greeted Betsy Palmer, Agnes Mercer, and Frank Barns. Betsy got on the bus wearing a fancy new pantsuit with a matching purse. Rumor had it Glen finally left town, at least that's what Mildred heard from Mark Olsen when he was on the bus just minutes before.

"Coming to the quilting bee this week, Mildred? We missed seeing you there last week. And by the way, so glad to see the bus running again. It's what keeps us together."

"Thank you, Betsy. How's the quilt coming along?"

"It'll move along faster once you're there," she said smiling.

Frank Barns got on after Betsy. "Glad to see the bus back in commission, Mildred." He dropped in some change. "Damn, we miss this old bus when it's down."

"Me too, Frank. Watch your step there."

As she approached the next stop her mouth went dry. She took a sip of water from her water bottle and sat up straight. It was the gang of thugs' stop. *They may not know the bus is back in service; in fact I'm sure of it.* As she pulled up she was relieved to find no one waiting.

As required, she slowed to the curb anyway and just then spotted one of them gyrating his hips and yelling at a woman passing by on the sidewalk.

"Mother fucker c'mere for a little fun, bitch."

Dreamer, the tall one, rubbed his crotch and followed her to the corner while they all laughed before stepping up to the bus waiting for the door to open. Leon, one of the original thugs, spotted Mildred through the window in the bus door.

"Hey it's the bus bitch," and he banged on the door. "C'mon mother fucker let us in. Come do a little lap dance, bitch."

She sat numb while they banged on the door.

"Hey bitch, open up. C'mon, we gotta get on the bus. Open the door."

She saw the light turn green and the cars next to the bus moved forward almost in slow motion. She sat tapping her finger on the steering wheel. Everything became quiet, silent really. She could see the thugs, their mouths moving and their fists raised as they banged on the door, but there was no sound.

In one sudden move, she jerked the bus in gear and gunned the throttle while swinging it into the next lane and driving full speed ahead, leaving a cloud of black smoke blanketing the thugs standing and yelling on the corner. She held her breath, hearing only her heart racing. Once she cleared the intersection, she wiped the perspiration from her face with her sleeve and settled deep into her seat hearing the cheers and clapping from her riders but mostly the bus, its grace on the road, the sound of the tires, the hum of the engine, and the road ahead. She glanced at the little card she kept above the dash. *One chance, work hard, be kind to everyone.*

"Not everyone," she murmured under her breath as she slipped the card from the visor and dropped it into the small waste basket next to her seat.

~~~~

That afternoon she started honking the horn about a half a block from the Bus Bay. When she arrived, Spencer was standing in front looking concerned. Within minutes they were laughing and hugging in the parking lot. At one point, he climbed up into the bus and then leaned out the door,

"Yep, looking good, looking good!" He hugged her again when she told him how she roared through the intersection without stopping for the gang of thugs. He made her repeat it over and over again and hugged her after each time.

"What do you think Supervisor Studebaker will say when he calls you in to the office after the delinquent boys complain, saying you wouldn't let them on the bus?"

"I'll say, 'what boys? I didn't see any boys.'" They laughed again and walked arm in arm to her car. "Actually, I'll tell him what you told me: that this is my bus not theirs. Studebaker wants to keep the peace at this point. I think everyone in the community and in the mayor's office will agree. Those boys need to start walking since the bus is now off limits."

Spencer squeezed her shoulder. He couldn't stop smiling. "You have yourself a good evening, Miss Mildred. A real good evening."

"You too, Spencer. A real good evening too."

~~~~

The sun lingered over Myers Junction a little longer that day before turning the sky to a deep orange with white wispy streaks.

Mildred took in the beauty of it all as she drove into her driveway and walked up the steps to the old wooden porch. She noticed Buster's water bowl was empty. She knew he'd been sleeping there as he does every afternoon when the sun warms the porch.

Inside, she poured a glass of *chabliss* and put her uniform on a hanger and her shoes near the bed ready for the following day. She reached down, adjusting them a little so they'd be perfectly parallel.

In the closet she reached for the box. This time she put it on the bed and pulled the lid off. Her tap dancing shoes were the *show tap* type used in Broadway musicals. The sound of the tap striking the floor was a form of exaggerated percussion making it more exciting to watch and hear, according to what she'd read. She bought them at Thelma's thrift shop a few years ago when she needed some cheering up. Thelma said, "Go ahead and buy 'em even if you never wear them."

Thelma always knew what to say to Mildred, like when the members of the high school drill team donated their marching uniforms to the thrift shop after getting new ones. Mildred happened to see them in the shop, and her eye went immediately to a pair of red, white, and blue, shiny satin shorts in her size.

"Try them on," Thelma had said. "And try on this sequined top." When Mildred saw it sparkling in the light she made up her mind to buy them both even if they didn't fit. But that was a few years ago and now for the first time, Mildred put them on and stood in front of the mirror, arms hanging at her side. *Darn, it's the blouse.* She tucked it in and then threw her shoulders back. *Bingo!*

Turning twice in front of the mirror she was pleased. The satin shorts made her legs look shorter than they were but she thought the shiny fabric was a delight when it caught the light. She did a little shuffle step in her stocking feet and giggled. Reaching for the tap shoes, she ran her hand over the tops giving them an imaginary shine and smiled before slipping her feet into each one. She tried them out on the oak floor and nodded. Fluffing her hair, and with one last look in the mirror, she grinned as she marched out to the garage with her portable player and recording.

Taking a breath, she turned the music on and warmed up with a little shuffle while trying to remember her favorite Ginger Rogers steps. Picking up the tempo, she did some step-heel turns while swinging her arms and then stumbled. But she caught herself and continued, laughing as the flesh under her arms seemed to dance to its own rhythm. She closed her eyes and pictured Fred Astaire and Gene Kelly. Spreading her short fingers, she arched her back and stretched her hands high to the sky as the rhythm took hold.

"Come and meet those dancing feet, scooby do, scooby do." She imagined the bright lights on stage as her feet tapped to a steady beat. Tap, tap, ta, tap tap. "Hear the beat of dancing feet," she sang off key moving faster and faster, now with rhythm, now pulsating, and energized by the sound of her own dancing feet.

Picking up the pace she broke free, her feet pounding the garage floor louder and louder with a boisterous outpouring of energy, emotion, knowing this is who she really is, the sparkle in her eyes dancing with her

Lifting her chin she let her shoulders move with her body, leaning forward, arms swinging wide, feet tapping faster . . . and leading the chorus line to center stage with the wild cheers of the audience, the spotlight turned to her.

"Five, Six, Seven, Eight," she shouted. The sounds, the touch, the visceral sensation of her taps pounding the floor, thrilling, titillating, and moving freely now with the beat of her dancing feet. Nothing can stop her now, she has the rhythm, tapping faster, in total control and she knew it. Finally at last she knew it.

Made in the USA
San Bernardino, CA
03 June 2020

72676013R00156